ST

Vicky Allan grew up on a farm in Northumberland and studied to be a vet at Cambridge University. In 1995 she won the *Vogue* talent contest for writing and she now writes for *Scotland on Sunday*. She lives in a flat in Edinburgh with her cat.

STRAY

Vicky Allan

FOURTH ESTATE • *London*

First published in Great Britain in 2000 by
Fourth Estate Limited
6 Salem Road
London W2 4BU
www.4thestate.co.uk

1 3 5 7 9 10 8 6 4 2

A catalogue record for this book is available
from the British Library.

ISBN 1-84115-252-8

Typeset by MATS, Southend-on-Sea, Essex
Printed in Great Britain by
Cox & Wyman Ltd, Reading

for Christopher

'animal, vegetable
or mineral?'

No company compares with the company of cats.

It's their talk that gets me.

For all our thousands of dialects, not one human tongue translates it well. In English, we have just a single word, *miaow*. In French it's the same, just spelt differently. In Cat it's *Mhrrrnhhh*, *mrrhhh*, *miiirrahhhhi*, *brrwwaaaoo*, *row*, *miiouuu*, *rrhhheeeaoooou*, *weeiiiaoueeeee* and millions of other words which I couldn't begin to transcribe. There are Cat murmurs and greetings and squawks and whispers and rants and ravings and swearings and gossipings. There's a short, sharp *eahh* from the back of the mouth. There's a lingering drawn-out whistle-like sound. There's a long, ostentatious wail. Listen hard and you'll hear sounds of anger, sounds of love and sounds of happiness. The Cat vocabulary is as vast as our own.

Mrrrrrrrrhhhhhhhhh . . . I let it slide softly through my throat.

My physiology dictates that I speak poor Cat. I

3

have a human throat, a human tongue, a human voice-box. All these things are stacked against me. Yet, when I hear a cat utter a plaintive *mhrnnnnhhh* ... I can't help but attempt to return the call. *Mrhnnnhhh* ... I roll it around my mouth, forcing the *rrrr* across my palate into an *nnn*. I mimic as well as any other human. I'm no great actor, but at times I capture the hollow feline *aow* sound with a surprising deftness and ease. Sometimes the cat voice squeaks out involuntarily. Other times it becomes forced and weighed down by my human accent. I feel like a phrasebook speaker in a foreign land.

Behind their still faces are these cats laughing at me?

They do laugh. I'm sure of it. For them, I make as good entertainment as a parrot. They're amused at my random repetitions. They think it's cute and endearing. *Ahhh, poor petal, but at least she tries ... Let's see what else we can get her to try and say!* I suspect they must be delivering me their rudest words. Then they'll roll about with laughter as I make my attempt. *Heee heee ...* you little monsters *... heee heee.* Probably I'm capable of saying no more than two or three words in Cat. That's my limit. Yet still I repeat the sounds over and over again. Maybe someday I'll get through.

Maybe some day ... I'm not stopping yet.

You see, I have a calling – a voice that came to me in childhood. And, yes, it was a feline voice. At the age of ten I once heard a cat speak to me. In a clear voice it said to me, 'You know what you want. Just

4

try it.' Sometimes I imagine it was a mishearing, an echo of some abstract noise, a whistle in the wind that opened my subconscious. Sometimes I even imagine all this work is based on a fleeting delusion. Probably everything I have done since then has been driven by that moment.

That single occasion.

As an adult, I can't help but think of all that as childish dreamings. A juvenile fantasy. Now, trained by scientific thought, I can no longer believe what I heard was grounded in reality. I giggle at myself even as I tell you it. What nonsense. If anyone else told me a story like that I would laugh. Whether my own experience or another person's, I need more proof. I ought to ditch the whole idea, but I don't – I use it. I use it to provide some excuse for my obsession with the feline species. I use it as a quaint little explanation for my endless probing into the language of cats. A part of my story.

My calling has led to a great deal of disappointment. Since then I've been forced to seek out the company of cats more than is right. I have sat for hours, staring at cats, almost willing myself to dissolve and float inside one of their bodies. And in all that time I've not heard a clear voice. I've hung on every squeaking utterance, kept my ears primed every second. I've read the papers of the great Mildred Moelk on cat phonetics. I've studied, taped and mimicked those subtle intonations. But, no luck. Where's the sense of it all, when you just end up spending your hours wondering whether that *brapp* means 'Switch the telly on', or if *braowww* is more than just a sign of discontent and means 'It's well past breakfast time'? What's the use?

For all these fumblings and uncertainties, I can't escape it. I can't break free. All this time I've clung longingly to the idea that I might hear that call again, hoping that it would save me from something. From the emptiness. The isolation.

We all fear being alone. We all find our different ways of dealing with it. Some people search the skies endlessly for hope of first contact with an alien race, others turn to New Age cults, drugs, gambling, compulsive eating, God even.

Me, I just sit around with cats.

the stray

Men are more difficult to fathom than cats, so I'll be perverse and start with the man. This was before I met Purrl.

It all happened so fast.

'Mind the dog . . . She bites.'

That was the first thing I heard him say, as he squeezed deftly between the pincering doors of an underground train. He drew his breath in quickly, almost laughingly. There was something too brash, too attention-seeking, about his tone to take his warning seriously. Too deadpan too. Particularly when the dog was such a soft, soppish Weimaraner. We all ignored him – me and everyone else in the carriage. No one laughed and no one moved aside for the large, sleek-muscled, doe-eyed dog. He sat down opposite me, underneath the dust-grafitti that said, 'Frankie was murdered.' He smiled.

I like a man who smiles.

I barely glanced his way at first – I was so locked in my own boringly banal thoughts. The truth was I was feeling pretty dead that Sunday morning, not exactly hung-over but touchy and sad. I was a lonely girl, travelling home on a lonely line. No sweaty Saturday-night fling, just a homely dinner with my happily in love friends Sophie and Paul. The dinner was a downer. It was all too much: too much happiness on display, too much touchy-feely under the table, hot chilli, tequila and warm, knowing smiles. It was all so lovely it had to be meaningless. And to top it, I'm sure in the morning, when they woke up and found me still on the sofa, they wished I wasn't there. Some friends . . .

I was vaguely distracted by the dog. She lay on the ground, her dusky brown limbs taking up most of the aisle and her front claws almost reaching out to my feet. With her head on top of her paws, she looked up at me and raised a brow as if to warn me off. Actually, I was intrigued and stared a little longer. The carriage jolted. She shifted restlessly, letting out a long groan, a wiry lament which strained into a low-pitched whine, a song to the clanking rhythm of the train, and, picking up on the flow, my eyes floated from the dog to its owner's feet, to scuffed-up suede shoes and a denim leg. His socks were odd, but his jeans looked new and pressed. What kind of man was this?

My thoughts drifted . . . Sometimes, when I'm on the underground, I play the old guessing game – the one I used to play with Mina. The one where you try and guess who a person is just from the way they look. My sister was good at it. But then, she always had a way with guessing, just like she had with all things. Mina was a golden girl. She just knew.

I often imagine I'm still playing it with her, being tested by her. Her voice goes round and round inside my head as if she's right next to me, even though I know she's not. And it's not that I'm preoccupied with her, it's just, well . . . there are some people you can't bury. Their life is part of every cell in your body, part of every adenine, guanine, thymine and cytosine, every strand of your DNA. They keep coming back in the smallest, most inoffensive thoughts – like tiny, insidious tentacles of memory. It's the family thing. You can't forget family. Family is there in everything, no matter how hard you try to escape it.

You first . . . That familiar whisper creeps out from somewhere at the back of my brain and I wonder if it's my own voice or hers. *How about that man with the glasses?* It's always men I try it out on. I'm not interested in women – neither of us ever was, even at that age. We'd already had an overdose of the female with each other. No, men are the stuff of the game . . . and not every variety of man. We have a type – or rather two types. Mina goes for bright, flashy types with gadgets and gleaming teeth and I go for the drips, or so she says. Average height, with dirt-brown ear-cropped hair, his skin is pale from lack of air and he wears little gold-rimmed glasses often stuck carelessly together with tape. Maybe he's a musician or a lab technician or a librarian. I never find out. He's very anal, likes reading Russian

11

novels, cares about the environment and eats organic vegetables.

Or so I guess . . . But not this guy. This guy sitting opposite was different. He wasn't my usual type.

Question one? Well, question one was a cinch.

Straight off I could tell he was a dog lover. But then, wasn't question one always the easiest in our game? For Mina and I there were only two types of people in the world. 'Dog lover or cat lover?' came first before name, age, profession or what disease they were going to die of.

Of course, most men are dog lovers. The dog is about the only animal other than woman, that they're even remotely interested in. It's one of those left brain, right brain sorts of thing. Men are canine. Women are feline. Men hunt in packs, fight like warriors and will obey their leader when ordered. They're naturally attracted to dogs not cats. As Jemima used to tell me, cat haters are invariably men: Adolf Hitler, Julius Caesar, Alexander the Great, Napoleon Bonaparte, Dwight Eisenhower. All men with some kind of power complex: dictators and egomaniacs.

Maybe it was the Weimaraner that gave him away.

The fact that he had such a big, handsome dog with him said canine, canine, canine. I let my eyes drift back to his face, to his neck and the faintly stubbled line of his chin. He was looking along the carriage, his eyes upturned thoughtfully and his lips slightly open. Though I'm shy, I can't help

12

looking at people. I find my pupils cling irresistibly to their faces, to the spots and pimples and contours of their cheekbones. I am fascinated by faces. Like this face. It had a Latin look. A bit like a heated-up version of the young Marlon Brando, but with more edges. Warmly tanned skin, dark hair, darker eyes . . . I studied his lashes, long like they'd been slicked with mascara. His hair was thick and curling. His lips were full and ripe – almost too ripe for a man. I wondered what they'd feel like against my skin . . . Breath-stopping . . .

Suddenly two dark, darting pupils met mine. Suddenly his face had turned towards me, sending panic fluttering up through my face. I glanced away quickly, faking a wandering, thoughtless, day-dreaming gaze and pretending my eyes had caught on the advert above. Then I bided my time. How long would it be till I could legitimately allow my eyes to return to him again?

The train slowed a little, quietening its shattering roar, and I began to mentally prepare myself for the stop. Here was where I changed lines. With very little more ride-time, I needn't worry too much about facing him. There was a winding-up noise. We slowed and slowed and came to a stop. But instead of entering the bright, white light of the station, we halted in darkness. There was only the blackness of the tunnel out there in this temporary pause.

When I did drop my gaze he was still staring at me.

I looked down and blushed slightly. I had been caught in the act.

Seconds ticked past. I felt I could almost hear them. *Tick . . . tick . . .* as I looked restlessly from side to side, avoiding his gaze. *Tick . . .* as I shuffled anxiously. There I was, staring at the floor, committing to memory the glistening wetness of a dog's nose. I thought I could almost hear this man breathing.

More seconds passed. Minutes even. I don't know how long.

'Have you ever thought the train might have stopped for ever and you'd be down here just waiting and waiting, always thinking it would move on?' A voice broke through the silence. 'Ever thought that?'

I looked up. 'Huh!' I laughed, almost out of surprise, glancing around, uncertain if he was talking to me. It seemed he was. I thought about it for a second. 'Mmmm . . . yeah. Kind of.'

'So, when would you start to go mad?'

At this point it would have been reasonable to ignore him, but instead I humoured him. 'I dunno. Who knows? Would you ever?'

'Mmmm. Maybe you wouldn't.' He was talking absent-mindedly, almost as if it didn't matter whom he spoke to. He could have just as well been talking to his dog as to me. 'I wonder what's happened?'

'Somebody under a train, signal failure, driver just completely lost it and decided to give up his job and get out here. It could be anything,' I suggested,

14

still nervous. I looked down at the Weimaraner. 'I like your dog.'

'Mmmm ... She's a love. Biggest sop I've ever known.'

I bent forward and scratched the hair on the back of the dog's head. 'Not neurotic? Most Weimaraners are.'

'Neurotic? Maybe sometimes ... Though neurotic's not the word I would use for it – just affectionate, really affectionate. But that's all part of her appeal.' The dog had raised her head and was beginning to snuffle around my legs. 'She seems to like you,' he said.

'I guess so ... Most animals do. What's her name?'

'Zara ...'

'Zara ... mmm ... nice.' I smiled, ruffling up the fur around her face. Suddenly I was a little tongue-tied. Suddenly I was at a loss.

There was a bang and a shallow fluttering vibration and the engine started up again. And then the train was moving, clattering its way towards the station with only seconds to go, seconds that were conducted in complete silence except for that thundering noise of wheels against tracks and air whooshing. Seconds of wondering why I couldn't think of anything to say.

We both got off at the same stop . . . him first, me following him out of the door, vaguely embarrassed.

'Is this your stop too?' he asked, laughing.

15

'No, just changing. I'm only going one more stop, but it saves a bit of a walk. My head's not quite up for hiking today. Tequila night last night.'

'Mmm . . . I've had a few of them.' He nodded. 'You live up here then?'

'Yeah, just up on Dover Hill. Do you?'

'Uh-uh, just taking Zara for a walk in the park.' He smiled again, cocking his head to one side thoughtfully. 'But I'm often in the area . . . We could meet for a drink, if you like.'

So effortlessly upfront, it caught my breath. I was taken aback but charmed, not sure whether I liked his directness or not. I hesitated. 'I suppose we could. Yeah. Maybe we could.'

'Let me take your number and I'll give you a ring.' He was fishing inside his pockets with his left hand, gripping his dog's lead with his right. Zara was getting impatient, pacing on the spot.

'OK.'

'I've got a pen.' He brought out a biro, but stood there flustered, still raking through his jacket. 'But no paper.'

'Me neither.' I shrugged.

'Typical. I guess I'll have to do the usual scrawl on the back of my hand then.'

Usual scrawl? That implied he often took down girls' numbers.

He seemed to sense what I was thinking. 'Uh . . . Not that I normally do this. I mean, just like work numbers or friends' numbers.'

'Oh, yeah.' I nodded.

16

He laughed, then raised one hand to his head, making a two-fingered pistol point. 'Poofff! What an idiot!' The dog was tugging hard now at his wrist and barking. She was clearly eager to run. 'Quiet, Zars!' He pulled her in again. 'I'd better get going before she has a fit. Anyway . . . I'm Josh.'

'I'm Milla.'

'OK, Milla – nice name – so what's your number?'

'434-6751 . . .' It just came out. 434-6751, with one digit wrong – like I always use whenever I'm trying to put off a man. There I was. I'd done it again. And this time I wasn't even sure if I'd wanted to.

'Great . . . I'll give you a ring,' he said, as he was dragged along the platform by the dog. 'I will definitely.'

'Oh, err . . . Josh . . .' I called after him.

'Save it! I'll call you. 434-6751. I'll call you.'

Another missed opportunity. Another ship that didn't even pass in the night . . . This is how I find my bliss.

Purrl was a completely different kettle of fish.

I first met her on a fairly routine house visit. Routine, that is, apart from the fact that maybe, just maybe, I felt a slight pang before I arrived, and definitely, yes definitely, the suspicion that food might be on the agenda popped into my brain before I even left my house. It's true mere deduction could have led me there. Yet sometimes I wonder if, like Jemima Spall, I get an inexplicable sense of an animal long before I even meet him or her – say, on the way there or as I'm entering the house, or even as I'm talking to the owner on the phone. This time it came in the form of a nagging stomach-ache.

'The cat's behaving oddly. I don't know what to do,' Rowena's voice lilted down the receiver.

My stomach growled.

'I've got a window tomorrow. I could come round if you're free then,' I said. My life, in fact, has so many windows it's practically a greenhouse. 'Usual fees.'

My stomach whined.

'Yes, fine. See you then.'

Rowena Benson sat in a huge jade-green armchair in her front room, thighs spreading over the cushions. Her earthy face was attractive in an over-ripe way, cheeks hanging low, large eyes glistening. Her brown hair bobbed around her face, moulded into obedience with hairspray. The neatly pressed maroon shift she was wearing smelt of fabric conditioner mixed with floral perfume. Everything about her was tightly under control. Everything she touched was clean and preened and smelling of furniture polish.

Roland stood next to his wife, bouncing their month-old baby on his chest, rocking him backwards and forwards and backwards and forwards while making gentle cooing noises. He marched up and down for several minutes until little Marty quietened down.

Meanwhile, Rowena smiled proudly. 'Rol's so good with Marty – much better than me.'

18

Noticing that I hadn't helped myself to any of the cakes laid out on the coffee table, Rowe placed a pudgy grip round the plate of chocolate brownies and offered it to me.

'No thanks,' I said. My stomach was still growling – a warning, perhaps.

'Go on, be a devil.' Her fleshy plum-painted lips spread across her face extravagantly. 'It's a delicious batch.'

The sun was filtering through the front windows, casting long shadowy spears over the coffee table. Rowena seemed to glow in that light. She placed a vast slice of the brownie on her plate, then licked the cocoa powder off her fingers.

I bit my lip disapprovingly, but Rowe just grinned back. 'Got to keep my energy levels up – what with the breast-feeding.'

'Of course,' I said, trying to resist the baby talk and get down to business. I asked her about her cat.

'Oh, Nilli . . . She's a bit shy. Funny little thing. And, well, she's just not eating.'

'Not eating?'

'Mmmm . . . I've tried everything: fresh calf's liver, tuna, smoked salmon, venison and redcurrant saugages, even . . .' She paused and grimaced. '*The tinned stuff.*'

'No, not the *tinned stuff*,' I echoed. 'She must be getting her food elsewhere. When did the trouble start?'

'It's been ever since we had Marty. First she

started wailing in the middle of the night, and then there's this . . . She just stops eating.'

'Since you had Marty?' It was all slotting into place. I put it to them that she might be jealous.

'Of Marty?' asked Rol, leaping on the suggestion. 'Yes, isn't that what I said, darling? Isn't it?'

'It is quite likely,' I said. 'This kind of thing sounds like a classic case of attention-seeking behaviour. It's a bit like a hunger strike. She probably just wants a bit more love.'

Jealousy, of course it had to be jealousy.

Cats, after all, have feelings. It's a fact that few owners take into account. For instance, when expecting a new baby, parents will often take into account the feelings of an older sibling. They'll anticipate distress. Children by nature get jealous when their parents pop another sprog. Cats, however, are rarely allowed this liberty. When, after being the baby of the house for an extended period of time, they are suddenly ousted by a bawling, helpless mini-human, it's not surprising if they feel it as an affront to their dignity. They may even appear to behave irrationally. Mummy and Daddy have got another child and one that absorbs them much more than the furry variety. Poor old pusses, they can so easily find themselves in the doghouse.

Rol led me through their barren hallway. I followed slowly. For some reason I was apprehensive. Before

20

I even reached the kitchen I felt the saliva gather in the back of my throat.

'I think she might be Siamese or something,' he went on. 'She's very dainty, but she was so scraggy the first day she came in. Rowe saw her scratching away at the kitchen window, all pathetic and rain-drenched, and we let her in, and she's never left.'

What I felt when I went into that room was something rare.

Occasionally, just very occasionally, you meet a person or an animal and you feel something inside you click. That was one of those moments. I'd seen thousands of cats before, but this was different. A sharp tremor slid down my back and my finger-ends began to tingle. Before I'd even glimpsed the animal, my breath seemed to catch in the back of my throat. I don't know what it was: a chemical reaction, a touch of *déjà vu*? But I like to think it was a form of love at first sight. I believe in those kinds of things. Yes, I believe in love.

Some humans like to laugh at the idea of passion, or friendship or love, between animals. They think true love exists only between human souls. Not true. Not only are dogs, cats, geese, horses and so on capable of intense love within their species, but they are also capable of similar relationships with humans. Love is an animal thing. It's an evolu-tionary device, common to many species. Parrots are so inclined towards love at first sight that we've developed a name for it, 'the thunderbolt'. I wonder if that's what happened when I first saw Purrl. Were we, like two parrots, suddenly sealed together for life?

The room was silent, apart from the steady buzz of the fridge. On impulse I turned immediately to the left and found myself gazing straight into a set of cat's eyes. Purrl was sitting bolt upright on a wicker chair in the corner of the room by the patio door, poised like some Egyptian statue. She was skinny and ragged, with a coat of pure-white fur and the coldest pink eyes. From her large triangular ears, I could tell she was clearly an Oriental, probably pure-bred. But she was also that incredibly rare thing, an albino, a pure, pigmentless white. Most albinos die in their early years – they're generally too weak and sickly from the start – but Purrl, while smaller than your average moggy, was full-grown and, given a good diet, she could easily bloom.

Those eyes, they cut right through me.

'Come on, little Nilli, you silly billy,' whined Rol, waggling his fingers at the cat.

I bent down to move one of the stools that was blocking my path to her, then paused. I felt intensely self-conscious. The cat was staring at me. I got the feeling she was warning me not to move an inch further, not to step over her line, to invade her personal space.

'She's gorgeous. An albino, you know. It's very rare,' I said, transfixed.

Being careful not to make any fast movements, I shifted the stools out of my path and approached. I was worried that I might spook her, but I needn't have been. Purrl showed no sign of alarm, and slowly I reached a hand out to her. Could I break the spell? Would she crack?

That first touch of her fur sent a thrill shooting up my arm. I breathed in quickly, unable to do anything for a few seconds, oddly paralysed, as if stunned by an electric shock, breath squeezed from my lungs.

Rol stood by, his hands folded over his chest, studying my movements. 'Do you think she's OK?'

'Mmmm . . . yeah,' I murmured. 'Yes . . . yes . . . with a bit of care. Though we *do* need to get her to eat.'

I crouched in front of the stool and brought my face down to her level, but looking downwards. Slowly, I levelled upwards and gazed into her pure-pink irises. Generally cats don't like you to stare at them. People often make the mistake of eyeballing a cat in the hope of making friends, but the animal world doesn't work like that. They think you're an aggressor. Me, I tend to slightly avert my gaze for about ten seconds, signalling submission, before facing the cat. I also try and keep on their eye level. It's like a negotiation, a compromise of communication between the feline and human codes. I'm showing I understand, and that helps.

Or at least most of the time it does. With Purrl it was different. This time I was floored. Looking into her eyes knocked my senses for six. For once it felt like it was her that was analysing me, not the other way round. Was she seeing right into my soul? The dynamics were so different from those I was used to. I was the weak element, she was the strong, groping around inside my head. But only for a few seconds. Then there was a silence, a wall. It was as if she hadn't liked what she found. She gave her mouth a double lick of the tongue – a sure sign of feline displeasure – then spat out a cold, threatening hiss.

She deftly leapt down into the shadows under the table, where she quietly wove her way between the table legs, watching me.

'Awkward, huh?' I said to Rol.

Rol nodded. 'She's an odd one.'

'Do you . . . uh . . . think I could have a bit of time on my own with her?' I asked.

'Yeah. Fine. I'll go through and check on Marty.' Rol bent down and thrust his face under the table. 'Now you be a good little pussum-wussum, ey, Nilli.'

The cat just stared back blankly.

Rol sighed. 'Help yourself to any food. There's some fresh meat in the fridge and some tinned stuff in the top right-hand cupboard.'

Alone now, I could sense her.

I could feel my way to her problem, be there with her, bring to bear all my powers of empathy. Because empathy is what it's all about. To get to a cat, you have to think like a cat. You have to put yourself inside their skin, test out their bones,

24

stomp around inside their senses. Really go there. It takes a bit of imagination, a little bit of logic and a lot of learning, but it all adds up to some kind of grasp of the feline. Empathy is nothing new. How many human counsellors and psychologists have talked about it? And there's an art to it – it's not like I picked it all up the first time I met a cat. Empathy is a thing you get better and better at.

If you don't try it you never do it. Gabriel hasn't. Gabriel doesn't believe in empathy. He thinks it's impossible to get inside the head of any other human being, let alone an animal. But I know differently. When you've understood another person as completely as I understood Mina, you know the possibilities – same DNA or different. And the possibilities are mind-blowing.

Right at that moment, there, at the Bensons, with this cat, the whole empathy thing was hotting up. I was picking up a strange energy from Purrl. Neither exactly negative nor positive, it was just *there*. *She* was just there. She filled up the room. I could sense her loneliness calling out to me. It was plain to see that I was right, that she was jealous – she was jealous because she was so alone.

I had decided to give her the floor. Sitting down on the lino in the corner, I surveyed her environment. As my gaze slipped over the walls, floor and surfaces, I tried to work my mind into hers. Step one of the empathy routine: being there. *This is her territory . . . This is it . . .* It occurred to me that this cat had not been outside the room for a long time. The absence of a catflap in the patio door, the well-used cat litter by the bookshelf in the corner, the lack of even the trace of muddied paw-prints on the floor all told me that this was a cat in retreat. *These walls, these windows, they were the limits of her range.* Most rural cats take in a territory of about twenty-five acres, most suburban cats just 0.2 acres, but this cat . . . this cat had gone for even less. A retreat. But from what?

I looked around for more signs, tried to imagine the daily passage of her life. I breathed in the air, holding it, smelling it. With male cats I can sometimes even sniff out their favourite patches, their daily route around the house. A nose to the floor can tell me so much. I've developed a discriminating palate for feline scents. With just a sniff I can distinguish one set of cat urine from another. The smell of the Siamese has a slight ammoniacal tang, the Burman is more vinegary and Persians whiff of rotting flowers. All cats smell different, just like all humans. They each have a perfume of their own. All except this cat. With her I smelt nothing, a strangely scentless patch. I was intrigued.

Yet I did detect some things – signs here and there – but they weren't what was bothering me. There was something bigger than that, something more interesting, something I could feel. Yes, I knew she liked her wicker chair and a drink from the sink, and that she loved to sit on the window-ledge behind the gauze-covered goldfish tank and watch the fish. That was all the standard stuff. But it was nothing compared with the energy she was giving out, the sense of suffocation. There was a neediness there that sucked me in. I don't think I'd ever had empathy like this before.

I guess I must have tried to block it out for a while, just do my usual routine. I knew she was playing with me, so I let her. I let her sit on the chair till she got bored, then pretended to ignore her when she began her parade along the far edge of the kitchen cabinets. I was patient. I sat and waited. I waited and I watched and I waited, ever aware of her toying with me. She was a flirt. To begin with she behaved as if she wasn't interested, only every now and again casting a short glance in my direcion. Then, gradually, she became more curious, bolder and more reckless, darting short penetrating glares, eyes sucking me up. At one point she wandered along the back of the wall by the window, slinking behind the goldfish tank. She pretended to be watching the fish darting to and fro in the water. But I knew she wasn't. I could see her gazing through at me.

I, in turn, tried to look as casual as possible, breathing deeply and relaxing into my thoughts. I tried to empty my mind, focus on the texture of the lino, immunise myself to the feelings I was picking up. But I couldn't. I knew I had to face up to them. I had to move on. Step two of the empathy routine: showing you're there. Ten times as hard as just empathising with an animal is showing that you do, giving out your signals, telling them you understand.

And yet, wasn't I already doing it? Didn't Purrl already seem to know I was there? Maybe all this conscious effort I normally went to wasn't even necessary. The routine went on. The distance was maintained. Then, just as my own patience was beginning to ebb, she appeared to grow tired. She turned decisively and began to traverse the space between us. Slowly but boldly. As I sat in silence, she approached. She sniffed the air, then cautiously placed a paw on my leg. *Magic*.

I gave her a greeting murmur – 'mhrhrhrn' – short and light and friendly.

There was no reply.

'Mhrhhhnnhh,' I tried again, hoping if nothing else to amuse her.

She stretched out her long neck inquisitively, big eyes staring at me. She let me stroke her. Perhaps she was playing me on, perhaps she felt sorry for me.

Her fur was as soft as silk – so soft that I felt only the slightest tickle on my fingertips as they glided over her body. I could feel every perfectly formed bone. I traced the line of her ears, rising to acute points. I let my fingers drift along her back, feeling through to her spine and ribs, smoothing her hairs over her skin. She was thin. I repeated the action, this time pressing more firmly, testing her muscles. I stroked downwards across her face, scruffing up the fur underneath her chin, catching on something hard, a collar with a small, metallic disc. *So, she did come from somewhere* . . . I read it. 'Purrl', engraved in delicate curling letters. No number, no address, just a name. Purrl . . . Not like Nilli. *Purrl* . . .

Cat sense. That was all it took, the cat version of common sense. Within minutes I'd made my deductions. First, there was the attention problem. If the Bensons were going to hold on to this cat, they were going to have to devote a little more than their quick five minutes' feeding allocation a day. Just in the short time I'd spent with Purrl, her spirits had already lifted. Then there was the food. I'd understood that she didn't like the food that the Bensons were feeding her. She didn't like it because it was cold and dry and straight from the fridge. Is it surprising? Jaws used to claiming the warm blood of a freshly killed mouse don't take kindly to a slice of half-frozen turkey, even if it does come from the local delicatessen.

When I put a plate of warmed-up liver down on the floor, she pounced on it, responding generously to my logic. I'd rationalised my way to an answer and she was now willing to eat. But I knew it was more than that. Purrl was thanking me for breaking through her isolation. She was eating because we'd made contact. Contact is the thing. Contact that makes life worth living, that takes away the boredom. Just a moment can mean everything. I'd felt it too.

When I left she clung to my shoulder, claws sticking into my jumper as if trying to stop me from going. I could see it in her eyes as well. Even when

I'd turned away I could still feel them boring into the back of my head. A magnet in the room pulling me back. I left feeling strangely off-key. It was so heightened, so unreal. Those pale eyes had burned their way into my memory. That odd grace had fired my imagination. I was sure I'd be hearing from the Bensons again.

At home that evening I played with Tibbsy. I stared into his warm eyes, hoping for something. They glinted back playfully. Empathy, *empathy*, I thought, searching slit black pupils. But Tibbs wasn't going along with this. He squirmed and pulled away and started jumping on my chest and brushing his cheek against my face and clawing me, just like he always does – a ball of energy. He wanted to play. And maybe I wanted to play too. The simplicity of play.

~

Milla often tells me that she thinks I'd make a natural cat person. Not that she's obsessed with cats, of course, as she constantly reminds me, but there is a similarity in the appeal of cats and birds – though I don't quite see what that is.

We're close. I'm probably the first person she told about Purrl. And Lord, did she rave on. She was doing her natural-cat-person argument, trying to persuade me that I would really fall hook, line and sinker for the creature, just as she had done. It wasn't working. Much as I love her, I didn't come round to listen to speeches

30

about cats all night. That evening was particularly bad. It was beginning to turn into a monologue about one single cat. 'I feel like an infatuated teenager,' she declared, sighing and flopping on the sofa in front of me. I laughed. She looked petulant. Insulted almost, then laughed at herself.

For all that, she was, I admitted, sure to be right. If Milla said there was something special about a cat, then there must be. Milla after all could work a kind of magic with cats. Despite the seeming lunacy of her interest in the creatures, one thing you couldn't take away from Milla was that. Put her with a cat and things would happen. The cat would blossom. For instance Tibbs. He would otherwise be a dull, sluggardly slob of a cat, but in Milla's hands he turned into a playful ball of life. She had a way. When most people talk about a person having a way with animals they simply mean that person isn't scared of animals. My way with birds is like that. But Milla's 'way' is very different. There is an energy to it. It's as if she only ever comes alive in that moment. Some people do it with other people; she does it with cats.

I remember her telling me about her secret, as she called it. It was a typical child's story, one about her sister and her cat and how her parents never paid any attention to her and how she was never really that popular at school, but I listened, just like I always listen, and it was interesting, in a way. We were having one of those late-night, cheap-red-wine, revising-cranial-nerves types of session and for once it was Milla not me who had already had a few glasses too many. Not so much that she'd do anything stupid, but she kept getting her Latin names

31

mixed up . . . terms like exoccipital became oxeccipital. She was giggling a lot too. I'd asked her a question about the path of the fifth cranial nerve, which she clearly didn't know the answer to, and she avoided by coming back with another question. It's not very subtle, but it works.

'If you were an animal, what kind of animal would you be?' she asked.

She had an annoying habit of asking the most stupid questions as if there was something profound about them. Her clear, pale eyes would level themselves at you, goading you into an equally childish answer. 'Just try not answering me!' she seemed to be saying. This was one of those times and I knew where it was leading – Milla's questions were always questions she wanted you to ask her. Their logic was always transparent: I'd say bird, she'd say cat, she'd tell me the only creature in the world that has ever understood her is her cat, I'd smile, feel like leaning over and kissing her but, as ever, wouldn't, she'd say why start a relationship with a man if a cat's better company? I'd say, who's asking? And she'd imply what the two of us have is as good as it gets but there's no way she'd share her life with a man. Given the choice between a man and a cat, the cat wins.

Still, I answered the question. 'Battery hen.' It was a pathetic, half-hearted joke. I could see she was getting bored, but I didn't want her to go. I wanted her to stay. 'And don't think you're going to slither away like that . . . Path of the fifth cranial nerve or the cat gets it.'

'You're so irritating,' she tutted. 'I can never work out whether you've really got it, or if you're just very good at playing me along.'

I laughed slightly and started to pick at the piece of rubber that was peeling off the side of her trainer. Gorgeous Milla – it seemed right that she kept her distance, kept her secrets to herself. I could understand that as much as she could understand me holing myself up with my books on bird diseases. It didn't stop me wanting to know more though.

'Tell me then . . . Why not tell me?'

And for once she told me.

~

L ove, in my experience, has always been a bit of a punch in the guts. A huge, savage blow to the innards that leaves you winded and incapacitated. I was beginning to feel something like that already, as I sat, legs practically horizontal, in the dentist's chair.

Love, so they say, is partly about torture – and the dentist's drill is the greatest of all torture weapons. So, why shouldn't I find love at the dentist's?

Only weeks after the incident in the underground and after years of dental neglect, I had finally come to terms with the idea of going for a check-up. It was now time to face up to the realities of life, teeth and paying for dental care. For too long, I had been living in cowardly fear of the drill and the anaesthetic needle. For too long I had mumbled incoherently when my mother asked if I'd registered at a dentist's yet. Now was the time for my caries to be exposed, nerves to be tweaked and molars to be picked out. Now was the time for descaling and flossing. Now my cavities would be filled.

The truth is I would never have gone for that check-up if it hadn't been for one batty old client of mine, Lady Kitty. She somehow latched on to my fears when she witnessed me wincing over a lemon sorbet dished up to me on a house visit. 'Oooh, darling,' she'd said. 'A lady should be able to eat ice cream, one of the few pleasures in life.' And I suddenly found myself confessing that I hadn't been to the dentist's for the last five years and lived in mortal fear of men in white coats (something to do with my sister, I explained). Besides, I had my excuses. Only six months earlier I'd tried to book an appointment but found I'd been struck off the National Health list. That's what happens to people who stay away too long. According to the awkward old cow who answered the phone, my teeth no longer existed – the records had been lost or burned or dumped or whatever. I was a dental nobody. No National Health dentist would take a look at me.

Lady Kitty had the perfect solution. She'd been 'dentophobic', as she called it, herself for years and avoided them like the plague. Kitty had thought her beautiful teeth would last for ever, but then she'd lost three in the course of a month and realised that drastic measures were called for. Luckily she discovered this marvellous new surgery close to her home. It had the latest treatments – laser therapies, orthodontics, oral rehabilitations, the lot. Its staff were young. They were sympathetic and they knew how to calm a hysterical old lady. In fact they specialised in nervous cases and complementary treatments. Oral Magic was the practice's name and Kitty was under its spell.

When I trekked down Ivory Road to Oral Magic that day, it was for my second appointment. I'd already failed to turn up for the first one, my excuse being that I had flu and didn't want to pass it on to the unsuspecting victim who would be peering inside my mouth. They clearly weren't fooled. They knew it was nerves. All people, they say, who miss appointments are scared. It's transparent. Why else would there be so many cancellations?

Ivory Road, despite its name, is one of the scummiest roads in a posh area. The clinic, a newish simple building, looks oddly clean against the rubbish, rising up like a gleaming new crown against a row of plaque-caked and cracked teeth. A gang of kids with skateboards hanging out on the road gave me the once-over, setting me on edge. But I was OK. Oral Magic was magic. Inside was like heaven – all white and shiny and filled with nice clean people. Not the sterile whiteness of a geriatric hospital ward, but the smooth, comforting whiteness of a gallery space. Paradise. And the smell . . . It smelt like lavender oil and musk and beauty parlours, not the usual mouth-washy disinfectants.

'Dr Pride is running a little late,' said the smiley, deeply tanned receptionist. 'Would you like to take a seat for a while?' She pointed to some comfy-looking leather sofas arranged around a glass magazine-strewn table. The wall was covered with glamorous photos of beautiful faces and sparkling polished teeth. Huge shiny grins, smug and unbearable, hemmed me in. All I could see was dentibrite perfection. Whiter than white, among all these pearlies there was not one speck of plaque, not one hint of decay. I began to repent my sins. The error of my ways – the toffees, the Coca-Colas, the cakes and the pastries, the cigarettes, the half-hearted brushing and overall lack of flossing. These things catch up with you.

So, my teeth . . . How exactly do I feel about them? Most of the time I don't feel or even think. Some nights, I'll admit, I go to bed without brushing them and wake up early in the morning to find my mouth tasting of dead things, and my teeth tacky and plaque-smeared. Other times, though, I'll go through periods of manic brushing. I've tried dry-brushing, electric-brushing, finger-brushing, hard brushing, soft brushing. I've had herbal tooth-pastes, stripy toothpastes, stain-removing drops, tartar-control toothpastes and sugar-free gums of every variety. I've done brushless three-o'clock-in-the-morning finger smears across the front of my mouth. I often forget my toothbrush. I forget. I forget easily. I've never been big on routines.

There, in the waiting room, I grinned to myself, testing my mouth out. A blonde girl with braces sitting opposite me noticed and mugged back. Her pristine mother didn't see. The girl was sat there in her big black chair, swinging her legs and clacking her teeth together. *Zitface*, I thought, but kept quiet, wishing the noise would stop. For an instant I felt like walking over and pulling out every single one of those clicking braced teeth. Instead I ran my tongue around my mouth again.

These, then, are my teeth, soft and buttermilky – not the brilliant white of a Hollywood starlet, nor the dank yellow of a twenty-a-day smoker – just creamy-coloured, like old piano keys. If I run a tongue around my mouth I can feel the damage of the last twenty years since I swapped baby teeth for adult dead ends. There are holes. There are cavities. I have a gap – between my upper incisors – glaring out at me every time I smile. My gap is large and insolent. It refuses to be ignored. *Mind the gap*, it says. Sometimes I play with it, forcing the nail of my little finger into the space, running the tip of my tongue inside so you can see a pink sliver of flesh. How big is my gap? How much can I push inside? How much tongue does it take? In the geography of my mouth, it seems like a vast canyon. My obstinate gap.

As for the rest – the mapping of the rest of my mouth – there are many faults. I have irregular fangs. I have fillings. I follow them round. My tongue tip catches on a grazing point in my upper-left molars, where raspberry seeds and tomato skins get stuck and I have to prise them out using a cocktail stick or a fingernail. I worry that might be the edge of an expanding cavity. Then, on my lower jaw the surfaces are smoother, yet I am aware of another

37

nitch. But it's at the front that I start to get my fear of dying, of getting old, getting smashed in, toothless and impotent. It's there that my bite will fail – in my left central incisor. There's something too delicate about these lower teeth, too thin and tapering – like withering stumps on bad soil. I'm scared, if I push my strapping upper incisors against them, they might crumble, crack or simply fall out. The enamel is weak – it has been since childhood. The side effect of a heavy dose of antibiotics, or so my mother says.

But I've got good gums. That's one thing I have got – pink, fleshy and shiningly healthy, just like my mum's. Strong, robust gums run in my family. They never bleed. I can peel back my lips and know my teeth will never be blighted by a blot of vampiric blood. When I smile I flaunt them.

On the table, the dental-care leaflet *Make War on Decay* caught my eye. It was in one of those pamphlet holders, waiting for some militant tooth-brusher to take it away. The pictures of soldiers battling over a landscape of huge white mountains, some wielding gigantic toothbrushes, others paint-guns loaded with toothpaste, made me suppress a small giggle. The dentibrite boys in blue were fighting to the end against the nasty red-uniformed bacterial regiment. The drama that goes on inside your everyday mouth. I began to imagine the life and death scenarios that were taking place over my gums.

'Would you like a glass of water while you're waiting?' asked a nurse.

'No thanks.'

She smiled, revealing a set of immaculately white teeth. I half-smiled back, my lips sticking together as if by a resisting film of glue. I put down *Make War* and tried to distract myself by reading the restaurant reviews in some style magazine.

'Actually, I think Dr Pride is ready for you,' she interrupted. 'Would you like to follow me?'

I was taken on a tour of the white corridors and ushered through an open blue door into a room where a white-coated back was bent over some dental equipment.

'Hello, err, Camilla.' The man was studying a piece of paper while absent-mindedly introducing himself. 'I'm sorry we're running late.' He turned towards me. The slightly curling dark hair, the fleshy lips, the sparkling eyes all looked so familiar. A hand thrust out welcomingly.

Dr Pride was young and smiling and had warm, olive skin and long, full lashes. I cast my mind back to my man on the underground with the dog and felt my stomach flip. It was him: the one with the Weimaraner. Here he was. The same guy, but in a white coat, looking crisply clinical. This was a switch around. *Another chance at the game. Round two and I already had his name and profession.* My brain raced, my voice stuck in the back of my throat. 'Hello.' It came out croaky and barely there. Screwed up again . . . My mind was a mush.

He frowned and did a double-take. 'I'm sorry . . . Milla, isn't it? Of course, Milla.' A hand grasped mine, firmly and warmly.

'Yeah ... I'm sorry, err, I can't remember your ...'
I lied and watched his smile drop a little.

'Josh. It's Josh.'

'Of course,' I said. 'Quite a coincidence this, then!'

'Mmm ... Quite a coincidence,' he replied, shuffling his file of dental papers and taking up a professional composure. 'So, I guess you haven't been to the dentist's for a while? No records.'

'Just a couple of years. My old dentist's closed down,' I muttered too quickly.

'Mmm ... The last person who said they hadn't been in for a couple of years turned out to have not been for twenty years. There were only two live teeth left in his mouth.'

I laughed a little too loudly.

This was a potentially difficult situation. The false number – 434-6751 – flashed through my brain. Perhaps it would be better not to mention it. Glancing round, I noticed that the room was decorated with soothing minimalist prints and warm, peach-coloured curtains. There was music, Muzaky slush of some sort, playing in the background. I wrinkled up my nose.

'Mmm ... The music's a nice touch, though it's likely to cause more pain than the drill.'

'I can change it if you want,' he offered.

'Don't worry ... This will do.'

He gestured for me to take my jacket off. 'I'll hang that up for you.'

I immediately felt slightly self-conscious at the old jeans I was wearing. His hands brushed over my shoulders as he took the jacket from behind. I felt a tiny electric shock fizzle through my body.

'Is that my electric chair then?'

He lowered the chair. 'Take a pew.'

I cautiously sat down and within seconds found my legs tilted upwards and a blinding light shining in my face. I could now see only a silhouette shrouded in a halo of sterile white light. I blinked demonstratively, screwing up my nose.

'Is that a good position for you?' he asked teasingly. There was a softness in his voice that relaxed me.

'Well, I've always been a fan of the missionary.'

'The classics are always the best, but I can adjust it if you like.'

'Well, OK, but I think I have a personal preference towards keeping my feet below my centre of gravity.'

'Right . . . just hold on there and I'll tilt it over.' He started fumbling with a knob on the side. 'I'm happy to try it any way you like. There. If you can just put up with it for a couple of minutes we'll be fine . . . So, shall I just have a little look and see what's going on in there?'

'I guess so.'

Josh gathered his shiny metallic implements together. 'Don't worry, I used to hate dentists myself. I suppose this is my way of getting over it, getting my revenge. Now I get to be in control.'

He was holding a set of forceps – the kind they use for removing teeth. From the position I was in they looked enormous.

41

'You are *not* using that on me.'

'Sorry, just putting them away,' he said, reaching towards his tray. 'I thought you might prefer this.' It was one of those hook-like metal probes.

Personally I would have preferred nothing. Or just a quickie – an open and close of the mouth, a 'that's perfect' and out within seconds. But it clearly wasn't going to happen.

'I thought I was coming in for a dental check-up, not an induced delivery.'

I opened my mouth wide. Christ knows what it must have been like down there. A huge pink abyss, teeth, fillings, saliva, tiny bubbles clinging to reddish membranes, slime, remnants of today's corn flakes that I didn't get rid of in my morning brush, huge silvery fillings and a deep, dark, cavernous cavity. The lot.

'Mmmm . . . You've got beautiful gums,' said the dentist. 'Not a spot of peridontal disease.'

'Yea, Uy gnow,' I garbled. I felt myself beginning to blush.

'And you've got great canines. Perfectly shaped, almost like a dog's.' He turned away and made some notes. 'So, do you like dogs?'

Dogs? Canines? *Right, dogs . . . like Weimaraners.* We were playing some kind of game then. I laughed nervously, realising what he was getting at.

I had to say something. I couldn't go on pretending. I had to confess. 'Err . . . Dr Pride, you remember how I gave you my phone number . . .'

Too late. He thrust a mirror in my mouth before I could get any further.

'Listen, I know it sounds stupid.' He peered inside my mouth, avoiding my eyes. 'After all, I asked you for it. But, well, I'm a dentist, as you can see, and I have to wash my hands, really thoroughly . . . Oh, hell, that's a pathetic excuse. I just forgot to transfer the number, and gradually it wore off so I could barely read it all, and I couldn't work out whether one of the numbers was a 7 or a 1 and I thought about phoning both but didn't. I still might have done though!'

He took the mirror out of my mouth again.

'You didn't?' I asked. 'You didn't phone?' My stomach constricted as I realised the guessed number he was talking about would have been mine, the correct number. 'No, that's right, you didn't.'

'But I wish I had.'

'You do?'

'Well, no dentist could forget a smile like yours.'

A short silence followed, while I blushed. 'I think I should mention that I was a little nervous about coming here.'

'Sorry, I wasn't getting a bit carried away, was I?'

'Actually, I was just about to say I'm fine now,' I lied.

'Really?'

'Yes.'

'Well, in that case, you won't mind if we get on . . .'

This time my mouth opened as if by remote control.

My heart was racing and breath had quickened. I felt the blood surging round my body, rushing to my skin. I wanted to gulp, but my mouth was open. His face was close to mine. His head was practically inside my mouth. He was so absurdly close and if it weren't for the mirror implement in my mouth, I felt sure I could have just reached up and given him a kiss. I could feel his breath on my face, his hands almost brushing against my nose.

Gulp . . . His hook was scraping away at the bottom of one of my teeth, gouging away at my mouth. I was just thinking of gnashing my teeth down on him, when I heard a whisper. Soft and fluttering. '*You might not realise this, but when I got up the escalator and walked to the park I suddenly decided to turn back and try and talk to you again. But, of course, you'd gone.*' His voice was deep, low and whispered. My stomach somersaulted. 'You may need just one tiny filling at the back there.' I could feel the probe sticking in my tooth, catching in the decayed part. The saliva was welling up in the corners of my mouth.

The dentist's I'd been to as a kid had never been like this. Mr Bart had been a doddery old man who liked nothing better than to get out the needle. Mr Soanes had had a passion for the drill. Together, they put the fear of death into me. I remember the time when I was thirteen years old, and Bart must have got the anaesthetic wrong, because he tried to

44

whip one of my teeth out, only I could feel every single yank at it. I screamed in agony, but only heard him saying, 'Don't be silly, Milla, it's just one little tooth.' Dentists have always made me feel nauseous.

'Are you all right?'

'Gno,' I garbled.

'OK . . . Let's take a breather!'

I picked up the glass and slooshed the water round inside my mouth, then spat in the metal bowl-sink at the side of me, feeling a little self-conscious. He stood over me for a few seconds just watching.

I leaned back. 'OK.'

'Just one more look and that's it.' There was a slight moment of hesitation, as if he didn't quite feel any contact with me was right, then he inserted his thumb into my mouth. He ran it around my gums, feeling up where my wisdoms were budding through. I felt the warm slide of his skin against my gum. 'That's strange . . . Your wisdoms are late, very late. There's still no sign of them.' Then he whispered again. '*Maybe we could meet for a drink sometime, or go for dinner.*' He pulled away, as if he'd said nothing, and made a half-smile. Was I imagining things? I tried to stop the crimson flow of blood to my face. 'Yup, just one filling. I'll put that down, upper-left second molar. As a special client, I can try and fit you in sometime next week.'

I felt intensely awkward. *Say something, anything, but say it now . . .*' I . . .'

45

'I was . . .' he said at the same time. Then gestured for me to go on, but I'd already nodded at him.

'I was wondering if . . .' Was wondering . . . Was wondering . . . A flurry of broken words came tripping out over each other.

It was then that the nurse walked in.

'I think we'll put Miss Hall down for sometime in the next couple of weeks. I want to get her done as soon as possible,' Josh said. He placed his hand on my arm and I felt a tingle flutter down my back. But all remained professional and he scrawled out a spidery trail on an appointment reminder sheet handed to him by the nurse. 'I'll see you then,' he said, thrusting it quickly into my hand. 'See you soon.'

I walked out into the street, and saw crowds of perfect teeth. There are teeth all over the place: chomping and biting and cracking and grinning and grinding. In everyone's mouth they chatter away. On the street, it's not so bad: some have gaps, some are crooked, some are nicotine yellow, some are dentures, some have crowns, some have braces. Some, like mine, are just average. On a billboard I glimpsed a perfect smile, an anonymous model flashing her perfect pearlies. Wasn't it enough that she earned thousands and thousands, without having beautiful teeth to boot. I was disillusioned. With teeth like mine, how could I possibly stand a chance with a dentist?

My mind was in a whirl. The humiliation! I'd given too much of myself away. I'd given the back of my throat, and a blush and a stammer and a pint of saliva. *Can a dentist be struck off for cavorting with his client?* I wonder.

I'll have to ask Gabriel.

~

I knew something must be going on. It was so obvious. Although Milla didn't tell me directly, I could tell she was distracted because she stopped phoning so often and appeared abnormally cheerful and energetic when she did. Life for her was good – and that could mean only a man or a cat.

I know what Milla thinks of me. Milla thinks I'm the fount of all knowledge just because I read a lot and remember it. I'm all work and no play. I work too hard. 'You should learn how to relax, Gabe. Slow down, there's a whole world out there.' And it's true, my work is important to me, the most important thing in my life, though my mum would probably say I'm just an old-fashioned romantic looking for love and all that will change when I find the right woman.

Maybe so. Actually, for a brief moment I had thought I'd found the right woman in Melanie. I was fooling myself, but you only realise that in retrospect. Melanie was a distraction that could never live up to my expectations. She could never be as good-looking as Milla, as clever as Milla or as difficult to pin down as Milla. I always preferred working to spending time with her anyway.

~

So, maybe my teeth aren't so bad, after all.

'Did you know George Washington had dentures?'

Josh, on our first date, nervously making small talk as he stood gazing into a glassy cabinet of eighteenth-century false teeth. Ochrous and brown-stained, those old-fashioned falsies still looked like they might come to life and take a bite. 'There's a portrait of him, one of the famous ones, and apparently he had only one tooth left in his mouth. The artist had to pad his lips out with cotton.'

'Mmmm . . . Thank Christ for medical progress,' I murmured, thoughts distracted by the sight of the metallic Erada, a form of early dental drill that looked like an elaborate torture device. 'The pain they must have gone through back then.'

Yes, the pain. The teeth. The pain. After just a couple of minutes lingering in the dusty corridors of the top floor of a science museum, I was rapidly becoming aware of a psychosomatic ache in one of my lower-left molars and I was desperately trying to think of something to talk about other than teeth. It was all Sophie's fault. Sophie had advised me that a museum was a good place to go on a first date. 'It's so perfect,' she said. 'Even if you have nothing else to talk about, you can always make facile comments about the exhibits. Fills up the awkward silences.' Perhaps I'd chosen the wrong museum. The Archimedean drills and tooth-extracting forceps were reminding me of the dreams I'd been having over the last week. Trust my dentist to have found the dentures display.

My dreams, since my appointment, had featured a lot of teeth. Or, more specifically, they'd been haunted by a huge, terrifying drill. The diameter of the bit was the size of my mouth at full stretch. It roared like a full-scale pneumatic. It whirled so fast that, as it touched the edges of my mouth, it peeled away a layer of skin. It was so long it touched the back of my throat and made me want to retch. And now, here in the museum, every time I looked at anything vaguely dental, I started to feel queasy.

'The stuff I'm practising will seem barbaric in a hundred years' time,' Josh commented. 'Look at this . . . a tooth transplantation. I can't believe they tried *tooth transplantation* back then! Lunacy.' He turned and glanced at me, smiling, his dark eyes twinkling under the ceiling spots. The light was warm and flattering and I felt my guts twinge as his smile grew.

'You really are obsessed with teeth, aren't you?'

'Me? Not at all. Do I seem it?'

'Just a little.'

'Well, I am standing in front of a rack of dentures, and it is my job, and just remember, you brought me here.'

'Mmmm . . . my mistake.'

He grinned. 'Sorry. Am I turning into nerd of the year? Shall we move on? I swear I won't mention anything remotely dental for the rest of the afternoon.' He touched me gently on the back, guiding

49

me towards the next set of cabinets. The pressure sent a tingle fluttering down my spine.

Cabinet H4 contained the equipment relating to eighteenth-century obstetrics. This was safer ground.

'So, Milla,' Josh said, leaning forwards and frowning at a large set of rusted iron forceps, 'you know loads about me. You know what I do for a living, that I have a dog, that I am *obsessed*, as you, with teeth – but I hardly know anything about you. What do you do?'

I laughed, looking up from the cabinet and finding I'd plunged straight into those deep brown eyes. 'Guess.'

He shrugged helplessly.

'Give it a try! What do I look like?'

'Beats me . . . Astronaut.'

'Very funny. Go on, guess . . . properly!'

'MI5 spy.'

'Come on! Play the game.'

'I dunno . . . I'm useless. Just tell me! I'll never get it.'

'Cat therapist.' I never know quite what to say, so I just blurt it out.

'I didn't think people did jobs like that.'

'Well, I do.'

He let out a light, low chuckle and screwed up his eyebrows, thoughtfully appraising me. 'Cat therapist? So, what does that involve? Sitting in an armchair asking a cat to tell you its latest dreams?'

'Not quite, but almost. You know, I just go and

sort out any problems people have with their cats. It's quite simple.' I was being deliberately cryptic, playing at being mysterious, hoping to draw him in. We were walking now, barely looking at the exhibits, staring absent-mindedly at the abstract shapes in the cases.

'Well, it can't be that simple. It's not as if you can just sort out a cat's problems by talking to them like humans.'

'I have my ways.' I tried an enigmatic smile.

'I suppose that means you get all soppy and wet over cats.'

'Not exactly soppy. But I am a bit of an animal person. I like cats. I like dogs,' I lied, not wanting to ruin my chances with this handsome dog owner. This wasn't the time, I suspected, to say I like cats and solely cats – that I don't really take to dogs, that I think dogs are a biological mistake. 'You're a dog person, Josh, I can tell that. It says a lot about you.'

'Oh yeah, what?' he said, pausing to look at a rigid iron orthopaedic cage. 'I'll bet that was uncomfortable.'

'Mmm ... For instance, you're Zara's pack-leader.' I could see his reflection in the glass of the cabinet, fragile and fleeting, his white shirt like a ghost on the glass.

'That's good to know.'

'And,' I said, 'dogs appeal to people who like power. I reckon you're a power freak, Josh.'

'I hardly feel it,' he said, pressing his nose up against the glass to read one of the labels. 'Orthopaedic correction frame, used as a demonstration model for students . . . Looks like a cross between a set of armour and an S&M suit . . . Actually, you're wrong. I'm not a dog person at all. In fact, until I got Zara I wasn't really a pet person of any sort.' He turned back, allowing me to see that his smile had dropped a little. Suddenly he looked troubled. 'Zara was my best mate Colin's dog. That's how I got her.'

I nodded encouragingly, sensing there was more.

'Getting on to the grim stuff now, aren't you?' he said, smiling helplessly. 'Well, no point holding it back . . . Colin died in a boating accident about two years ago. I was looking after Zara at the time. We were very close and he loved his dog, was utterly devoted to her. I couldn't see her go to anyone else. I had to take her.'

'Oh, God,' I muttered, my voice echoing through the room pathetically. 'It must have been awful.'

'Yes . . . He was fished out of the water after falling overboard. It was a stupid, pointless accident. He'd been mucking around, peeing over the side of the boat.'

'Sorry.'

'Don't worry! It's OK . . . I don't mind talking about it. Anyway, to me, Zara was Colin personified. A little bit of him reincarnated. The one bit I have left.'

'So you're a converted dog person now.' I tried pushing the conversation in a new direction, stopping to examine a new display. We were in the section labelled 'Quacks and Alternative Remedies'.

'Yup – a Zara person,' he said, half-smiling. 'And I'm not a power freak in the least little bit.'

'So you say! But still, I'm not so sure. Maybe we can find out in here.' I pointed to the large case of bald white busts in front of me, illustrating the various phrenological types. 'Maybe your bumps will tell us.'

'Quick-tempered, lazy, stubborn,' he read out, skimming over some of the labels. 'I don't think any of those fit . . . Where's charming, patient, angelic? I'm not sure anybody would be able to make any sense of my head.'

'Come on, I'll bet we can work something out.'

'Well, I do have one *very* odd bump.'

'Really?'

'Yeah, really weird. I've had it since I was a kid.' He placed his fingertips on the top of his head. 'Just about here.'

'What kind of bump is it?'

'Here,' he said, bending his head towards me, taking my breath away. 'Feel it.'

Josh took hold of my hand and raised it up to his head. Just the sensation of his touch against my skin sent a brief shock through me. It made me smile a little. Was this a seduction? Was it an excuse to make me touch him? Or was it a simple clinical demonstration? His fingers rested on top of mine, guiding them through his hair to the spot. That hair was soft and silky, like it had just been washed. Downy. My index finger skimmed across his warm scalp.

53

'There,' he said, pushing down on them so that I was massaging my fingertips in circles and I could feel an outward-jutting ridge. It was hard and bony, as if the skull had been slightly misshapen. 'Feel it?'

But I was no longer interested in that. Yes, I could feel a bump, but what fascinated me was not the bump, but the whole head, the whole body, the whole Josh, everything about him, every story and every stupid joke. All I could do was try to control my breath and not look flustered as I faced his smiling eyes. I tried to look as nonchalant as possible.

'Yes, got it,' I murmured.

He was still looking at me. I was aware of the fact that my body was close to his, just inches away, that the barrier of personal space had been transgressed and, though I tried to distract myself, I wondered if this might be the moment to reach up and brush those lips with my own, to start the something that was promised in us just being there together. I was, however, frozen to the spot, my nervous system paralysed, unable to make the leap of contact across the gulf between our two bodies. I couldn't move, though every axon, every dendrite in my frame was buzzing. My senses were alive and bared. They were attuned to everything. My whole surroundings. I suddenly became aware of the fact that the floor was quiet and so silent and deserted. Apart from a few kids scuttling in and out of the spotlit shadows, it was desolate – like a ghost town. Our breaths seemed loud and echoey and I felt like whispering. Speech messages pulsed from my brain to my throat.

A word almost came to my lips . . . but not quite soon enough and, without warning, he ducked out, breaking my contact. 'I don't think it means anything – I think I banged it when I was a kid, that's all.' And that was it. The spell was broken and suddenly we seemed to be moving, on the march again, accelerating through the medical ages.

Why the retraction?

I was confused. Perhaps I had misunderstood the signs. Perhaps he wasn't looking for love. Perhaps he already had a girlfriend.

That would be just typical. After all, interesting men always had girlfriends. All the single men I'd met lately had been the same: selfish, inconsiderate oafs. They'd had no imagination, were impossible to talk to and their idea of a good night was a couple of conversationless drinks down the pub, followed by an anticlimactic shag back home. Friends of mine had introduced me to bankers and City people, but they just weren't my type, and I never met a single man at work. The people I met through work generally turned out to be batty old dears with too much money to spend on bizarre animal treatments and gourmet cat dinners, and gardeners who weren't even good-looking enough to be a diversion. The last guy I went out with turned out to be something entirely different from what he told me. When we met, he said he was a photographer. It was only when, three months down the line, I bought him a UV lens for his birthday and he said, 'What's this for?' that I discovered he was an estate agent whose experience with cameras was limited to one old Instamatic his mother had given him on his twelfth birthday. That was it. I don't like being lied to. I stumbled out of his house in the middle of a football match and never answered one of his calls again. That was another dead end. Sometimes I'd look around and think that maybe there's no one in the world for me. Perhaps my expectations were too high. Perhaps I should have settled for Gabriel. Was there no one I considered good enough for me, who also thought that I was good enough for them?

Still, Josh must have known this was a date he'd committed himself to. There could have been no mistaking it for anything else. And besides, we were getting on so well. As Josh and I drifted among the ghostly masks, preserved specimens, strange pots and weird potions, the conversation flowed. His presence filled the quiet, low-lit hall, making me laugh and exciting me. Sometimes, in the glow of a ceiling spot, he'd look fierce and frightening, his blackish hair and darker eyes almost vampiric. Sometimes, in the corners, he'd look soft and pretty and gentle. Sometimes he made me tremble. He was teasing and funny, but not afraid to be open. He was handsome and strong-looking, but not too vain. He made me laugh. He told me I looked like one of the shrunken heads in the 'Curiosities' section. He told me about the time he'd fainted when giving blood. He told me he had a voracious appetite for science. He even confessed to having a crazed obsession with obscure sci-fi movies. In return, I confessed to liking weepies. We were charmed by each other. We were not too similar, but not too different.

We talked about families – always a good sign. 'So . . . got any brothers or sisters?' he asked, pouncing on a short-lived break in our conversation with a stock question.

'Not really. Well, one sort of half-sister you might say. It's a bit complicated.' I thought it was best not to go into the Mina thing. Not just yet. 'You?'

'Nope. Only child. I always wanted a brother though – you know, someone other than your parents to fight with. That would have been good, someone else to blame for all the bad stuff I got up to.'

'Mmmm . . .' I said. 'Brothers and sisters are good like that.'

Later, we found ourselves lingering in the mummification section. Josh stared for a long time at the curled-up, contorted form of a sand-buried Incan woman, while I studied the tiny cat mummies in the corner. The Egyptians, I nodded to myself, knew what they were doing.

'Egyptians worshipped cats, we turned them into fertiliser. That says a lot. Would you believe that back in the nineteenth century a whole load of

Egyptian cat mummies were brought over here and sold as fertiliser?' I muttered.

'Do you ever think,' Josh asked distractedly, 'that you wish you had a hundred lives to live? That you'd love to do everything, be everyone. Like say, for instance, this woman here. I wonder what her life was like.' The skinny figure was shrivelled and grey, covered by a thick, reddish shawl, and with a long plaited wig of hair. 'She looks pretty pained there, but then all mummies do – it's the way the skin shrinks back from their faces so they look like they're screaming. But what was her life like? What's your life like? What's anybody's life like?'

I laughed. 'Mmm . . . Sometimes I wish I had nine lives – like a cat.'

'I'd love to live that guy's life . . . The old guy round the corner with the spectacles and the note-book – looks like a historian or something. I'd love to be that kid we saw earlier by the magic masks . . . All of them. But somehow, I've just ended up being a dentist.'

'A dentist is a good thing,' I said, edging forward a few steps to stand next to him, to peer inside the glass case containing the Incan woman. Now I could see not only the contorted lines in her thick, leathery skin but also Josh's reflection in the glass. I could feel his shirt-sleeve brushing against my bare arm. I could smell him. I imagined I could sense everything about him. I wondered what it would take to get closer.

'A dentist is a square thing and you know it. It's not a grand thing.'

'Hey, hey,' I cried, turning to glance directly into his eyes. 'Listen to yourself . . . Who was the guy who was ranting on about teeth earlier? You're fascinated by your job. You know it's important. People need teeth. Where would we be without them? We'd all be gummy and toothless like George Washington if it weren't for dentists.'

He didn't laugh. He was looking pensive. 'Yeah, I guess it's true. And it *is* true that the first thing I notice about a person is their teeth.'

'Oh, really?' I said, feeling his dark pupils burning into the back of my eyes, feeling my heart leap inside my chest. 'And what do you notice about my teeth?' I pulled my lips into a wide grin.

He smiled, as if it was something he had thought about, noticed, possibly even was waiting for the opportunity to say. 'The gap – the gap between your front two teeth, that tiny, millimetre-thick space. I like gaps.' He nodded, his face coming up close to mine, studying my lips and teeth. I could almost feel his breath tingling across my face. He touched my arm.

There was a gap, a silence that needed to be filled by a kiss. It lingered in the air, floating there, threatening like a black hole to suck everything in – and I thought yet again that it might pass. It might be lost and we might go nowhere, but still instead of plunging and taking the initiative I opened my mouth to speak. 'I was thinking about having it . . .'

But before I had time to finish my sentence I found a set of warm lips clamped on mine, an electrical thrill running down my spine, a sweet warmth enveloping me . . . and I knew there was no point arguing. This was it. It was happening, so fast, in the middle of the day in a museum of all places. It was wet and woozy and it took away my breath. I was queasy with love and bold too, almost not like me any more. I pulled out, laughing, slightly embarrassed and still – though I knew it was a date, and these things are meant to happen on a date – slightly bewildered. In the distance I could hear a kid wailing, 'You said we could have ice cream!'

I could feel blood rushing, legs swaying. 'I don't want you to think I'm in the habit . . .' I began, but he put his fingers to my lips and stopped me.

'Come back to my place . . . Please.'

I was glad we went to his place not mine – even though I'd spent that entire morning rearranging my furniture, vacuuming the floor and sticking Jemima's china cats in random hiding places. This was all so unlike me, so very Mina-ish, and feeling Mina-ish is always a good sign. (Mother would be pleased with me.) I'd even gone as far as hiding the economy tomato soup at the back of the cupboard and placing all my most interesting books in conspicuous spots. But it was still better that Josh didn't see it. Better that I kept a few secrets. I preferred getting a glimpse of his smooth, ordered world to letting him poke his nose into mine.

When I finally got home the following day, I was even more glad. Coming back from fresh white sheets and neatly stacked shelves, my flat looked dirty and cluttered. It's a little embarrassing really – but I love this place. One of the few lucky breaks in my life, left to me by Jemima Spall, the author of *A Commune of Cats*, it's got something nowhere else has. And there's part of me that wants to keep it how it is, in her memory. My lucky break . . . Who would have believed it? How could I have imagined the events that would follow my writing to the eccentric, intellectual old spinster, telling her how much I had enjoyed her book? We met and that was it. I lodged with her for a while, bunking down in the front room of her flat. Then, finally, when she keeled over, found I was left the lot – in gratitude for my friendship. I loved the place. From the outside it looked dark and dingy, but inside it was a palace of mirrors, books and kitschy cat ornaments.

I suspected that Josh might not fall for its cluttered romance. That morning, I wondered if I fell for it myself. To add to the general mess, Tibbs had managed to knock over the vase of flowers I'd arranged on the table and dumped a dead mouse on the bathroom. I guess he must have been missing me. As soon as I walked through the door he was there at my legs, brushing up against my skin and scenting me – soft ginger hair on bare skin. Real warmth. I got down on my knees and rubbed noses, felt whiskers prickling over my face. He sniffed me. New smells . . . more new smells . . .

I like to fool myself that Tibbs knows everything. But I know he doesn't. He's just not that kind of cat.

Not everything in the cat world is as obvious as it seems to us humans. Sometimes we misinterpret. Sometimes we, arrogant know-it-alls that we are, translate a cat gesture as exactly the opposite of what it is. We see a 'no' where there's really a 'yes'.

Which is exactly what happened with the Bensons. It was inevitable that they would run into more trouble with Purrl – I'd almost sensed it. Out of the blue, I suddenly got the urge to give Rowe a ring. It was strangely out of character for me. I'm generally not that good at keeping in touch; unless someone calls me I won't contact them.

The phone rang about fifteen times before it was picked up and at first I thought I must have got a bad line because all I could make out was an abstract whine. Then I realised it was Rowe. I had to ask her to repeat herself. 'Sorry, I can't . . .' That was when she started shrieking and I realised I was in the middle of something.

'Milla! You brought this on me. Who do you think you are? That cat tried to kill my baby!' she screeched. 'That bitch of a cat!'

'What?'

'Nilli. She's lethal!'

Not able to work out what she was on about, or where this was coming from, I wondered if I should just quietly and deliberately put the phone down. Luckily, Rol decided to interrupt on their other phone line. 'Come on, darling,' he said to her. '*Hello, Milla!* Now, just put the phone down. *I'm sorry about this, Milla. I'm afraid you've called at the wrong time.* Put the phone down, Sweetpea.'

'Like hell, I'm putting the phone down! That cat's a mu –'

'Calm down, dear . . . Calm down, angel . . . Calm down. I'm coming through.'

The phone clicked off at one end and there was a long silence behind which I could barely make out random mutterings and wails. Eventually, unable to make any interpretation, I hung up. It wasn't until Rol rang back five minutes later that I was given the full story.

It had been a Saturday night like any other in the Benson household. Having tucked little Marty up in bed, the Bensons had settled down to an evening of TV game shows, hot chocolate and home-made caramel crunch biscuits. The only thing out of the ordinary was that it was a surprisingly quiet night. Marty seemed to fall almost immediately asleep and they barely heard a peep from him. At the end of the evening, when the game shows had run out and they'd found there wasn't an interesting late-night film to switch over to, Rol decided to go and feed the cat, while Rowe went through to check on Marty. All this was perfectly normal. However, Rol was surprised to find that Purrl, or rather Nilli, wasn't around: neither poised expectantly on the shelf above the food bowl nor sat regally on her chair. She was nowhere to be seen. He called out to her a few times, scratched his head and got on with the business of warming her shiny red lamb's kidneys.

It was then that he heard a terrifying wail. Rising like the howl of an animal, it echoed through the house and down the street. And it was coming from little Marty's bedroom.

When he reached the bedroom, it was just in time to see the cat hurtling through the air and slamming against the wall. Rowe was screaming, tears gushing down her face. Turning her back, barely noticing Rol, she reached down into the cot and pulled her baby up to her chest. 'My baby,' she moaned. 'My baby . . .' Hugging Little Marty into her breasts, she rocked backwards and forwards repeating it: 'My baby.'

It was Rol who saved Purrl. He was distraught and distressed, but he had the clear-sightedness to deal with the situation. When Rowe started kicking the cat he intervened. 'Stop that!' he said. 'You're being hysterical.'

'But, Marty,' she sobbed.

There was a muffled snuffle from her chest. Rowe looked down, appearing almost startled. Little Marty gurgled, then he started groaning, then he started wailing. 'He's alive!' she screamed. 'My baby's alive!'

Since then, Rowe had been determined that the cat should be put down. ' "It's only right, only just. It isn't worth the risk," ' Rol quoted her. ' "The cat is a natural-born killer." I can see her point of view,' he commented. 'And I only want to do what's right.'

64

Before I could say anything about what was and wasn't right, Rowe came back on the other phone with a fresh stream of vitriol. She hadn't wanted that cat around the house any more. She didn't want to hear its name again. She just couldn't bear it. Yes, she was being irrational, but surely everyone could understand. She was dealing with a murderer. 'So don't worry, Milla,' she said. 'Rol has already had her put down.'

It was a sad tale to hear. My sympathies went out to Purrl. The cat had found herself in an unfortunate situation. And it was all the more unfortunate, because it was clear to me what her motivations were. Far from jealousy, Purrl had been showing her affection. Cats do that sort of thing. She had been hugging Marty's face like a kitten to its mother. It was love – and that is surely no crime. No trial for her, though. Poor Purrl . . . she was only a cat.

I couldn't believe Rol would have had her put down. Not level-headed, dependable, cat-loving Rol. So I made some investigations. Rol was a little too cagey about the whole affair. Whenever I asked about it, he would act shifty and change the subject quickly. 'I did what was right,' he repeated again and again. But how to find Purrl if she was alive? I asked my vet friend Gabriel to get on the case. If anyone heard any news of an albino queen, it would be him. Gabriel might not have been much of a talker but he heard everything. Anything that he didn't catch drift of, quite simply did not happen.

*

It was then that I first began to dream about Purrl. During the nights my mind would conjure up images of her prowling the streets in the darkness, an ethereal white figure pacing the alleys and pavements, clambering across the roofs. Some nights, she would be there in my front room, sitting on the window-seat, watching me hauntingly. Other times she would just be there, big and almost terrifying, the same size as me. Once I dreamt I met Purrl in the form of a young girl, all skinny, with white-blonde hair like Mina. She's stood there in a garden, fishing in a tiny pond and giggling constantly. I watch her from a distance at first, then see she's caught this salmon that must weigh a lot, about twenty-eight pounds. 'That's a big one,' I say. She just smiles. 'I like fish,' I say, weighing the salmon up in my hands. 'I like them too,' says she.

~

Everybody has a problem. Mine – among others – is that I've never met a woman that I've liked quite as much as Milla. So it should be no surprise if I'm not entirely enthusiastic about any relationships she has with other men. Josh, for instance. It seemed so odd when Milla rang me up and went on at great length about this love affair she was having with her dentist. Milla was generally so reticent and secretive and not prone to this sort of infatuation at all, and I couldn't help thinking that something must be up. I wondered if she was having one of her twin moments. After all, you couldn't rely on her being entirely consistent – there were these occasional bouts where she started to believe she was her sister. Funny gestural patterns and alien phrases that would come out every now and again. Sometimes I'd catch her at it and she wouldn't even have realised.

A dentist. Professionally very suspect, I told her (half jokingly), then tried not to be too negative about the whole thing. Maybe I was just a little jealous. After all, normally she'd be stuck on some cat she was treating – but a man? As always, I remembered the stuff she'd told me about never sharing her life with any man and couldn't help feeling a little resentful. I blanked my ears to the sound of her voice and muttered frequent listless affirmatives to try and halt the flow, which she must have picked up on, because she changed the subject. To cats, of course.

There was that skinny white albino that she was trying to track down. What was it she called it? Purrl . . . yes, Purrl was the name. 'This is the cat for me,' she pronounced. 'I swear it. There's something about her that just sets my heart pounding. She's so beautiful. Come on, Gabriel. Ask around. I'm sure you can find out something about her.' It was funny that she said this, because I'm hardly the world's greatest detective. Yes, when it comes to bird diseases, I've got a keen eye and a good memory, but tracking down cats? It's true, sometimes I do catch the odd bit of news from old Ida, almost unintentionally, but these days Milla knows Ida as well as I do. She can go direct to source. 'I know you'll find something,' she kept repeating, and I felt the urge to put the phone down but didn't. The really irritating thing was she still hadn't asked about my mother, who'd just gone into hospital to have a mastectomy.

'I'll do my best,' I said, 'but, look . . . let me call you back later. I've got to go over and see Mum now. Visiting hours.'

That was just about frosty enough to work. She became apologetic and immediately did her best to cheer me up and make me laugh – the desired effect. No one can ever feel angry with Milla for very long, particularly when she's sensitive to it. And on this occasion she was. She kept repeating how good it was to talk to me, how I was her best friend and it was so good that we could always rely on each other. 'You know I love you, Gabe!' she cooed, but I couldn't bring myself to reply.

~

Gabriel, in fact, turned up nothing.

That is, nothing more concrete than a few fleeting mentions of a sighting of a white cat, which yes, upon reflection, did have something odd about it, but no, hadn't been spotted again. What I did find out about Purrl came from an entirely different source – my friend and dental adviser Lady Kitty Wendersby-Jones. The Divine Kitty, as she was often known, was an eccentric and grossly rich old lady. Once the belle of the City, she now lived on her own with about twenty cats, which she pampered from dawn to dusk. Lady Kitty's name, I think, wasn't even Kitty. Her bank account, I noticed, was under the name P. Wendersby-Jones, and when I once asked her what the P stood for, she looked at me bewildered, as if I was making up some wild story.

Kitty is a class act. She's the kind of old crank who

would greet you at the door draped in diaphanous fabrics and antique jewels, carrying one of her perfectly preened Persians and muttering some sort of Eastern chant. She's a moneyed old eccentric who lost her marbles years ago. Apparently she'd been quite a rebel in her youth – driving around with all sorts of young men in the twenties and thirties, staying up late and partying – and she'd been married a grand total of six times. But her cats were now her sole family. 'My kitties and I are spiritually one,' she would often say, and wandered round the house chanting, 'Puss, puss', from dawn to dusk.

On this particular occasion when I went to visit the Divine Lady K, it was a green day. 'Millsie, daarling.' She kissed me four times. 'I have entered *une période verte*. Green is the way.' In other words, she was dressed entirely in green, from her floaty mint kaftan to her viridian eyeshadow. Her cats all sported an apple-green ribbon, dinner was served on twenty perfectly lined-up porcelain plates and a 'Sounds of the Hills' tape played in the background. 'Green is the colour of peace, tranquillity and a oneness with nature,' she said, as she handed me a drink of Crème de Menthe. 'Let your spirit atune.' She was looking skyward, with her hands hovering in the air, then she gestured towards a fluffy creature in the corner. 'Pootie is atuned. I can feel her aura. She is in a pasture. We are both in a pasture.' Needless to say, Kitty had lately been to see a colour therapist, who had recommended that one of her pussums, a large

Siamese tom called Mr Skaratch who had taken to threatening the others and starting a good few fights, needed the calming influence of green.

The colour therapy had obviously yet to take effect and Mr Skaratch was the reason why I'd been brought in. The case aside, Kitty was, as ever, a fascinating source of information. When I'd finished with Skaratch, she made me seaweed tea and told me the latest cat gossip. She always had the best stories – and on this occasion I was not disappointed. Apparently only the previous week, she had become entranced by 'the most wonderful, enigmatic of creatures, a little goddess herself'. A small, white stray with incredible eyes and a scrawny delicate body had turned up at the Heights.

'You should have seen her,' raved Lady K. 'She had eyes that could seduce anyone, she walked like she had no weight. Like a dancer, she was. You know I was a dancer in my heyday, don't you, darling? Danced *Coppélia* even. So this little creature arrives and she sits in my conservatory for hours, not moving, just looking out of the window. And she is divine, truly divine. Honestly, darling, you would be entranced. And would you believe it? She stays for two weeks and I just think I have her. I think she's joined our little family, don't I, Pootie? We all did. Then all of a sudden – she's gone. So that was it. As I say, darling, a divine little creature.' Lady K was rambling as always. She rarely seemed to notice whether I spoke or not. 'She came, she went. Like a free-ee spirit. Which is what we all want to be, isn't it, Pootie? Serafina too. It's true. I forgot to tell you that, darling. Serafina has gone walkabout again. Just last week, suddenly she disappears. It's enough to almost drive me to tears. Deserting the family. A tragedy.' She lowered her voice conspiratorially. 'But this white cat . . . she was so much a real cat. She occasionally brought in her little gifts. She refused to eat the food I give to my babies, and instead she would regularly arrive with her own little gifts, her own prey: a half-alive mouse, or a little bird in its last throes. She was so beautiful, a true hunter. I *adored* her.'

Can you have any doubt? The eyes, the tiny body, the weightless walk . . . It was clearly Purrl. Nutter or not, the Divine Kitty was not one for fabricating cat stories. And anyway why should she? Purrl was simply living off her nine lives and had wandered down to Wendersby Heights. It's not so improbable. Just a little tale of a cat that missed the needle, and lost one life.

As I left the house I had the vague feeling that I was being watched. The sense of eyes out there, following me – but where? Getting into the car, I caught a glimpse of something in the mirror. The image seemed to imprint on my brain after the fact – a white cat crossing the road behind. It had stopped and turned towards me. I looked round to see what was there – nothing. Not even a piece of white paper fluttering in the wind.

71

the domestic

I'm jumping forward in time now – three, four months – because there's little story to tell. While I didn't see anything of Purrl, my relationship with Josh followed a fairly predictable trajectory. Predictable, that is, according to classic romance, but not at all predictable according to my experience. We had our dates. We had the most erotic dental session I've ever had in my life. Josh pretty soon admitted the second appointment was a false one, I hadn't needed a filling at all, and he'd just been trying to work out some way of getting me back into his clutches.

He didn't need to plan like that again. I became very willing to return to those warming clutches. Yes, we had our months of games and lusty spontaneous meetings. Yes, we spent our mornings in bed, followed by cooked ham and eggs on toast at three in the afternoon. Yes, we threw ourselves at love with a lusty energy, which was bound to dwindle just a little. But it hasn't . . . yet.

Even though I now know so many of his very

worst habits, I still find Josh perfect. He's so perfect I want to be him. I want to grow six inches and gather big wide shoulders just like his. I want a deep, dark tan like his. I want to dye my hair dark brown like his. (I've already had it cut in the same style.) I want to be strong like him. (I've taken up weight-training.) I want to have a head chock-a-block of useless facts just like him. I want to tell jokes like him. I want to dress like him. I want to speak Spanish like him. I want to be clever like him. I want to win arguments like him. If it weren't for the fact I want to have sex with him, I'd want to *be* Josh.

Though Josh is a dentist, he's not like most dentists, or indeed most people. He questions everything, analyses his patients, tells me intricate stories of their emotional lives. 'I think Mrs Wilmot should leave her husband. That's what she's building up to. That's why she's getting her veneers. She wants more out of life.' Josh believes in dreams. Josh is also a self-improver. He reads stacks – and tries to write sci-fi books. He sits in his corner at his computer and writes for hours late into the night, until I'm fed up with waiting for him to come to bed and drag him through. Bored? It's not that I ever get bored with Josh. Just mildly irritated. The thing is, when you've been with a person for a while you start picking at each other. You see your partner split in two – into the pathetic creature that plays your petty, childish games and the strong, wilful man who's far too good for you. But which one do you love?

These last few months, I admit, have been a little more domestic. In fact, I'm almost proud of my new-found homeliness (though perhaps it has come all too fast). We still have our moments of passion and we still feel queasy whenever we see each other, but other matters have started to take over. Like cooking, for instance. I never thought it would happen, but it has. Josh bought me a steamer and I became a kitchen convert. I can think of nothing more pleasant than an evening experimenting with spices and concocting a meal for my man: salmon steaks with avocado sauce, Armagnac prunes and crème fraîche, pears in port, rainbow trout in black bean sauce. I'm almost becoming a Benson at heart. I've put on about half a stone since I started seeing Josh, and that's even given I've started jogging every day.

So, there you have it. I'm in love. Josh and I are now a couple. We're an item. We get invited to parties together. We walk the dog together. We're frowned at in parks for our public displays of affection. We're asked to the kind of get-togethers I always used to hate. We gossip in the taxi on the way home. We analyse everybody else's relationships. Josh and Milla. *Say it again.* Milla and Josh. Sounds good, doesn't it?

Of course, I know I don't deserve this. He really is too good for me. I don't deserve a man as handsome, adorable and perfect as Josh. But somehow in some bizarre and unfathomable way he seems to have fallen for me. I just keep fooling him, keep acting like Mina, talking the Mina talk, smiling the Mina smile, telling the Mina stories – and it seems to work. In my crappy, underhand way I've got under that boy's skin and I feel like I've pulled a kind of hoax. Doesn't he know that he's sold himself short?

Josh soon moved into my flat with me. For a long while I had been able to spot those tell-tale signs that my Joshua was thinking of moving in: the pyjamas now kept in my drawers; the pile of dental-care books and sci-fi mags accumulating on my shelves, forcing my cat books from their rightful place; the PC housed permanently in my kitchen; the phone calls from his mates wondering why they haven't seen him in ages.

I remember the day that he suggested it. It's marked with a blue inky star in my diary – Josh's birthday. It all made sense. After all, the flat was mine – willed to me by the late Jemima Spall, in return for looking after her dear cat, Tiberius Mumperjack, in the manner to which he was accustomed.

There was plenty of room in Jemima's dark and dusty spaces: room for me, Josh, Zara and of course Tibbs. There was easily room for us all. We would be like one big family. I would put up with Zara and Josh would put up with Tibbs. It was as simple as that. Contented domesticity. For all too long, I'd been living on my own.

He was eating steak au poivre when he said it. A piece of hair hung down like a comma stuck on the side of his face. I wanted to swipe it away, but let it hang there. He hesitated before speaking, as if building up to something momentous. I almost thought I sensed a ring on its way. But no, my Joshua had more predictable plans. 'Gaps, honey,' he said, 'I've been thinking. You know how it seems we're really getting on so well. I just thought, I'm spending more time here than at my own place. My lease ends next month and I think I should just move in. There's plenty of room there.'

I was smugly thrilled. Not because he said, 'I love you', we already say that countless times each day – so many times, countless meaningless times. *Love, love, LOVE, lurve, love, Lovvve, luv, luv, love, love,* was the constant refrain in our lives. No, not for that reason. But because, for once, this was a real relationship. Someone in the world thought I was worth it.

He had his conditions, of course, and I had mine. 'I can put up with Tibbsy, he's almost like a dog, but I just don't want to be living in a house overrun with cats,' he said, as he picked a speck of basil from between my front teeth. 'You know it provokes my asthma.' Wielding a cocktail stick like a surgeon, he carefully extricated the specimen.

He preens me, we preen each other, like two animals. Josh inspects my teeth regularly and makes sure they look respectable. He's a dentist, after all. It humiliated me at first, all this bird-like picking and poking, then it irritated the hell out of me and now I recognise it's just part of Josh's way of looking after me. It's an expression of the fact that he cares for me.

'Fine,' I said, without thinking – and quickly ran a tongue over my now spotless teeth. 'That's OK, so long as you understand that I don't want this place overrun with your sci-fi and football friends.'

'Understood.'

And that was that. We started on the tiramisu.

Fine, I'd agreed. I'd gone along with his request. But something was nagging at me: the fact that he'd mentioned the cat thing. I'd always known cats would come into his conditions, of course. Men, on the whole, just don't appreciate them. My mother warned me so. 'Don't mention the cats. You'll never find yourself a man if all you do is babble on about cats.' And she was right, in a way. But I was sure Joshua could tolerate a cat or two. If I was willing to walk Zara every other day, then he could put up with a few cat hairs. Asthma or no asthma.

Of course Purrl didn't die. My feminine-feline intuition is never wrong.

Five days ago she first appeared at my window. I was washing the dishes at the time, and staring absent-mindedly at the bubbles breaking across my fingers and contemplating a face as wrinkled as my hands. The caked-on sauce of last night's meal began to shift from the plates. I was thinking of tonight's dinner and what I could make next. I was thinking of Josh and his daft theories about the future.

Mrrrnaouhhh, I heard quietly and lightly, as if from nowhere.

Miirrhhnaouh. I listened. I recognised the sound. It wasn't a Tibbsy call – no, this was a different, but still familiar cry.

I looked up from rice grains swirling in water and cocked my head to one side. I stared out of the window. There was no one there. Strange . . . Was I hearing things? Maybe I really was going mad. Sometimes I felt, after too much time spent with Josh, that I was entering a delirious madness. I would start to feel that I was in this haze, not just of love and happiness but also of near-hysteria. Love-delirium. I could imagine myself gobbling him up, tickling him, teasing him, taking him on.

But not today. Today I was normal Milla. I was almost like single Milla, the Milla I always used to be: cool, calm and collected, or so I thought. Josh had got in late last night and had left straight after breakfast. We'd had our usual: mushrooms on toast – toast lightly done, mushrooms fried in butter not oil. (He cooks. I wash up afterwards.) Josh had rushed, while I took it slowly, reading the papers as I went. I didn't have an appointment till lunchtime, and only had to take Zara for a walk, so I was in a leisurely mood. Perhaps I'd been day-dreaming.

I peeked out of the side window into the yard. Nothing there. The radio was on. Maybe all I'd heard was some interference. I returned to my dishes.

Mihhrnhhh . . . I looked up again.

81

Then, suddenly rising up into my field of vision, in a weightless jump, a small white cat landed on my window-sill. It was Purrl. I recognised her immediately. That angelic flash of cat. She was just as skinny and as flawless as she had been on that first day I'd seen her.

Two pinkish eyes peered in. They met mine across the kitchen sink. Staring directly and un-flinchingly, looking me up and down, they challenged me. I stared back again.

My breathing seemed to stop. The whole world halted in its tracks. How long was it for? I think several minutes passed. I was locked in her gaze, transfixed by her presence. For an eternity I seemed to be staring through the glass, staring at Purrl, this cat that I'd so long wanted to see again. It was inexplicable, but I was strangely attracted to her. Why did she draw me like this? She was remark-able, it was true. But what was *so* special? My eyes reached out to her. Then suddenly there was the flutter of a bird in the bushes outside and the spell was broken. Purrl started and looked around – then looked back again.

'Are you coming in, baby?' I asked.

I reached for the catch on the window. It was sticking slightly and I tried to loosen it, aware of the blur of the cat moving, a pale phantasm flowing across my retina. A white streak flickered past my eyes. I looked up and she was gone, like a ghost that was never there.

*

Maybe, after all, I wasn't feeling quite myself. In fact, maybe I was in such a strange, unfamiliar mood that I almost might have imagined all this. I certainly would have thought so if it weren't for a telephone call I received from Ida Little. Ida, you see, is another one of my cat cranks. Sixty-two years old, she's part of a network called Missing Moggies, a Neighbourhood Watch of the cat world, with spies all over the country looking out for cats that have gone AWOL. I met her through Gabriel – she's one of the nuts that comes down to their special Wednesday-evening drop-in.

Ida calls me regularly, to see if I've got the low-down on my street – who's moved in, whether they have any cats, any strays on the prowl, etc. This time she was breathless. 'Millie,' she said in a con-spiratorial whisper, 'I have some news for you. You will be pleased, darlin'!'

'Pleased?'

'Yes. Remember that case you mentioned to me months back – the skinny white cat. Well, I got some info from my contacts at the Governing Council of the Cat Fancy and I put it together and I sent it to all my best spies in the area. And now, all of a sudden, something happens. Mrs Frankl, just round the corner from you, gives me a call. She'd seen it sat on the wall in front of her neighbour's house. Now, what do you think of that?'

'I'm impressed, Ida. Very impressed.'

My mother phoned that evening. She had it in her

head that I'd said I was coming up at the weekend, but then she's always inventing that sort of thing. The truth is I never want to see her. Can't bear to spend more than a couple of hours with her. Sometimes I wonder what connection there could possibly be between the two of us. Oh yes, we look vaguely alike (or would do if she didn't put so much gunk on her face), but that's as far as it goes. From time to time I suspect that I am not really her daughter – I was just placed in her care for a while on this earth. My mum and I don't think the same, we don't act the same and we never agree about anything.

Anyway, she had a new boyfriend (*another* one). 'Milla, honey,' she said, 'you wouldn't believe the nice young man I met recently.'

Generally he'll be half her age – one of those lechy boys with a fantasy about the older woman that never lasts. I can just see him dribbling and drooling over her body, boasting to his friends that he's pulled this sophisticated older bird with plenty of money. It flatters her to be pursued by them, but when it all goes wrong and they go off with a younger model, she's left feeling like a dirty old hag. And I'm the one who has to pick up the pieces. Still, she was feeling 'up' when she phoned.

'He's terribly sweet and he's so good to me. You would love him.'

'What does he do?'

'Gym instructor.' She lowers her voice and mutters under her breath, 'He's even got his belly button pierced. It's terribly exciting, don't you think? I was almost thinking of having it done myself.'

I shudder at the thought of a sparkling gold ring locked between the folds of her tummy: a little metallic incrustation on her slack skin. 'I wouldn't know.' Josh is hardly your body piercing sort, and Mother knows it. She's always been a bit down on him because he's a dentist. She'd like me to hitch up with a biker or 'one of those druggie, arty types' or anyone that she could shock her life-drawing class friends with. I don't know why she confides in me.

'So, how's that funny boy of yours, Joshua?' she asks. 'When are we going to see him, darling?'

'Mother . . . I don't think it's a good idea. He's not into that family thing.'

'Because I was just thinking it's about time we should be hearing wedding bells. You know, by the time I was your age I'd been engaged four times.'

'Yes, Mother. I know.' She's told me so many times. Not that she wants me to get married, just engaged. I must be such a disappointment to her: a daughter who's never even been proposed to once, who has these brief little relationships that never amount to anything and possesses minimal charm.

There she sits with her white-blonde hair – *or is it grey now?* – her Chanel lipstick, her *pale and interesting* moisturising foundation and her thick black kohl eyeliner. She tosses her locks from side to side and twiddles her perfectly manicured fingers. And here I sit, all pretty-plain. Mother, an ex-Avon lady who set up her own house-to-house cosmetics business and always longed for a daughter to instruct in the art of face-painting, must have felt her heart sink inside when she was left with me.

'Of course, Mina would have been just like me. Even when she was a little toddler she always managed to charm the boys.'

Mother is always pushing those buttons. She can't hold back – always trying to tip me over. I try to be so calm and rational all the time, but it becomes too much. It just keeps overwhelming me. And Mother knows my lack of control, the constant possibility of me approaching the edge of a tear, the smarting, the stinging, better than anyone. She works it. It's always that way with her. *Mina this . . . Mina that . . . Mina the other . . .* When's she ever going to let up? I stand in silence, not reacting. Though I feel like putting the phone down, somehow I never can. Somehow she always keeps me there.

I sigh . . . and she changes the subject.

'So, how are things with the cat business?' she asks, in that sliding tone of voice that suggests, well, OK, she'll give up on the exciting stuff and talk work with me.

'Oh, fine,' I answer, but I know she's not interested. The truth is, my mother always hated cats. She thought they were unhygienic and smelly. That's probably why we don't get on. I've always believed you should never trust a person who doesn't like cats – even if it is your own mother.

*

It's too late already in life for me to change some of my bad habits and the following morning I was late as ever for my lunch with Gabriel. Although he'd asked me to be sharp ('I know what you're like, Milla, never punctual'), I got delayed while taking Zara for a walk. She was wildly hyper and kept running off across the other side of the park, barking madly, jumping up and being chased by dogs half her size – but that wasn't really why I was late. It was that gratuitous half-hour trip I took round the neighbourhood in the hope that I might spot Purrl. Gratuitous and pointless. Sadly, no sign.

Gabriel had already ordered in the Italian restaurant when I arrived. 'I'm afraid I've only got an hour and a half,' he sighed. 'We've already lost thirty-three minutes and twenty-two seconds of it. And I've got a colonic carcinoma to remove after lunch, which I'm not too happy about – it's Jess's patient and she's off with the flu. The sooner I can leave behind this mammalian crap and stick to my birds, the better.' He was looking vaguely distant, vaguely agitated. His grey-peppered hair stuck out in all directions like a cornfield that had been wrecked by storms.

'Sorry, Gabriel,' I said. 'Don't be such a sourpuss. Something happened to me this morning,' I lied – a minor white lie, just a transposition of time.

Gabriel got up from his seat to kiss me on the cheek, in that blundering, half-hearted way he always does. I pulled away awkwardly, laughing nervously, then sat down at the table next to him and picked up the menu. I felt on edge.

The trouble is I feel too sorry for Gabriel to get really close to him these days. I guess it was always a little that way, but it's got worse recently. He's always been the kind of person who's in a perpetual state of indignance, full of slights balled up inside so tight he's not aware of them any more. Stuff that was once emotion is now hardened to rock. The real Gabriel is floating somewhere about his body, where *those people* can't get to him. It's true he is different with me – he relaxes. With me he becomes enthusiastic and over-loud and extrovert, as if compensating for his hours of silence. A bit of the elemental Gabriel seems to erupt from inside. But even that elemental Gabriel seems unhappy these days.

~

It's only natural if I'm a little down on her affair with Josh. I can't help it. I simply wish I was him. Is there anything so bad about that? Actually I don't have any particular feelings about the man, not ones that aren't informed by a mild jealousy. I've met him a couple of times and in a strange way wanted to impress him – probably just to score points with Milla. It didn't work. I feel bad, because I may have been slightly awkward, but it didn't matter, because he was so busy talking and being charming. He tried starting a conversation about some football player, but I wasn't sure what team he played for and murmured something unenthusiastic, so, after a few false starts, we just ended up talking about convergent evolution in teeth and the colour of their new sofa. I can't understand why Milla's fallen for him, but that's her business. Don't interfere. Best not to think about it too much. File the whole thing off as a nesting phase. From a biological standpoint it's obvious why she might have chosen Josh – handsome, alpha-male type, reliable genes, probably smells right, right pheromones, etc. There's nothing I can do about it and I've got enough sense to know that if I interfere it will only turn her against me. I wouldn't do that anyway. Just sit tight and ride the storm.

Funnily enough, some things haven't really changed. When we meet on our own, we almost pretend she isn't having a relationship. It's very tactful. Milla's oh so careful not to mention him and I don't generally stray on to that territory, though sometimes I do end up pressing the point and hearing all the swoony love talk that I don't want to know about. Like that time at Pavelli's. That was an uncomfortable occasion. I could see that warning look in her eyes . . .

Milla was late. That was probably what set me off in the first place. Milla was always *at least half an hour late – I had to account for it in my arrangements. Late . . . I should have guessed she would be, only this time I couldn't help associating it with the fact that she was in this state of happily wedded bliss. I should have seen it as just Milla – nothing new. Pathologically late Milla. But I didn't. I got worked up. On this occasion we were meeting for lunch (dinners had become lunches since she'd started spending all her evenings with Josh) and there was a problem – I was supposed to have the afternoon off, but Jessica had taken ill and I'd promised to come back and deal with her cases. I should have phoned Milla to say I'd only got a couple of hours, but didn't. I sat there, ploughing through the basket of bread and butter. The waitress was nice – ruthlessly clear skin – and must have seen I was waiting for someone and probably thought I'd been stood up. There was something so sympathetic about the way she kept trying to have a conversation.*

Of course, when Milla did arrive I barely mentioned it. She came swooping in, drenched with rain, hair pasted to the side of her face but still glowing and full of apologies. Beautiful as ever. 'Gabriel . . . so, so sorry. So sorry . . . Mmm mmm . . . very sorry . . .' For a few minutes I forgot any anger, kissed her gently on the cheek. And there I was again, sitting at the table, doing the small talk about cats and birds . . . I won't mention Josh if you don't . . . Let's just pretend it's only us two . . . Only for some reason Josh was really on my mind that day.

~

Gabriel's pizza arrived. He barely looked at the waitress, shyly keeping his head down, eyes averted as he always does. She asked him if he wanted pepper, he nodded and then she gave him a stormy sprinkling, crunching in circles over the plate. When she'd left he started to wolf it down. He has no self-consciousness in front of me. He does what he likes. Gabriel and I go a long way back. He's probably the person who knows most about me on the planet and he's the only person I've ever told about Mina. He's the only person who knows my secrets.

Gabriel was at vet school with me – but much older. He was doing a PhD in avine heart aberrations and was shy and lurked around in the cafeteria on his own a lot and, because I was a bit of an outsider myself, we hung out together for a while. Nothing happened between us. It was a difficult time for me and I was having a crisis: both in my career and emotionally. Did I or didn't I want to do this for the rest of my life? Gabriel tried to persuade me yes, but it came to the exams and I was down on enthusiasm and ended up being lumbered with resits. 'Stop throwing things away when they get hard,' he told me. 'You've got to learn to deal with stuff.'

I didn't contact him over the summer vacation – my decision, 'throwing it all away' and all that. Still, he was the person who pushed me through to finish one more year, even though I was sure I never wanted to be a vet. He also tried to persuade me to stick it out to the end. Not that it worked . . . His words held little sway, because it was round about then that I read a small book by the biologist Jemima Spall. Immediately I was converted, ducked out of the course and wrote to the seventy-two-year-old, saying I wanted to meet her. She wrote back saying she would be delighted and that was it. I'd made up my mind that a cat behaviourist was what I wanted to be. Why bother with human thought, when you can be inspired by cat thought? Gabriel thinks I'm an idiot of course, but he likes me a little too much, even loves me, all the same.

As for my cats, it's not as if he doesn't understand where I'm coming from. I think he knows it only too well. Just as much as I love cats, he loves birds. They're his obsession. Gabriel even looks like a bird. Birdboy Gabriel . . . His nose, long and thin, could easily have earned him the nickname Beaky at school, if it weren't for the fact that the kids had already given him a whole string of other names: Birdy, Birdman, Budgie, Tweety. No wonder he spent so much time with his birds.

He gulped back a mouthful of wine. 'So, how's Joshua?'

'Fine . . . You know, still sticking his head down other women's mouths.'

'Have you told him everything yet?' he asked, his fingers running hyperactively up and down the glass stem.

I shook my head. 'I don't really see the point.'

His fingers were still playing over the now empty glass, making faint ringing sounds.

'Stop that,' I muttered. Gabriel's tics get to me – they always have done. He's all arms and legs all over the place, eyes like he never knows quite where to put them. It's amazing that he has the coordination to do surgery.

He sighed, reached over to the bottle and poured himself a little more wine.

~

Perhaps I was a little distracted . . . There was that motorbike accident I'd driven past on the way over and the problem with the painkillers that kept disappearing from the drugs cupboard . . . But Milla was going on and on about that cat.

We'd been chatting for about half an hour and I felt she was being really distant. All this talk about the cat. It did sound intriguing, but then Milla could make a mystery out of anything. It felt like she wasn't looking me straight in the eye. That was odd. You know it when Milla really looks at you – it's like a shot right through you, until you get used to it and start to hold it and enjoy it and wish for it all the time.

'How's Joshua?' I asked, for once breaking the code.

A vaguely mischievous smile flickered across her face, but she suppressed it. I suspected she might be laughing at me. Not that I cared. What I really wanted to know, in a roundabout way, was whether she'd shared all her secrets with him yet. If they were really that close that he knew all about Mina and all about her mother. No one could really know Milla and not know all that. So much of what she is relates back to that – especially to her sister. Few people even know she exists, but I've even been to the care home to visit her. I've seen pictures of them together from when they were about seven years old. They were surprising. The obvious sparkle that Mina was supposed to have so much more of didn't seem obvious. Quite the reverse, Milla, smiling there on the right, seemed to glow out of the frame.

I didn't want to let the subject drop. 'Don't you think you should at least introduce him to your mother?' and 'What's your problem?'

She started out shrugging my questions off, but soon got angry. I thought she was living a lie. She thought it was all the more true because she'd got rid of all her childhood hang-ups. They weren't real, she said. The point was that it wasn't a problem any more. She'd dealt with all that – so why even acknowledge it existed. Her clean-slate, blank-slate theory. I could see her getting more and more flustered. 'You haven't got a clue, Gabriel!' she finally said. 'You think the rest of the world is screwed up, but it's not. It's us. Just face up to it.' And it was a bit of a slap in the face after all this time of listening to all her problems.

I poured myself a glass of water and for the rest of the meal didn't speak a single other word.

Neither did she.

~

Tibbsy was beginning to worry me. When you know a cat well, then you pick up on the tiniest deviations in their behaviour.

Like Tibbsy hiding under the bed when I came back that evening . . . He refused to budge for about an hour and a half, his blank eyes staring out reluctantly from the darkness. I lay there in the shadows, sizing him up, trying to bridge that empathy gap, to show him I understood. But he didn't seem to get it. I could only assume that something had spooked him – but what? When I eventually did tempt him out from his hiding place, I could feel he was shaking. Tiny tremors flowed through his body as he sat on my lap.

Josh brought my coffee and sat down beside me. 'Is he OK?' he said, tickling the cat underneath his chin. I nodded. 'How's my little Tibbsy-wibbsy?' he murmured. Josh was a sucker now for old Tibbs. Things had definitely progressed on the feline front, there was no doubt, and my little ginger moggie was clearly third in his affections – after me and Zara of course. Even though too long spent stroking him would lead to his breath becoming slightly wheezy, he still found Tibbsy's company irresistible (who wouldn't?). So much for Gabriel's pronouncement. Josh was rapidly becoming a cat person. You could tell by the way he'd started burbling nonsense at Tibbs – the same sort of childish nonsense he'd started burbling at me. Not only was it *Tibbsy-wibbsy*, it was also *Dappy-gappy* and *Choco Pop* and *Sugar Puff*. Sugar, sugar, sugar and more sugar all round. There was something about all this syrupy stuff that slightly irritated me – but I let it lie. At least it meant he was happy.

Josh bent over and kissed me on the side of the neck. 'Mmmm, Gaps . . . You smell good,' he said. A tingle fluttered down my back. I felt the warm, damp pressure of his lips on my skin. 'Do you think he'll be OK?' he murmured, his voice barely audible.

'Of course he will,' I said, feeling my body quicken under his caresses. I sighed, '*Shooooo, baby*,' gently shifting Tibbs from my lap and pulling Josh towards me.

Tibbs stumbled off looking dejected and we moved into our routine. And it *is* a routine now – a

95

little dance that we've perfected over the months – over and over again, like a natural, irresistible rhythm. It's so comfortable. Josh's face loomed over me. 'Poor puss. Rejected in favour of a man,' he said. 'Are you sure he'll be all right?'

I drew his lips on to mine, 'Mm-hmm', and began undoing my blouse. 'But,' I said, suppressing a small giggle and taking whispered pleasure in a word, 'there's another pussy I think is in need of attention.'

Josh smiled. 'Oh, is there now . . . ' His lips traced the line of my jugular. His fingers trailed along the inside of my thigh. 'Well, let me see what Dr Pride can do for this particular little animal.' Josh's mouth edged its way down my chest. 'Mmmmm,' he murmured, his tongue drawing along the curve of my breast, his fingers sliding . . . *Mmmm* . . .

Before I go too far, let me diverge a little . . . *Pussy* . . . It's rather a curiosity *that*, don't you think? That a woman's private parts should be called her pussy – that we should have our own little pet down there, our own personal piece of feline. I've often wondered where this expression comes from. Who invented it? Of course, common sense takes us a long way in linguistics. Pusscat. Pussy. Pussum. Puss. The word Puss itself, in the feline sense, probably derives in some loose way from the name of the Egyptian goddess Bastet, or Pasht as she is sometimes called. But the sex bit? The associative leap? Why the elision of meaning between cat and woman? Why the reduction to a female sexual part? I suppose if kitten equals flirty young girl, it is not hard to reduce her to her basic essential parts and the puss lurking below. Anthropomorphism isn't necessarily misleading. After all, there's always been something inherently sexy about cats. Cats are the embodiment of sex and sensuality. They've got the life force.

Not that I'm really a 'pussy' person. I would never normally use the term – except sometimes when joking and often just innocently. Pussy is the kind of thing you read about in porn magazines, or on flyers pinned to the inside of phone boxes. Leyla with her thirty-eight-inch chest always seems to have a hot, wet one. It's almost sweet and affectionate, for all the fact that I'd rather ignore mine. A fact which one pussy-obsessed ex-lover of mine failed to take into account. Me, I like it all over. I never did manage to teach him any better, and pretty soon he moved on to other feline pastures.

But that's not the problem with Josh. He would never err in that way. Josh and I are faultlessly in tune. The rhythms and responses of our bodies just fit, like two pieces of a jigsaw puzzle. For some magical reason there's no desire of his that isn't matched with a complementary desire of mine. Or at least, if there is, he never expresses it. Which brings me back to the bedroom and a fast but breathy climax.

Our five-minute passion routine over, Josh rolled over and picked up *Clones from Carnos*, his latest sci-fi mag.

'Do you have to?' I asked.

97

He shrugged and smiled so cutely I couldn't argue.

'I was thinking,' said Josh, lying back on the bed and staring into the air, 'that in the future . . .'

'Ha! You and your future. You've probably been thinking about it for the last half-hour. So what's going to happen in this future?' I was considering whether cats and girls are interlinked in all human languages.

'Well, in the future, if we were to have virtual sex – like there is in this magazine – and instead of really making love people just got wired up to some machine, people would get so bored with love-making that they'd stop it entirely. Either we'd have to do the test-tube baby thing, or the whole of our species would die out.'

'That's stupid,' I groaned, lifting my legs in the air and shifting into a yoga-like pose. 'Sex is all about real flesh, real bodies. It's nothing without the mess of it all. It would never catch on in the first place. People would never get bored.'

'But if it did . . .'

My legs were now above my head, toes stretched into balletic points. I strained. 'Are you saying you're bored with sex?'

'Bored? No. It's just a theory.' He props himself up on the pillows and flicks over on to the next page. 'Could you put the kettle on, sweets?'

'Sure thing, babe.'

My mother called again. She's thinking of having the house converted so that she can have Mina at home. 'Obviously it will cost, but I think I might be able to get a grant, and a carer would come round every day to help.'

The idea of my mother lugging Mina round the house seems laughable.

'Don't you think it's about time you came up to see her, honey?' she says. 'It must be over a year since you last visited her. I know it's hard for you . . .'

She's wrong. It's not that it's hard for me – just pointless. Mina's not even there any more – or if she is she'll never reveal herself. It's like she's got herself locked in her own game of hide-and-seek, stuck in the cupboard that's the best hiding place in all the world. She'll never come out of her hiding place for fear of losing. I know her too well. I can almost hear her laughing.

Thursday evening's Big Shop Night – in the car, down to the supermarket, get a whopper of a trolley and pile in the food. It's trip of the week – like a regular jaunt to an amusement park. We have our routine. Normally we have a good few recipes planned, and we've some idea what we want. That Thursday it was sole and mussels in lemon sauce, Oriental pork with lentils, and lamb shanks in apple and horseradish, plus I decided to buy some extra fish. But half the joy of it is not knowing; it's the spontaneous discovery, the special offer reduced by ten pence that gives you an excuse to buy something totally fresh, like escargots at three pounds a packet or salmon mousse at one pound fifty. In the trolley, join the queue, through the checkout, spend a fortune and back in the car. Then it's straight home again, like any long-married pair. Which we practically are. We're partners these days – partners in the crime of coupledom.

Yesterday, we got home, laden with bags and bags of food, carried it out of the car, fumbled with the lock, headed down the hallway and lugged it into the kitchen. Josh got through the doorway first and hesitated, then dropped his bags straight on the ground. They landed with an egg-cracking thud. There was a stunned pause.

'What?' he said, turning to me, with eyes raised into the top of his sockets. 'What is that?' He was already in a bit of a grouchy mood. He'd had a bad day at work and the tone of his voice said, 'Don't mess.'

'What is what?'

He pointed to a white bundle of fur curled up in Tibbsy's bed. My heart did a double-flip. My jaw dropped. It was that singular, unmistakable, irresistible piece of feline perfection, Purrl. There was no hanging about with this cat.

'That.'

'That's a cat.'

'Yeah ... I know that's a cat. But do you know what?'

'What? Don't look so grumpy! What?'

'I've never seen this cat before. It's not Tibbsy, is it? Not unless he's suddenly metamorphosed. I mean, it's not all fluffy and chubby and ginger, is it? What is it doing here?'

I shrugged my shoulders. 'I dunno . . . I guess it must have just wandered in through the cat flap.'

Dropping my own bags on the ground, I approached the sleeping kitty. 'Hello, baby.' I bent over to stroke her and she woke up with a fright. Her eyes barely opened. Her legs stretched out, mouth opening in a yawn. She looked like some new-born kitten. Foetal almost. Maternal instincts roused, I gently wrapped my hands around her.

'You call that a cat?' said Josh. 'That's the weirdest-looking cat I've ever seen.'

'Well, what else would you call her? She's not a dog, is she?' I picked her up in my arms. For some reason, this time it was so much easier than any other time. This time she was being friendly. With a light hand, I stroked her across the forehead and tickled her under her chin. She was gorgeous, a rare beauty.

'Don't you think it's a bit worrying that any old cat can just come in and take up nest in the house?' said Josh, grasping a carrier bag and wandering over to the cupboards.

I heard him bang it down hard and start thrusting tins on to shelves, but I was much too absorbed in my new friend. She had me mesmerised. Her eyes searched my face, seemingly taking in every detail.

'Well, don't you?'

'Don't I what?' I murmured.

'Think it's odd?'

'No,' I said. 'Normally they wouldn't. But this isn't just any old cat. I know this cat.'

'Don't tell me . . .' He clanked a tin of tomatoes into place. 'Don't tell me . . . You've adopted a new cat. I thought I was just getting to grips with Tibbs, and you've adopted a new cat.'

'I haven't exactly adopted her,' I said. 'But –'

'And this one's an ugly-looking thing too. It's not as if it's even a cute cat. Being forced to buy chocolate ice cream instead of toffee pecan was bad enough, but coming back to find the house is gradually being overtaken by stray animals . . .'

I hate Josh when he gets in one of his moods and I'd seen this one brewing all evening. The minor tiff over orange or red sweet potatoes had been the first sign, followed by the tantrum about the chocolate biscuits, which I said I didn't want in the house, because I knew it would be me who ended up eating them. It would be no good for my anti-fat diet. Then there was his picking on my driving all the way home. Big Shop Night had so far been Big Sulk Night. 'So, go on . . . explain!'

'Well, I just think she's decided I should look after her.'

'You mean she's a stray you've befriended.'

'Well, kind of. Actually she's a cat I've known for a while. I think I've got some kind of weird affinity thing with her. Something you wouldn't understand, Josh.'

'Mmmm . . .' He slumped in the seat in despair and looked at me with pursed lips from under his

102

long fringe. He stared at the cat questioningly. 'Maybe . . .'

'Listen, hon. I know she looks a bit strange, but actually that's a kind of feline beauty. And she is the most incredible cat. You've always said you like the freaks and weirdos of this world. I'm sure you'll grow to like her. Go on . . . Let her stay for a while. She's just like one of those freaky-looking catwalk models. You'll soon realise how beautiful she is.' I stroked his hair and bent forward to kiss him.

'I dunno, Mills. I just don't take too well to this cat thing. I think I'm getting allergic to them – all this wheezing I've been doing – and to be honest I feel a bit weird with all these animals in the way. It's like we've already got kids.'

'Come on, Joshua, it'll be OK. I swear.'

'Well,' he said, shaking his head. 'OK, OK. But, you know, much as I like them, I don't want to be living with a whole household full of cats. Just promise this isn't the beginning of invasion of the strays. Like *doo . . . doo . . . doo-doo . . . doo . . . doo . . .* suddenly we have sixty of them setting up camp in the kitchen. This is the only one.'

'Of course it's the only one,' I said petulantly. 'Like I said, she's just a very special cat.'

'I just don't want you turning into some Brigitte Bardot type with throngs of kittens clinging to your heels. It's absurd . . .' He paused and smiled. 'Though obviously if you looked like her I wouldn't complain. Just the cats part. That's what I don't want.'

Smarmy bugger. 'Very funny,' I said resentfully. 'Are you trying to say I'm fat? Well, get stuffed.'

Our first argument and it was over a cat. Somehow it just didn't seem acceptable; he'd only been moved in a couple of days and was already laying down the rules. It wasn't right. How were we supposed to survive years together if he wasn't willing to make a few compromises? Didn't he understand that it's pointless going into competition with a cat? It's clear from the start who'll win – always the cat; always, always the cat.

But I didn't lose faith. You see, I have confidence that Josh will change. He'll grow to love Purrl in the same way that he's grown to love Tibbs. There is no question of that. Cats are irresistible animals and Purrl is one of the most irresistible of them. Slowly and surely Purrl and I can change him. I know they say you shouldn't try to change a man, but what is the point of a relationship if not to change each other just a little bit? Change is good. It's what loving should be all about.

the feral

Beginning today ... Tuesday, 29 April, I'm smitten ...

I am fascinated by the curve of Purrl's left patella, the way it slides under her skin. The undulating way her tiny muscles ripple across her slip-thin legs. More than anything else, I am fascinated by that part of her body. The details would be imperceptible on a long-hair. On a fat cat there would be no way you could make them out. But on Purrl, it's all there. Every detail. In just one day I have become mesmerised by her. I have become captivated by every tendon, every ligament, every vein, every bone. Purrl, in all her physical glory, has seduced me.

There's something entrancing about the way a cat moves, the way it slinks low and noiselessly across the ground, leaps from on high to land softly, absorbing impact, or stretches into a sinuous curve. Even a klutz of a cat like Tibbs moves with a deftness beyond even the most skilled dancer, a Nureyev or a Baryshnikov. Their *grands jetés* and pirouettes are something to behold. But the most graceful cats, Purrl and her like, have an effortless fluency that is unmatched by any other creature on this earth. They move like divine spirits, paws fluttering weightlessly across the ground. Purrl glides, she hovers, she floats, she pounces. You wouldn't actually believe that she was a corporeal being. More like a ghost, a phantom, a rushing wind. *Ssshhhhhh . . . Watch her go!*

It's already way past feeding time and Tibbs has not yet arrived for breakfast. This is very unlike him. He's a stomach-led cat, always here on the dot, without fail. You can set your clocks by him: eight a.m. to the nearest minute. Always first to the bowl, never loses his appetite, that's my Tibbs.

Lately, he's been eating a little less, but there's been no wavering in his routine. He demands that I am reliable, makes sure I stick to my promise of food with regularity. That is what an owner is for – to be there at eight, even on a Sunday morning, rain or shine, in sickness or in health, for richer or poorer, etc. It's a marriage with only one real commitment: food. *Do you, Milla Hall, take this cat, Tiberius Mumperjack, to feed and to fuss over for as long as his stomach demands? I do.* I have. I'm here. Have I ever let you down?

Tibbs always comes pattering through the cat flap at one minute to, his tail curled up like a question mark, his big, cushioning paws skidding across the floor. He makes a beeline straight for his red plastic bowl, waiting with hungry anticipation for Gourmet Rabbit to be opened and fall into its rightful place. If I'm not there, he claws the mat like a wild cat, frantically digging his claws into the wiry fabric. He mews and cries with impatience. It's *time* now, and he wants it. No waiting around. He's king. He's master of the house. His wish is my command.

But not today. There was no mewing or pattering or clawing today. There was no Tibbs, and no food eaten. All the shouting and calling I did from the backyard could not tempt him in. Maybe he'd found a new friend, maybe he'd got a good catch last night. I'm worried that something might have happened to him. Like a neurotic wife whose husband hasn't come back at the usual time, I have the darkest thoughts in my mind, and it's not just because Tibbs didn't come in this morning, it's also because last night I had a dream about a cat, a simple yet haunting dream. This cat could have been any cat. It could have been Tibbs or Purrl or little Mopsy or any other cat I've known – though I can't help feeling it was Tibbs.

My dream was full of cries: faint, drained whines from a shadowy figure in the darkness. The voice was trapped inside a wire cage. The cage was dark because it was surrounded on all side by huge bales of straw, a thick, suffocating prison blanket. The space was claustrophobic and small, barely big enough for a cat, never mind a human being, yet somehow I could see in there, I could hear the desperate grate of the cat scratching at metal, starting slow and low, gradually getting faster, screeching like a chalk across a blackboard and rising to a crescendo of panic as the cat tried to push its way out, not realising that there was no hope. The straw-weighted lid could not be pushed upwards. Then more cries for help, but I wasn't really there. I couldn't do anything. I could see it all, but I was powerless, a paralysed observer of the scene, neither inside nor outside, just two hovering eyes. There was nothing I could do. I had deserted and betrayed my cat. 'Tibbs!' I called out in the middle of the night, waking Josh, so that he switched on the bedside lamp and shook me.

And now, with Josh gone, I go outside and start yelling again. 'Tibbs . . . Tibbsy! Where are you, baby? Come and get your food!'

The front doorbell rings and I jump up madly, thinking it might be Josh. But it isn't. He's off at his parents for Sunday lunch and probably won't be back till late.

The Prides invited me too, but I didn't want to go. I already feel like I've done my share of sessions with them. On this occasion they had a window in their ever-hectic lifestyle into which he might just fit. Josh jumped to it. They beckon, he runs, like an over-enthusiastic puppy. He's so desperate to please. He's a mummy's boy – with both his mother's temperament and her Latin looks.

Josh's parents are rich. His mother was Spanish, brought up over here, so I guess Josh is a hotch-potch person too. His father is a doctor, a brilliant oncologist, specialising in some obscure form of cancer, and so brilliant he makes Josh insecure, which amazes me. I can't get my head round the fact that Josh, despite all his brightness, still feels he doesn't live up to his father's expectations – he's still not good enough, never good enough, would only have been good enough if he'd outshone his parents and gone on to be a heart surgeon or a brain surgeon. Josh once explained that for his father, having a son was simply an opportunity to create an extended, more talented version of yourself, one not hampered by your own parents' flaws, your own inadequate schooling.

It didn't work out. Josh was never the child prodigy he was meant to be. As a boy he was sent to boarding school. He hated it at first, would sit in his room reading sci-fi mags, unable to cope with being away from his mother, his beautiful, entertaining Spanish mother. When he did see his parents, he would grab at them, stamp his feet, try desperately hard to make them laugh, till they were so exhausted they wanted to send him away again. And it still works that way. I know – I've seen them at it.

I've met them three or four times. On Easter Sunday we had a roast dinner and they talked about art and jet-setting and the exact meaning of the word plebiscite and other intellectual things – as well as how Josh could change his dentistry into a bright and brilliant career. I couldn't get a grip on the conversation. I drank too much, started slurring my words and saying stupid things. I was anxious. Josh was irritable. We left early.

'Who cares what my parents think about you?' he asked.

'You do . . . I do . . .' I said, and I was right.

The doorbell rings again.

Through the net curtains, I can make out the faint silhouette of a woman holding a cat in her arms. My heart skips a beat. There's a vague gingerish tinge to this motionless feline form. A gingerish, Tibbsish tinge. It skips another beat.

By now I'm frantic about my dear little puss. A whole day and a half has passed and still no sign, still no appearance. The Gourmet Rabbit has gone untouched. No sign of my cat, and all sorts of terrible thoughts have already passed through my mind: he's been in a fight with some territorial tom and had his face ripped; he's stumbling around half conscious from being knocked down by a car; worst of all, he's felt neglected here and he's gone to stay with a new owner.

I stayed in virtually all day for fear of missing him. All on my own, with Purrl – which in its own way was wonderful. She entrances me. I can spend hours watching her. But what about Tibbs? It's pathetic, I know, but something is making me feel so insecure. I reach the door, and somehow I can tell even before I've opened it what has happened. A

112

short cry catches at the back of my throat. I turn the latch, pull and open it. *What's happened to Tibbs? I hold on to the thought.*

Standing before me is Mrs Cohen, dressed in a blue wool dress and slippers. She lives three doors down from me and is a bit of a cat lover herself, and she's holding the cat. She's holding Tibbs, holding a limp ball of charcoaled ginger fur that is clearly lifeless. My cat.

The nausea of shock seeps through me. I start to feel dizzy, my stomach contracts and my legs sway. Tears seem to well up in my eyes, but stay there, clinging to the corners of my lids. I try to breathe in slowly. But I know it now. Yes, I already know it. *My Tibbs is dead.*

'I'm really sorry, Milla,' says Mrs Cohen, shaking her head helplessly. 'But I thought I better bring him round. I thought you ought to know.'

I reach out my hands to touch the cold, lifeless body and feel a small hiccup hit my oesophagus. '*Huc* . . . He's definitely dead?' I say, nodding slowly and pulling the lump of fur towards me, drawing it in and hugging it close to my chest. All I can think of is Jemima – how I've let her down. All I can think of is my failure.

'Yes, dear . . . I'm so sorry. I really am.'

Through a watery blur, I can see that Mrs Cohen is almost on the verge of tears herself.

'I . . . I just thought if it was me . . . well, you know.'

'No, you're right, you're right,' I say, as she puts

113

a hand on my shoulder in an attempt at comfort. 'Do you know how he . . .'

'Well, it's difficult to tell . . . But me and Bill, we found him by the electric pylon over our back garden. We thought he might have been clambering on the wires and somehow . . .'

Aaughh . . . Poor Tibbsy. My poor boy. My eyes are smarting and I feel a sob wrench my body, but try to hold it back. Mrs Cohen is looking at me with a strange pity. I kiss the slightly charred fur on the top of his head and step backwards into the hallway.

Half an hour later and I am now feeling dead to the world. Josh is not back and Purrl is poised smugly in the middle of the carpet, while I sit with Tibbs on my lap. What should I do with him? What do you do with a dead cat? I let out an ironic sob of laughter. What a stupid thing. What a bloody, callous, silly thing. Trust me to think of something like that at a time like this.

Purrl seems oblivious of all that's happened. She sits and stares at me for a while, and then begins to clean herself. I don't move. I just watch her. My heart feels numbed. She shifts around uncomfortably, as if trying to find the right spot in the pile of the carpet, then suddenly stands up as if she's heard something, pausing for a second to look around. Then she stalks her way towards the corner, pursuing some invisible prey, one of those ghostly creatures that only a cat can see. She misses it. Grabs again. Then tires of it and turns to walk slowly and proudly to the sofa, where she takes her place between the cushions. Shifting around, she tries to make herself comfortable, then folds her legs in front of her. I've never seen her look so relaxed. Her forelegs are folded neatly in front of her. Her ears stretch ceiling-wards and she breathes deep and long. For a second I almost imagine I hear her purring. I think I hear a glimmer of a light, soft *purrrrrrrrrrrr* . . . But then, maybe I'm mistaken.

Purrrrrrrrrrrrrrrrr . . .

I must be hearing things. Not a purr from Purrl? She never purrs.

I remember Tibbs bounding across the floor playfully, the way he used to lift his right paw to get attention, the way he used to make the smallest squeaking noises when he wanted to sit on my lap. Now, no more of that. I remember him hiding under the bed the other night, as if in terror of something unknown. I remember that he didn't understand Purrl, couldn't get to grips with her . . . If only my last thoughts of him hadn't been that irritation, my last behaviour towards him tinged with annoyance at his failing to be friendly to our newcomer. Perhaps I'd been giving too much attention to Purrl. As with all deaths, even a cat death leaves you racked with guilt.

Dead cats . . . Generally people don't have to deal with them. Take the animal to the vet's and they'll quite happily deal with the dead body, unless of course you put in a request to take it home with you. Then there are the cat deaths, the majority of cat

115

deaths, that take place away from home. The cat disappears and dies in some corner, in some shed, in some undergrowth, never to return again to its owner. That's the most noble form of cat death. It's their considerate way – not liking to subject their human friends to the agony of grief. They prefer to disappear ambiguously, to take a trip to their own deathbed somewhere and leave their owners wondering if they've passed away in some alley or just gone on a long journey. *Maybe they'll be back some time soon.* Tibbs will never be back. I know that. All his nine lives are spent.

He lies there . . . a floppy bundle of singed fur on my lap. The smell of burnt hair is overpowering.

The front doorbell rings but I don't move. It must be Josh. I hear his keys rattle, Zara barking in the background, the scratch of metal against metal and the click of the turn of the lock.

'Gaps,' I hear. 'Gaps . . . you home?'

I don't move. I don't say anything. I just wait.

The sound of Josh's feet swishes along the corridor. He turns and comes into the sitting room. I sit staring into thin air. Silently, I wait for his response. I avoid looking into his eyes.

'Mills . . . are you deaf? Didn't you hear the bell? You wouldn't believe what my father's up to now . . . I was . . .' He stops. 'What's up?'

I bite my lip and make a nodding gesture towards the dead cat on my lap.

'Tibbs?' He looks bewildered. 'What's happened?'

116

'I think,' I say, as I feel my mouth pucker and my chin dimple into an agonising grimace. I try to bite it back. It's as if my muscles are in spasm. 'I mean . . . well, you can see. He's . . .'

'Not Tibbs.' Josh stands there in the middle of the floor, not quite knowing what to do. His hand rises to cover his mouth. He starts to say something and then stops, staring at the cat on my lap. Josh breathes in deeply. 'No, not . . . Tibbs.' He crosses the floor to kneel on the ground by my chair, puts a hand to Tibbs's head and begins to stroke his fur. It all seems so sincere. Josh is almost as upset as I am. I can tell it's genuine. He feels for a cat.

We finally decided it would be best to bury Tibbs. After all, if a cat is treated like a member of the family in life, it should be given that respect in death. A difference of species shouldn't matter. And that shouldn't apply only to cats that die in the home, it should also apply to those that are put down. I've always been slightly shocked at the old vet routine of carelessly tossing Mr and Mrs Smith's favourite pet in the freezer with a couple of other dead cats.

The house seems quiet. It feels like some spell has been broken, and I can't help feeling grumpy with everyone, including Josh. I feel lazy too. I stand in the kitchen watching, while Josh digs a hole at the back of the garden. Like some great hero, he's decided to take the dirty work off my hands. 'I'll do it,' he quickly volunteered. I think he's worried it might be

117

upsetting for me, but I can deal with these things. Still, I like him this way. My sweet Joshua is behaving with all the generosity and tact that a true lover should have. Forget Josh the lad – Josh the New Man has come into his own. He's digging, while I'm watching.

It's like some secret conspiracy. I've made a little brown velvet bag to put the body in, with a drawstring at the top. It's put together from some old Jemima Spall curtain, and I've stitched the name Tibbs on the outside in embroidered black thread. I'm no great seamstress, but it almost seems quite neat. It's my one little indulgence. Just a small gesture as tribute to a cat that gave me many happy moments and an atonement to Jemima for letting her down. All right, it's not a coffin, but it's fitting, it's respect. And anyway Tibbs wasn't one for anything too fancy.

Josh is bent over the hole with a huge spade. I can see his muscles gently flexing under his white T-shirt. This is the side of him that's so often hidden from the world. Good, kind Josh. He looks strong and earthy as he delves into the mud – less the intellectual and more the man of the soil. Josh signals to me that he thinks he's dug deep enough and I wave to him to say I'm coming.

I grasp the soft velvet containing the cold, rigid corpse. I can feel the form inside, a smooth, hard object. It's no longer life. It's not even death. It's just a thing and I suddenly feel the pointlessness of this whole ceremony we're about to perform. I want to give up, but quash the feeling and grip the bag tighter. I walk up to join Josh, body in hand. The hole is just by the fence, underneath where next-door's ivy clambers over, and opposite the flower plot which I've been trying to keep going, but is now overgrown with weeds.

Josh smiles at me sympathetically, then stares back down at his handiwork. 'Do you think that's big enough?' he asks.

I nod. It's starting to rain, a warm summer shower, and I'm standing out in my bare legs and flip-flops. The water trickles down my forehead into my eyes. I know it looks like tears but it isn't. I'm not crying yet, though I suspect I should be. I've always cried at funerals. It's the hymns that get me going, all that sentiment, all those claims of some other land, some afterlife, and I just believe when you die, you die. Your molecules go back to the earth. Death *is* a sad thing. I sobbed my way through the entire week after Jemima's death. At her funeral I got through almost an entire box of hankies – mainly because I was so depressed that only her daughter and a couple of cat nuts turned up on the day. Only five people to watch a great woman go. Still, the cats must have been praying for her.

'So, what now?' Josh looks at me helplessly, then the spade against the garden fence.

'I suppose we just put him in.' I gesture pathetically to the hole. I'm feeling rather lost.

'D'you want to do the ashes to ashes, dust to dust?' he jokes.

'Don't be stupid,' I say, my throat closing up, half-smiling, almost (almost, almost) sobbing and attempting to kick him at the same time. 'That would be ridiculous. He's only a cat.' There's a sting in my eye, a quiver on my lip and a throaty spasm rising inside me. I try and hold it down, but suddenly it bursts and my face creases up and I find myself having to turn away from Josh, because I know I look ridiculous when I cry.

Josh takes hold of the bag and tries to prise it off me. Initially I resist. 'Come on, Mills, let me do it,' he says. 'We can't stand out here for ever.' And he takes it away and places it in the pool of mud that's developing in the hole. The rain is making a lake of our grave.

I stand there for a few minutes, staring at the soggy bag. 'Bye, Tibbs,' I say pathetically. Meanwhile, Josh runs in and gets a sheet of clear plastic from the kitchen and places it over the grave. He brings a cagoule too, but by now my dress is already wet through. With a muddy flourish, Josh starts shovelling the soil back into the grave. I stand there motionlessly watching. Shovel after shovel of earth falls on top of my Tibbs, and I feel the warm trickle of a tear run down my face. It mingles with the rain. 'Bye, baby . . .' I imagine his molecules running into the ground, flowing with the rainwater and joining the immense chaos of it all. 'Bye, Tibbs . . .'

They say God gives with one hand and takes away with another. Now all I have is Purrl. Funny how these things happen. I don't need to look for a replacement for Tibbs – though of course he's irreplaceable – I already have one. She's here, living with us already. My new baby. My only feline companion now is Purrl. All I have is her.

Every day I learn more about Purrl. I start to know her little habits, the way she likes things done. She's very different from Tibbs. Cats are. They're as different from each other as one man is from another. Now that Tibbs is gone and Purrl occupies his place as cat of the household, I notice Purrl's individuality all the more. Purrl likes raw organic pork, she likes the occasional piece of bitter, dark chocolate – which is strange in a cat – and she hates milk. She can't stand rock music but will listen to Beethoven and Debussy and doesn't mind the radio being on, provided it is tuned to the classics. Purrl doesn't really like drinking water from her bowl. She only does that if she has to. What she prefers is to drink from a running tap, like a fresh spring. Sometimes I walk into the bathroom and find her stood over the sink, waiting for water to come out. I switch the tap on and she laps it up hungrily, like she hasn't drunk in days.

Purrl likes watching TV. She also likes to stand on the bookcase by the front window and watch the world go by. She's fascinated by flies and spiders. Purrl is wary of Zara and, I think, slightly scared of Josh. She's graceful and gentle and beautiful. I adore her. If I were a cat I'd like to be her.

*

It's time now to stop waiting. To move on and get on with our lives. Though the truth is I'm hardly thinking of Tibbs at all now. That's not what preoccupies me even in the slightest. So, despite my reluctance and my current reclusiveness, we're having a dinner party. Josh thinks it would be good for me. He's worried that I don't get out enough, keeps dragging me out for walks with Zara. What does he know? Josh just wants to have a good time himself. And Tamara and Guy are hardly the ideal couple to cheer me up. They're so self-absorbed. They're more likely to make things worse. Still, tonight's the night and I've forced myself into chef mode. I've checked out my recipe books, got out the rice cooker and I'm thinking Japanese.

Tamara's throaty, cigarette-husked voice is already getting right up my nose. She's only been here twenty minutes and I want to slap her across those barely foundationed cheeks. Right now, she's droning on about some arthouse movie which she thinks is positively the most wonderful film she has seen in a long time. She absolutely adored the photography, the performances and that resonance . . . Tamara is precisely the sort of girl I've always hated. Too in love with the sound of her own voice.

Still, she's digging in well to the sushi. Which of course she *loves, darling*, being an art-world girl who has lunch in the local sushi place practically every day. Me, I tried it for the first time a couple of weeks ago. Before, I used to always hate the idea of raw fish, but recently I've come round to it. Recently, I've started to think that there would be nothing more mouth-watering than a nice slice of cold, raw fish. Josh thinks there's something slightly mean about sushi, but he agrees with me serving it, because he knows that Tamara and Guy will go for it. And they do.

Tamara and Guy are two of our four guests for dinner tonight. Tamara, late twenties and working in a swanky art gallery, and Guy, about Josh's age and earning a packet in advertising, are partners, and *Josh's friends* – positively not mine. Guy completes a very different picture of Josh from the one I know. But then I have painted a rather biased view. Though I know Josh inside-out, I often forget the gulf between us. Josh was a rich kid. It's how he knows Guy. They went to the same private school, were buddies from early youth, smoked joints in the dorms together and nicked cheap trophies from souvenir shops on school trips. They were rebels – or so they like to think.

Personally I couldn't quite be bothered with a dinner party, but Josh insisted. He convinced me that we do owe them a return dinner. Guy took us out to some posh place where he knows the management, and I guess it must have cost a lot. There was no way we could return that sort of hospitality. This was the closest we could go to something fancy – only I couldn't quite face another session just with Tam and Guy, so I've invited a couple of my own guests, Sophie and Gabriel. I'm not at my best at the moment, so it helps to be in familiar company.

So, here we are, the six of us. Sophie arrived early, to give me a hand. She's good like that – can always be relied on to pitch in in your hour of need. Tonight, however, she was more gossip than real practical help. She had problems. She always had problems and was good at making them into a whole show – the Sophie show.

'You'll probably find this ridiculous, but,' she began, then paused. 'Well, after all this time of saying I never want a kid, I've been getting this weird thing. Every time I see a baby in the street I start wondering how it would feel about me if I were its mother. That's fine. You probably get that. But I've also started to imagine myself as my own daughter. I don't know what started it. I've been doing it for the last couple of weeks. Maybe I was thinking about my mum – she's been put on another new set of drugs that probably will only make her sicker anyway. And I've been making speeches to myself about her. And I suddenly thought, what would my daughter say about me?'

'She'd find you square and embarrassing. Guaranteed. All daughters do.'

'Probably. Although this imaginary daughter of mine doesn't. Of course, instead of saying all the bad stuff about me, she sits there telling all her friends that I'm the most amazing, warm, loving person.'

'Are you trying to tell me that you're thinking about having a kid?' I swallow.

'Well, not really. But . . .'

'But?'

'One of the girls in 5B is pregnant.' Sophie sighed and picked up a sliver of salmon. 'Supermarket or fishmonger?' she asked.

'Supermarket,' I confessed. 'I know, I know . . . guilty, guilty.' Sophie is one of those organic obsessives who insists that everything she eats comes directly from source, grows her own vegetables and plans to settle down with a large garden and some chickens in about five years' time.

'You'll be sorry when you end up with bowel cancer. Still, it's good for you, this raw fish – full of amino acids and potassium and, I don't know . . . other stuff like that.' She swung around the room and perched her bum on the top of the fridge. 'I've also been getting letters from that kid in the sixth form about how he'd like to fuck me in the chemistry cupboard – lots of graphic detail.'

'Sounds a bit more pleasant than sticking a Bunsen burner up you in the bike shed, or whatever it was that last one said.'

'I guess so . . . You know, I've been taking that herbal remedy Paul bought for me.' Sophie poured herself a glass of wine.

'And?' I continued, chopping absent-mindedly.

'Seems to be working. I haven't had any colds or flus in the last four months and the school's been swimming in them. I feel like I've been wading through phlegm. Can't believe one of them hasn't hit me yet.'

'That's good.' I swiped my knife through the sharpener, metal grating against metal.

'Well, I don't know if it's the herbal thing or the exercise or the sleeping more. It could be any of them. I'm always trying to find explanations for why I'm fit one day and half dead the next. The immune system's a mysterious thing.'

'Four months,' I repeated. 'I guess that's good going.' I watched the shiny blade slivering through glistening pink flesh.

'It is considering I normally catch everything. You know me . . . I was a pretty sickly child – that's probably why I'm such a health freak now . . . You should take some.'

'Some what?'

'Of this stuff,' she said, rifling around inside her handbag.

'No, I don't think so. I'm not really into it.' I cut off a slice of the salmon and tried feeding it to Purrl. 'There you go, honey.'

'Really you should. You're looking a bit run-down.' She looked me quickly up and down, gaze scanning over my cheeks, eyes and hair.

'Am I? I hadn't noticed. Maybe I am feeling a little tired, but nothing that's out of the ordinary.'

'Trust me.' She squinted at me and pulled out a small brown bottle. My eyes followed it, small and anonymous-looking, over to the sink. Water from the tap, ten drops of dank brown liquid falling from a pipette and there, in a glass, thrust into my hand, was a pale yellow potion.

'Drink up.'

There's a brief silence at the table.

'Now what was that you were going to say, Mills?' Guy asks.

I've forgotten, but never mind. I did have something to say about the film. I'd been holding it in my mind, to drop into the conversation later, but it's gone now. If Tamara had stopped earlier I might have had a chance to butt in. But not now. Suddenly I can't think of anything whatsoever to say. 'Can't quite remember,' I murmur. People shuffle and look down at their food. 'Can't have been very significant.'

There's a momentary peace as everyone eats. Tamara holds her chopsticks daintily, pincer-like extensions of her perfectly manicured fingers. Sushi is her natural food. She would never consider using a fork. Probably she even uses chopsticks to eat her organic muesli of a morning. I watch her grasp a piece of mackerel between the slender wooden fingers, then elevate it elegantly to her mouth. It's like a prandial ballet. First the pincers close around the food, slowly and carefully. They grip with gentle pressure, then they lift. Up and down. Middle finger supports, index finger controls. Grasp, lift, release.

Tam's so perfect she reminds me of Mina – one of those people everybody adores. Not that she looks like Mina, because Mina, of course, looks like me. She just makes me feel like Mina always did. I can feel her summing me up as an also-ran, thinking, *What a loser,* then glancing over to Josh and wondering why he's with me. Josh is a winner. *Isn't he always?* He makes up for all my flaws. Tonight, he's dressed in black cord trousers and a mint-green shirt with an embroidered design. 'Cool shirt,' says Guy. 'Mmmm, very sexy,' says Tamara. This isn't his usual get-up. He's obviously made an effort – spent half the evening in the bedroom posing in front of the full-length mirror and trying on different combinations, while I slaved away in the kitchen. He can be such a tart. I know he's been looking forward to Guy and Tamara coming over – and not just for Guy. Tamara is a looker and she flirts with him a lot. Sometimes I'm still a little awe-struck by Josh.

Guy and Tamara looked very slightly lost for words on meeting Gabriel and Sophie.

Yes, *my* friends look like a couple of hicks next to them. Sophie is a hippie sort, but Gabriel is just Gabriel – plain and odd and old. He wears the same scruffy clothes all the time, barely aware of what he looks like and what other people think, his hair scruffed up all over the place. Guy held out a hand to shake with Gabriel, and Tamara gave Sophie a hesitant kiss on one cheek. They were apologising for their lateness ('Guy's new car wouldn't start'), but I knew it was more than that. It was clearly deliberate. Guy and Tamara never like to arrive at anything on time. It's a power thing, and it's pretty rude.

At least, chic or not, my friends arrived on time, even if Gabriel was already a little drunk and moody. He practically stumbled through the door. 'Just thought I'd start the evening early,' he said, eyes hitting me starkly. It seemed like he had something to say but instead he just thrust a new box of tetracycline into my hand.

'Good sushi,' says Guy.

I smile and nod. 'Thanks.'

'Yes, delicious,' says Tamara.

Finally the men have managed to get Tamara off the subject of Robert Redford and are trying to conduct a conversation about politics. 'We should stay out of the whole thing,' says Guy.

'Don't be such a fucking bore,' groans Tamara. 'You're so depressing.' And she launches into some tirade about Carl Andre and other art things. She may know her Oldenburgs from her Rauschenbergs, but she's an idiot really. She can't talk politics, makes gestures of boredom as soon as Josh mentions the election ('That's not dinner party conversation,' she says) and doesn't have a clue about the way the physical world works. Not that I really think all this is such a big deal. Personally, I barely participate in the arguments myself. I'm not that interested in politics. I'm not sure any one of us is – we just pretend. We are – *they* are – interested only in saying the right things, in having the right things; interested only in looking good. Really all anyone's interested in is *things*. People love *things*.

'Oh, shut up, Tams,' says Guy. 'Just because you don't have a clue.'

They bicker on for a while. Meantime, I watch Purrl wander into the room. I sense her coming long before she arrives. She cautiously enters, surveying the crowd. She's curious, I know. All afternoon she's been wondering what's going on. And now she wanders round like an invisible voyeur, lurking in the shadows, barely noticed by our guests. I think about drawing attention to her, of introducing her to Gabriel, Guy and Tamara, but decide not to. I can tell she'd rather go unnoticed. She's never seen so many people in here before.

Purrl watches. I can tell that she's watching like me, taking in every gesture, observing every shift in mood and silently scorning the stupidity of it all. She skirts the table, unfazed by the argument going on overhead. Our guests are engrossed. They're barely aware of the presence of my remarkable cat, though Purrl's long white tail dances in front of them, writing letters in the air, shifting from 's' to comma. Her back arches like an 'n'. Her head shifts from side to side, surveying expectantly. Then she ducks under the table and makes a beeline for me. I feel her brush against my legs. I hear a soft mew and sense her ready to jump. She leaps up on my lap. I stroke her. We both watch. Together we take in this little piece of theatre.

In between courses Tamara lights up a menthol cigarette and starts yabbering on about the gallery she works at. 'This band was in the other day, and you know what . . .' Sophie looks like she could easily throttle her and tries to change the subject to Third World debt. I sit quietly and say very little. What's the point anyway? All this pretentious blab, blab, blab takes us nowhere. I might as well sit back in silence and enjoy the sushi, which does taste good. *Then there's the skiing holiday she went on a couple of months ago.* Yawn, yawn, yawn. I can hardly get motivated about it. I'm in voyeuristic mode. All I feel like doing is watching. Purrl and I sit and watch like two little queens judging the world. Occasionally Gabriel glances at me – he's all quiet and boozily shut into himself. He says very little – he's too shy – but I have the feeling he could flare up at any minute. There's something in his posture that shows his straining. Can't anyone else see it? Gabriel is on edge.

Guy is the only one who can manage to drown Tamara out. While she talks of art, he talks of cuisine. He likes to think he knows about food, knows the menu off by heart for all the best restaurants. Never stops going on about it. *Yawn, yawn, yawn again.* Thinks he should be a restaurant critic. It's scary cooking for these two. I feel like every mouthful they're analysing my abilities as a cook; every flavour is a mark of my taste or lack of taste. Guy gets out some cigars, which he got in duty-free on his way back from Italy. 'Like one,

Mills?' he says jokingly. I almost think of taking one for a laugh, but decline. And anyway, what's he doing smoking when we haven't even had dessert? I cough gently but he ignores it.

'You know what you should do?' says Guy, blowing a soft trail of smoke. 'You should give up on this dentist lark and get a job in the City. You're not too old just yet.'

To Tamara we are all to be judged by our wallpaper, while to Guy every person is a salary. He drops pro ratas, commissions and bonuses all the time.

Tired of it all, I retire to the kitchen without a word.

'Need a hand, Milla?' Gabriel pipes up as I head down the corridor.

I can feel his eyes following me, but just shake my head, murmuring, 'No,' while secretly wishing he would come. My good friend Gabriel.

~

Milla is quite beautiful – or at least she seems so to me. The gap between her teeth, the smooth, kink-free hair, the slight scar in the corner of her mouth where she fell down as a kid . . . these are just some of the Milla things.

The dinner party? I was there. It was a bit of a strange affair. An odd combination of guests – as you often get when two members of a couple bring their friends together. There was a lot of talk of cars and salaries and interior décor and name-dropping, which bored me – and Milla too probably. A lot of the details are quite hazy, except to say that Milla wasn't quite her usual self. She murmured a lot and didn't appear to be listening to much of the conversation, which isn't surprising. Then there was this Mina-like tic of flicking her fingers. Still, she had this aura . . . there's always this aura.

She was looking pale and fidgety, seemingly distracted by the operations she had to perform as host – things like opening bottles and removing dirty plates appeared to absorb her. Rather than join in the conversation she fussed over the food or walked out into the kitchen or petted the cat. It was the first time I'd seen the cat, and for some reason I didn't really take to it. It was quite odd-looking, so thin it was almost barely there. At one point Milla got down from the table and crouched on the floor, staring at it for several minutes. Josh hardly noticed – he was too busy talking to the other girl – but it was strange. The two of them were head to head, just gazing at each other, like two cats in courtship or going in for a fight.

Then when Milla did speak, Josh would butt in and talk over her, as if he was scared she'd embarrass him. One mention of the word 'cat' and he'd start fluttering, creating a wall around Guy and Tamara of sophisticated arty talk. One instance stood out. For some reason the conversation strayed on to the subject of euthanasia. Milla just suddenly went off on one, saying that it was the only civilised option in certain situations, that she thought it was a weird world of double standards that we lived in. 'Sometimes people just don't want to be there any more,' she said. I couldn't help thinking it must have something to do with Mina. Josh either completely failed to pick up on her train of thought or simply didn't want to, because he changed the subject. He turned to Tamara and loudly asked her what she thought of the latest art exhibitions in town.

The food was good though.

~

An embarrassed clicking of chopsticks. There's tension in the air.

When I walk in the door with the desserts, there is an awkward silent pause. Guy pretends to have been talking about Chris Martyn, but I ignore it, I heard exactly what the last line said was. Josh was speaking and it ran something like, 'She's not been herself recently, been a bit odd.' Of course I know that *she* is me. Who else could it be? It's not even like I'm being paranoid, it was so obvious. They were talking about me. And besides I'm sure I heard Josh whisper, 'Tibbs dying really got to her,' to Tamara earlier. They both nodded sympathetically. *That* couldn't have been my imagination as well.

I sit down in silence, and enjoy their strained attempts at a cover-up. Only Tamara looks un-flustered. She takes a long, unfazed sip from her plum wine.

'I think he's very sexy,' I say.

'Who?'

'Chris Martyn.'

Briefly, I'm reminded of why I hate these couply dinner parties, with their conspiracies and plottings. People know each other too well. There's all those undercurrents which, if you're an outsider,

134

are so irritatingly difficult to grasp. Little comments that you can't understand. Jokes that just don't seem funny, but people laugh quietly and knowingly at. Whisperings between partners. I always vowed I wouldn't get so inward-looking and chummy. Why start now?

I start to pass round the desserts and am transfixed by the chocolate sauce on Sophie's ice cream. Its spindly trickles have spread out across the pale vanilla to form the shape of a spider: a huge brown blotch with head, body and eight delicate legs. It almost seems to move before my eyes. Irritated, I stick a spoon into the bowl and strike a dash through it, destroying the image. I look up and watch them chatter.

They're all laughing about the idea of marriage. Everyone, that is, except Gabriel, who's sitting there in the corner, silently destroying himself.

What about Guy and Tamara?

'Christ, no,' says Tamara. 'Me marry Guy? You've gotta be joking. He can't even wash his undies.'

Guy teases Josh, mockingly saying, *six months now*, as if it's a long time we've been going out, when it isn't. Josh just gives an embarrassed, 'Uh-uh. Not yet. And anyway, Guy, we can't give up on that idea of us both being bachelors together – getting the pad, smoking pipes and living like pigs.'

'Yup . . . total hogs.'

Gabriel blushes but keeps his head down.

Tamara laughs loudly and slaps a heavy hand

down on Josh's thigh. She leans across to whisper something in his ear – apparently about Guy. They both giggle.

'Don't you laugh,' Guy warns Josh. 'There's plenty of stories I can tell Mills about your teenage escapades.' He leans towards me. 'I can tell you things you wouldn't dream of that Josh got up to. I know the very worst of his childhood antics.'

Tamara takes a tired but elegant sip of her sake. 'Not that boring stuff again. *Guy*, we've all heard those stories too many times.'

Meanwhile, Gabriel has crawled out of his shell and is mumbling some sob story, which I assume is about Melanie, to Sophie – but I can't bring myself to listen. I've heard it too many times before. And anyway I'm too entranced by the way Tamara is entrancing my Josh. I feel a sharp pang. The Josh and Tamara thing is really bugging me. She's so obvious, can't keep her hands to herself. She keeps touching Josh, a little brush of the arm here and a trace of the thigh there, legs angled just that little bit too close to his, head bent that little bit too far forward. But I'm watching her. I see every single little gesture. And I see Josh touching her. They're both flirting out-rageously. Can't everyone else see it? They must be able to and that makes it all the more humiliating.

It's probably my own fault. Like an idiot I did the table setting with Josh between Tamara and Sophie and me between Gabriel and Guy. It was as if I wanted it to happen. It's strange the way girls fancy Josh. I mean, it's not like there's any mystery to him.

That's not saying he's shallow or superficial or anything. Some of the most mysterious people turn out to be about as deep as a puddle. No, how deep or not he is is not the Josh thing. What's brilliant and fanciable about him is less to do with who he is than with what he does to other people. He works some kind of magic. He makes other people see their lives better than he sees his own.

I look over to Guy, who also seems to be starting to get irritated, but he's used to it. He's tried getting me animated but failed miserably and doesn't seem inclined to persist, so he's moved on to Sophie. He's as bad as Tamara. I guess the two of them both normally behave like a couple of tarts, and Guy just feels he's missing out this evening. Hence the germinating irritation – a bad mood brewing.

'You're all so false,' I feel like saying, but don't. Instead I just start quietly humming some random tune under my breath. It's just a tiny tune, but it blots out the noise.

Josh notices, despite his absorption in Tamara's conversation, and gives me an evil look as if to tell me to stop behaving like a nutcase. I stop humming.

'I guess I better go and make coffee,' I say.

Josh nods.

~

I confess. I confess that I deliberately followed Milla along to the kitchen. I'd been watching her all evening and I couldn't help thinking that something was not quite right. Josh was so strangely inattentive and he flirted a lot with the other girl. Milla didn't seem to notice that so much, but I did, and felt irritated. There was one particularly weird moment when for some reason everybody had got off on some ironic half-philosophical discussion about what was the most important thing in life. Guy joked some kind of expensive cigars, his girlfriend said a French manicure, and Milla said 'love'. Josh just laughed and told her not to be so glib.

Suffice to say, I thought she needed company, sympathy. But I still can't work out what I thought I was doing. After all, Josh was just along the corridor, and for all the times, why this time? Perhaps because she seemed so alone.

So I made up some excuse about needing to go to the toilet and took a detour to the kitchen on the way. And there she was, Milla, standing there with her back to me at the coffee machine, singing to herself, some folksy tune, bare shoulders which looked so kissable. I couldn't resist. Shoes squeaking across the floor, I walked up behind. It seemed easy. So familiar. So comfortable. And really not a big deal at all.

~

Gabriel comes and finds me. He's a little drunk, and the first thing I feel is him slipping a hand up the back of my skirt. I let out a light squeal. But I'm slightly drunk too and it feels nice.

'Not enjoying the party?' he asks, all full of Dutch courage, as his hand glides along the back of my thigh. Taking my breath away, it drifts over my knickers. 'What did I tell you?' He cups my buttock with his hand. 'Didn't I tell you,' he says, turning me towards him.

I'm reminded for a second of our student gropings and I feel a surprising kick inside. I don't really expect to feel this now I'm going out with Josh. But then, he's upstairs being a tart with Tamara, why shouldn't I? Besides, Gabriel and I are good friends. It's just a friendly thing.

'How much have you had to drink?' I ask.

'Not much,' he drawls. 'Just enough.'

I try pathetically to push him away, but find myself laughing. Gabriel looks so silly when he's drunk, all badly coordinated and gangly. He lunges forward and our lips collide. My breath catches and I hesitate – then let go to it. Gabriel's soft, sake-breathed lips are against mine, Lip to lip, wet and comfortably familiar. It feels surprisingly good. *Mmmm* ... he groans softly and involuntarily, as if some long-lost part of himself has been rediscovered. I almost think he can't hear himself, that no one can hear us. For a moment I stop thinking about Josh. Just for a moment I let it all go. It's a couple of seconds before I come to my senses, before I bring myself to push him away, and even then I don't quite manage it in time. Too late?

'Er ... herm,' I hear from behind. It's Sophie. 'Just making the coffee?' she asks, raising her eyebrows.

We break off, looking slightly embarrassed, but giggling. 'Well, you know, it's a big job.' Gabriel is looking sheepish. He avoids Sophie's eyes. I'm just finding it funny. I know she blames me, thinks I abuse Gabriel. She'd like to protect him from me.

'Maybe you should come back up to the table, Gabriel. You're missing out on the liqueurs,' she says. 'And maybe *you* should actually get on with making that coffee.'

I shrug helplessly. 'Thanks,' I say.

'*Aaaaeeeeeeyyyaaahhhh!*' A shriek cuts through the air, and though it's difficult to tell initially whether it's a dog, a cat or a human, I suddenly realise it's Tamara. 'Ugh!' she cries. 'It's disgusting.'

I bite my lip and half-smile at Sophie, who cocks her head as if to say, 'Well, go on then – sort it out,' and find myself reluctantly trekking along the hall towards this small terror. 'Do something about it, would you?'

As I enter the room, I see Tamara's face frozen in mid-grimace.

'What's wrong?' I ask.

Tamara stares at me resentfully. 'That cat of yours . . . you should see what she's done.' A long, emerald nail points at the ground, at Purrl, who is sitting there, proud and contented as if she's got nothing whatsoever to do with it. And on the floor, next to my cat, is a large, barely moving lump of fur. It's a grey, pink-nosed mouse and the terrified creature is squeaking.

'She's brought you a present,' I inform Tamara.

'A present?' she whines. 'That is *so* foul.'

'It's a little dessert for you.'

140

Tamara looks drained and possibly on the verge of being flustered, though she would never admit it. 'You mean she wants me to eat it?'

'Who knows? Probably she'll just eat it herself.'

Purrl gazes back at me haughtily. Meanwhile, Tamara launches herself into another fit of hysterics, and Guy tries to fan her with a paper serviette. It's slightly unreal. I almost imagine she looks like she's going to faint, and Josh dashes to the rescue too, handing her a glass of water, which she practically bats out of the way in her desire to stay looking cool.

Josh looks at me threateningly. 'Mills . . . I think you'd better remove that mouse from the room.'

'OK.' I shrug my shoulders. 'But it's not going to do any harm. I mean, Purrl's already half-killed it.' And I bend over and pick it up gently and carefully between my fingers. It makes little effort to escape.

Josh smiles helplessly. 'It's going to be OK, Tams,' he says. 'Just breathe slowly.'

'Don't worry! I'm OK,' she wheezes. 'I'm perfectly fine.'

I move towards the door, bringing the mouse up to her eye level. 'See, it's all right,' I say. 'Purrl just wanted to have a little play with it before she ate it. I'll put it out of its misery.'

I march through to the kitchen, slamming the intervening door behind me.

When I walk back in, everything seems to have returned to normal. Tams is still swooning over

Josh. Guy looks like he wants to go home and Sophie's got on one of her animal rights crusades.

Gabriel has come alive for a few seconds, to mouth off about cloning, which he thinks would be highly beneficial to medicine and has no problem with. Tamara suddenly looks delighted. She's clearly obsessed with the idea of having a clone of herself. *Wouldn't it be great to have another perfect person in the world like her . . .*

'You'd hate it,' I say. 'And anyway, what's the difference between that and having a twin? It's not as if two clones really are the same people, it's not as if they're going to be able to relate to each other, is it? I should know. In fact, you're probably all clones yourselves. Apparently half the people in the world started out as part of a twin, they just lost their clone early.'

They all stop talking and silently turn and look at each other, as if I'm losing it. But I'm aware of the fact it's the most relevant thing I've said all night. I shrug my shoulders and smile. 'It's not a big deal.'

Guy, who is utterly bored ('fucking science'), cuts through the silence to tell Josh he's just bought a new car. He's starting to really irritate me. 'Stunning steering, great engine, purrs like a pussy.'

'I hate cars,' I say, hoping to shut him up. There is a hushed silence. 'Stinking things, polluting the atmosphere, killing people and destroying things – and all because people can't be bothered to walk.'

Guy lets out an embarrassed titter. 'Guess you

142

won't be coming for any rides out into the country with us then,' he says.

Tamara throws Josh a look questioning whether I'm serious or not. 'I think it's a beaut.'

I look down and stroke Purrl. It's pointless arguing. For a few seconds I listen to the folksy CD in the background. I close my eyes.

When I look up, they're all laughing at some kind of joke. All except Gabriel, who seems to have fallen asleep. Tamara is giggling uncontrollably and holding a cigarette just as delicately as she'd held her chopsticks. I realise I haven't even heard the joke, let alone got it. What had it been? I pretend a belated laugh, like I've just suddenly got it, but I haven't.

'I'm surprised you find that funny,' says Josh.

'Well, you know,' I mumble pointlessly.

'My last boss had his licence taken away from him the month after he passed his test,' says Guy.

'Ouch. I'll bet that hurt.'

'And the test examiner told him he'd done an immaculate test.'

I'm feeling a little queasy and wish they'd all go. 'One of my friends was hit by a car,' I say. 'I went to visit her in hospital. She can barely speak now. The only way I can tell she understands anything I say is that she laughs at my jokes – my stupid, pathetic jokes.'

The silence is now complete. Everyone stares at me. Josh kicks me under the table, hard, as if to say I've overstepped the mark. But I don't care. I don't care for Guy and Tamara's spit-worthy expensive

143

liqueur and their fashionable ways. I don't care at all what they think of me.

I slump in my chair and stare him out. 'I'm not apologising,' I say. 'It's the truth.'

'I think maybe you should have a bit of a lie-down for a while,' Josh says. He's trying to suggest that I'm too tired or too drunk. I refuse. I'm not missing the end of the party, not leaving Josh and Tamara unwatched.

'Don't worry, Josh,' says Guy. 'I think we should be getting back. I've got an early morning tomorrow.'

'Yes, yes,' says Tamara, who for once looks slightly at a loss for words. 'Lovely sushi though, Mills.'

'Yes, great sushi.'

Josh gives them their coats and bags and takes them to the door. I stand at the end of the hall and watch them say goodbye, observing Tamara as she kisses him firmly on the lips. I almost think I see him whisper something to her.

'Well, I guess I'd better go too,' says Sophie.

Gabriel is slumped in the corner. He could stay overnight but I order him a taxi. Better to get him out of the way, send him back to his own bed. Poor Gabriel. I almost feel like bending down and kissing him, but don't. I pinch his nose and wiggle it a little and he opens his eyes. 'Milla . . . Milla . . . You and me,' he drones, as I help him to his feet to take him to the taxi. 'You just can't take the fact that we're alike . . .'

'Don't be stupid, Gabe.'

'I'm not stupid. I know it . . . An' I know why.' He nods pathetically.

'Gabriel, I think it's time to get in the taxi. Time to go home.'

'Right, Milla, right . . . Ger in the taxi.'

Through the haze of half-sleep – a dream about cats and other things – I hear Josh come into the room. He doesn't switch on the light. He's been clearing up. I was too tired and drunk to help, so I just skipped the toothpaste, pulled my dress off and stumbled into bed in my undies. But he got on with the chores. He's never one to leave things till the morning.

I sense Josh undressing, listen to the shuffle of clothes falling to the ground. He pauses and sighs, lingering by the bed, watching me through the darkness. Then he pulls back the duvet and tumbles in.

'Mmmm . . . sugar,' I murmur, rolling towards him.

He says nothing. I pull in closer, drawing myself up, like a monkey curled around the horizontal stretch of his body. He feels sweet and warm and smells of alcohol and I snuggle in. Josh is silent. He sighs again, pulls the duvet over his shoulder and wriggles out of my grasp. In a second I find him turned away from me. I'm facing the mountainous mass of his back.

'Hon?' I whisper. For some reason I feel a desire to tell him all the stuff about Mina, to explain myself. I want him to understand about Mum and

Dad and Mina and me. I want to explain myself. 'What's wrong, hon?'

He doesn't answer. There is a long, ominous silence, though I think he can't have fallen asleep yet and I'm sure he must have heard me.

It seems odd that he should be like that, funny that he's in a mood with me. After all, I wasn't the one who was sweet-talking Tamara all evening. True, there'd been that skirmish with Gabriel in the kitchen, but Josh didn't know about that. Josh didn't have a clue. On the face of it, it should be me in the bad mood.

I wait a few seconds and run a hand along the length of his side, pulling myself towards him again. He shrugs his shoulders, shaking me away.

'Come on, sweets,' I say, 'what is it?'

Silence again, then an exasperated, 'Nothing.'

'Yes, there is,' I say, pinching a little stretch of flesh around his waist. He wriggles uncomfortably.

'No, there isn't,' he sighs. There's another pause and then, 'Just go back to sleep. We'll talk about it in the morning.'

I lie there staring at him in the darkness, watching the dark shadow that is his body rise and fall infinitesimally with his breath. He's like a stranger. 'Go to sleep,' he murmurs again, voice low and barely audible. This is weird. Normally he wants to have sex, but not now, not tonight. Tonight I'm the one who's feeling out in the cold. I'm the one who's being given the unflinching cold shoulder. I try kissing the back of his neck and he shrugs again.

146

There's no doubt that I've done something wrong. But what? I run my mind back through the events of the evening, the arrival of Tam and Guy, the sushi, the marriage talk – and find myself completely guiltless. Or at least virtually guiltless. Maybe I shouldn't have said that thing about cars and maybe I'd been a bit quiet, but I had been as good a host as could be expected. I was sure of that.

Josh remains motionless. His will keeps him steady against me. I can feel him refusing to move and a frustration rises up inside me. *Why's he doing this?* I wonder if crying would work, would gain me a little sympathy. It could be worth a try. In fact, I do actually feel like crying and tears start to well up in my eyes. I sense the water collecting in the corners, running noiselessly down my face. Before my throat and nose are even ready, I let out a loud sniff. It reverberates through the silent room. I wait to let him hear it, which I'm sure (despite his impression of a deep sleeper) he does. And when he doesn't respond I sigh, sniff again and let a tear drip on to my pillow. I turn my own back to him.

'Well, OK then,' I mutter. 'Be like that.'

The living, breathing mass that is my Josh does not move. It keeps on refusing me, keeps on snubbing. I feel like punching him, but instead I just lie there, breathing loud and tearfully until I fall asleep.

G'morning . . . I wake up and stumble through to view the remains of yesterday: half-empty bottles of wine, the occasional unwashed plate, the smell of alcohol left open and a damp purple stain on the tablecloth. The clock says ten, which is late, which means we've slept in, but I don't wake *him* up. I decide to leave that to Zara. *If he wants to be like that, he can be like that.* I haven't forgotten. My eyes feel sore and puffy and Josh's strangeness last night is bugging me. *Ugghhh.* I bend over to reach into the fridge. My head aches. Maybe I've got a hangover too. I forgot to drink any water before I went to bed and I feel fuzzy. I'm a wreck.

I pour myself a grapefruit juice and wander through to the bathroom. *Yuk.* I look disgusting – with those ugly bags under tiny half-open piggy eyes. I haven't looked this bad in years: not since Mum told me that Dad was giving both of our birthday presents to Mina, because I had been causing too much trouble. Mina, she said, had always been their favourite anyway.

Now a make-up job is in order. I can't have Josh seeing me like this. Though I'm not much one for make-up, at times of crisis my mother's training comes into play, with a little bit of kohl and cover-up. I dip a finger into a pot of cucumber-scented moisturiser and try massaging it into the stinging skin beneath my eyes.

There's no good excuse for it. I can barely work out why I've been crying, except that Josh was strange with me last night. My head swims. *That* surely didn't merit all these tears. I wouldn't normally react like this. I mean, I've been with Josh for a while and by now I'm used to the routine. We all know he has a tendency to be strange from time to time and this is one of those times.

The moisturiser makes little difference. My skin's a bit softer, but the soreness is still there. It almost burns. The mascara just seems to emphasise the mess around it and I look like I'm trying to cover something up – precisely the effect I am not looking for. What a pigface.

Zara starts barking and I know she must be waking Josh up. Though the incessant yapping is thudding through my head like a hefty mallet, I smile. It *is* funny how normal things seem in the clear light of day – how ordinary. The thundering thoughts that raged through my head in bed last night are now dull echoing thuds. All that mess seems like stupidity: the jealousy, the rejection, the over-dramatised pain that raged through my silent tears. It was all really unnecessary. I mean – Josh and I are in love. There *is* nothing wrong and there *was* nothing wrong. It was just one of those semi-sleep madnesses that sometimes catches a person. We'll be fine this morning.

Back in the kitchen I switch the filter coffee machine on. If I give Josh a strong, black, bitter Colombian coffee, just the way he likes it, that will be enough to make up. *Bigness* . . . I feel pleased with myself because it's a generous gesture. *It's big of me.* It's not me who's done anything wrong, so it shouldn't be me who makes the effort, but I'm willing to do it. I breathe in deep as the strong aroma of freshly ground

149

coffee beans wafts through the room.

I hear Josh heading straight for the toilet: the sound of trickling water, a few sighs and a yanking flush. He stumbles through in his pyjamas.

'Morning, love,' I say.

He doesn't answer – just heads straight over to the coffee machine and inspects it. It's still making plopping noises. 'Coffee not ready yet?'

'Couple of minutes.'

He sniffs and grabs a bowl, then fills it with muesli.

'You made a good dent in the washing-up last night,' I comment. 'There's not too much left to do – just a few serving dishes.'

'Mmmm hmmm.' He goes to the fridge and takes out the milk.

'Do you think it went all right? I mean, the party.'

Josh sniffs again. I listen to the long sloosh of milk pouring over cereal, then, 'No.'

'Oh, right,' I say and sit down, feeling the headache begin to swell again and my eyes start to sting. 'I see.'

Josh turns to me, dark eyes wide. He stares upwards for a second, then sighs. 'I know you don't like Guy and Tamara, but there was no need to be so rude to them.'

Mmmm . . . I guess they call this a lover's tiff. 'Well, sweetheart,' I say, 'if you hadn't been all over that ditzhead Tamara, things might have been different.'

He glares at me. 'I was not all over *that ditzhead*,'

150

he says defiantly. 'And she's not a ditzhead. She's a friend. I invited her to my party, so I talked to her. If you didn't take her so much at face value you'd find she's got lots of interesting stuff to say. You're just jealous.'

'Jealous? I am not jealous. What have I got to be jealous about?'

I know I seem a bit slack, but I do have a routine. Take this: every Monday I go to the Alice Elman rescue centre. It's a little contract I have with them. I go over and help out with any behavioural problems once a week, advising new cat owners and looking at any trauma cases. I'm generally away for the whole day. Purrl knows I do this. She's been here for five weeks and she's now clearly aware of what weekly routine I have. She knows Thursday night is Big Shop. She knows Saturday morning is Clothes Wash. Purrl is clever and she knows these things.

Today I wake up and, legs on automatic, head for the bathroom. Before I even enter I am overwhelmed by a strong, sweet, nauseating odour. I reel under the stench of what is immediately recognisable as cat sick. It practically knocks me out. *Cat sick*, it's a perfume that I'm intimately familiar with. It's heavy, acidic, and it catches you in the back of the nose like a bottle of vinegar. I retch slightly. I hold my breath for a second, but the tart pungency, the whiff of fetid flower and stomach juices, lingers in my passages. The back of my throat closes involuntarily. Then I see the vomit-damage, scattered in tiny reddish-brown pools all over the white-tiled floor. Accumulations of regurgitated meat. So much vomit for such a small cat. *Poor Purrl.* I feel another wave of nausea flood through me as the stink rises again, fizzing in my nostrils. There are pools in the bath, pools in the sink, pools on the mat and pools on the tiles.

Closing the door quickly to block out the stench, I look around for Purrl. I breathe a quick gulp of fresh air. 'Purrl . . . Purrl baby,' I call. 'What's up, my love?' I look in the living room, but she's not there. 'Hey, sweetie?' In the kitchen, she's lying on the floor, stretched out and motionless. She lifts her head and lets out a soft moan. 'Poor honey . . .' Her white body wriggles across the lino. Weak and tired, she stumbles to her feet. *Miaouh* . . . Her eyes look drained and colourless, her coat flecked with small brown splatters. I bend over and pick her up. *Miaouh* . . . she calls again. The smell catches me.

Purrl groans. *Colic*, I suspect, and wonder what could possibly have caused it. My mind races through the possibilities. Poison? Apart from any chemicals, which it's unlikely she's come across, there's is a chance that she may have eaten a mouse that's been poisoned, but even then all the symptoms aren't showing, and besides there was no sign of any mouse in the gunk she'd thrown up. I find myself wishing I'd been a better student.

I put her down and pick up my cat owner's almanac. I should know this kind of thing. It should be hidden away in those files of half-learned facts and figures now consigned to the wastebasket of my mind, but however much I dredge around in there, I can't seem to make much of those wasted years. I turn to the appropriate page. *Colic n. periodic spasms of pain caused by the stretching . . .* and read on. Poison seems unlikely but can't be ruled out, particularly given that she already seems to be perking up. Part of me wonders if it's all a bit of a show.

I decide to let her be for half an hour and clear up the mess. Josh will be waking up soon and I don't want him to stumble into the bathroom just yet. Purrl and I would be even less popular than we are already. Even yesterday he was groaning about red, itching eyeballs and rasped breathing and complaining that I must have let the cat on the bed again. He grunts angrily when Purrl claws the sofa, mutters grouchily when she leaves paw-prints on the lino and moans constantly on about the cat hairs everywhere. Sneezing loudly and fakely, 'That cat,' he mutters, 'it's provoking my asthma.' Josh is such a wimp, I can't imagine what he'd do at even the slightest whiff of a little cat sick.

Out come the rubber gloves, the disinfectant and the bucket of near-boiling hot water. I steel myself against the smell, swallow and venture into the bathroom. Grasping a large pad of kitchen roll, I wipe up the first pool of vomit. It makes me feel weak. I think I can't take it, but hold back the feeling. In the bin goes the first load. Followed by another wad and another pool. Then another and another, till I hardly feel a thing and all I've left to do is wash the floor with disinfectant, which is the nice, clean, sterile, easy bit. This is the bit that I enjoy. It's so purging, so cathartic to make things clean, to get rid of the dirt, the bacteria and the poison. I feel cleansed by the act of scrubbing, purified by bleach, wiped clean . . . fresh and new.

As anticipated, Josh has little sympathy for Purrl. He wakes up, goes through to the bathroom, washes, sniffs the air and calls through to me. 'Mills,' he says, 'do you think –' breathing deeply – 'do you think there's a funny smell in here?'

'Disinfectant,' I say.

'Why does the bathroom stink of disinfectant?'

'Purrl was sick.'

'Oh,' he says. 'Is she OK now?'

'Almost.'

Josh shrugs and wanders through to the kitchen, where Purrl is sitting.

He bends down towards her and speaks in a voice that doesn't sound like his own. 'You poor baby . . . Looks like you've had a bit of a hard night.' Then he glances quickly at me and says, 'Look, Mills, I said that I'd be into work early this morning so I'm in a bit of a rush. Can you deal with this yourself and maybe . . . do me a favour and walk Zars?'

I sit down with Purrl. She may be looking perkier, but I can tell she's still got a sore stomach. I invest-igate my personal feline drug supply cabinet, find a packet of pills and calculate her dosage as half a tablet.

It's already coming up for ten and I decide it would be best to phone Marjorie and say I won't be coming into the Elman centre till tomorrow. Marje won't be happy. It's not that she really needs me, it's just that she does like to feel in absolute control of everything.

'Well, what time do you think you'll grace us with your presence tomorrow?' she says, vaguely irritated.

I tell her probably not till ten, because I'm not feeling well. 'Must be a mild bout of food poisoning,' I say.

She shows little sympathy and murmurs, 'Oh dear.'

There's some tacky talk show on television. Today's issue: man's best friend. *Bloody dogs.* An ugly woman in a black wig whines on about how she used to come second to her husband's dog, which doesn't seem surprising given her grumpy demeanour. Even a pot-bellied pig would be better company than this witch. I switch over. Who wants to hear about dogs? I flick through the channels. Schools programmes, no . . . adverts, no . . . OK . . . Fred Astaire movie. That'll do. From her spot on my knee, Purrl stares intently at the screen. Purrl likes nothing better than to do this, and she's already starting to look healthier and happier. Within seconds she's perky and alert. You'd hardly believe that there'd been anything wrong with her.

Purrl loves television. She particularly loves movies and, contrary to Josh's claims, she's perfectly aware of what she's watching. She can see it all. Josh thinks cats are just intrigued by the flickering shadows on a screen, but you can tell it's more than that. She's so picky, my Purrl. There are two things that she'll always watch: cartoons and musicals. Two things she'll tolerate. For instance, if you're watching some stupid current affairs programme, she'll barely look at the screen, but as soon as you switch to *Roadrunner*, she'll be back on her seat, watching intently.

She digs her claws into my leg, as if in agreement with my every thought. I don't stop her. No, I like it. I thrill to the pain of those little pins puncturing my skin. *Ouch . . .* the claws dig in again and again. Purrl pads away at me as if I'm her mother – not to hurt me, but to love me. She's massaging away at my legs as if they're nipples. She's stimulating the milk flow: a kittenish reflex action, which shows she's relaxed. Silently, she sits there as, on my left leg, one slender white paw opens and stretches, then contracts on the purple fabric of my trousers. I can see her salivating with pleasure. Small droplets form on the corner of her mouth, expressing bliss.

The day happens without me noticing. Suddenly it's five o'clock and I find I haven't done anything – other than walk the dog and put the rubbish out –

and Josh is back, brandishing crisps and beer and other junk food.

'How was your day?' I ask, like the well-trained wife.

'Fine.' He shrugs. 'The usual . . .' and he slumps down into the sofa. 'How was yours?' His shirt rides up his stomach, exposing a small stretch of brownish skin, and I wonder if maybe he's developing a beer belly.

I used to think that the reason Josh and I hit it off was because we had a similar sense of humour. It was the only way I had of explaining the fact that, despite our many differences, we worked. All the laughter we shared. Now I'm not so convinced.

Not now I've discovered that Josh finds the crisp joke funny.

'What's red and white and spins round and round?' I asked, as I tried to explain the reason why I was refusing point blank to eat the solitary cheese crisp he was attempting to stuff down my throat.

'I dunno . . . A red and white Frisbee?' He shrugged.

'Uh-uh! A kitten in a washing machine.'

I waited for his response, assuming he would be as shocked as I had been. But instead he started to laugh . . . a very gentle, breathy giggle, the kind that, barely making any noise, can be perceived only in the creasing up of his face, the short jerking movement of his head, the quickening of his breath. Josh often laughs without making any noise. He looks so ridiculous he almost makes me laugh.

157

'That *is* actually quite funny,' he said.

'What?'

'Sick, but funny.' He was giggling away to himself. 'Funny because it's so pathetic and so sick and really not funny at all. Ha! That's what makes it funny. The fact that you think it's pathetic.'

Laughter's a funny thing . . .

No one's ever made me laugh as much as Mina. Partly, it was infectious – I just automatically started laughing as soon as she did.

Mina still laughs a lot now. Or at least, by that I mean Mina in her current state, which generally I refer to as 'Not Mina', because I refuse to believe it *is* her. I don't think she's actually there. Why should I? In the whole of the last fifteen years I've seen no sign. No, this is 'Not Mina'. It's my way of distinguishing between the real Mina, who's hiding somewhere, and this other person, who's a stranger, though quite nice.

'Not Mina' guffaws loudly echoing through the hallways of the home. She sometimes cries with laughter. From a distance it sounds like she's sobbing, but actually it always turns out she's laughing – she never really sobs, or wails or weeps, or any of the other things you might expect her to do. Last time I went to visit, I wandered into her room, where she was watching something on TV, her back turned to the doorway. She looked round from the screen for a brief second, saw that it was me and turned back to watch the slapstick

158

omnibus that was sending her into fits. I was too dull. Another boring person. I'd just tell her dull stories about my life as if she didn't understand English, slowly enunciating my words, animating the whole thing with huge gestures, helplessly trying to entertain. Trying too hard. Why bother with that when there was laughter to be had? It was infectious. I sat and watched the whole omnibus with her. I belly-laughed my way through the afternoon – wordlessly bonding. Being there with her.

'How about we go out for dinner tomorrow?' Josh slips his hand round my waist and pulls me towards him, as if to move in for a kiss. 'Hey?'

I shuffle toes on top of his, platforming me on to his eye level and feeling the rough suede of his shoes under my socks. Trying to avoid his eyes, I nuzzle into his neck. 'I don't know,' I murmur. 'I'm not really in the mood.'

'Come on, babes,' he says. 'You haven't been out for ages. Let's go out somewhere. Let's go and have a nice dinner. I'll take you to that Greek place you really like.'

'It's a waste of money. We might as well cook here.'

'We don't need to save money,' he says, leaning in towards my ear. 'Money's there to be spent, not saved. Haven't you got the hang of economics yet, hon? Come on, Millsie . . . I just feel we haven't done anything special for a while.'

'I know,' I whine. 'But not tomorrow. Maybe Thursday.'

Josh sighs. He brushes the hair from my forehead. 'OK. Promise we'll do it on Thursday. Promise.'

'OK.'

He sneezes. 'Bloody cat hairs.'

I know I promised Marjorie that I would go in, but I'm not so sure any more. You see, I'm standing here at the doorway, all ready to leave: bag in hand, car keys in pocket, thoughts tuned to working matters. I'm standing here and Purrl isn't looking too well again. The poor baby looks so weak and ill and she's making that sad mew sound which says, *I'm not too well, Milla, please stay home* . . . I can see it in her eyes too. They plead. They tell me, *Mummy, I hurt inside. I don't feel too good.*

Purrl could melt a heart of stone (unless it's Josh's heart). She's irresistible, and I just can't help falling for her every time. I know it's not right to give in to her, but she pleads so well. Against my better judgement, under some spontaneous compulsion, I phone up and cancel. Thankfully, I don't have to speak to Marjorie. Instead Julie picks up the phone. 'Oh, Mills, you poor dear . . .' She witters on, giving me motherly tips and advice about how to get well quick and make a hot toddy, and ending with, 'Have you been to the doctor's yet?'

'No,' I say. 'But I'm sure I'll be better by tomorrow.'

I put the phone down and pick up Purrl, who

perks up immediately. She rubs her face up against my arm. She licks my hand. 'Yes, baby,' I say. 'Mummy's going to stay home.'

I look through my movie collection and pick out a subtitled Italian horror film which I taped from the television.

That dog ought to be put down . . .

Just as the tension really starts to mount, our enjoyment of the movie is interrupted by loud barking noises. *Damn the bloody creature.* I press pause.

The dog is pacing along the hallway. She's howling like a wolf.

I wander through and, *sssssshhhhhhhhhhh*, try to get her to quieten down, but she doesn't. She just keeps pacing. 'Quiet, Zara,' I mutter, and give her a couple of dog biscuits. She gobbles them up and I wander back through to the living room. I hit play.

Within seconds she starts up again. This time, it's even louder. 'Zara . . .' I growl. 'If you don't shut up, I'm going to wring your neck.' We're so close to the end of the movie and it's really not right. Why can't Zara just sit down and watch it with us? Typical of a dog. Dogs are so needy, so wanting, so frantic, so famished, so craving, so over-eager, grasping, ardent and rabid . . . so unlike cats. Even Purrl, the most highly strung of cats, doesn't have that frantic wagging, panting, pacing energy. Dogs are such crap telly watchers. The day they breed a dog that prefers an evening in with a video to a game of fetch

161

in the park, then I'll consider adopting the canine species. Until then, they can stick to the dogs' home. *Leave us alone, bitch!*

She stops howling and starts making that pathetic whine. 'SHUT UP!' I yell. I'm fed up with Josh leaving the dog in the house for me to look after. 'KEEP YOUR TRAP SHUT!' She's not my responsibility and I can't be bothered with her. I've got a sick cat to look after and a big needy dog just gets in the way. To me, Zara's an unnecessary addition. 'I'LL PUT A CLAMP ON YOUR MUSH, MISSUS!'

Contempt is infectious. I can't help picking up on Purrl's dislike of Zara. The dog is an evolutionary dead end, a perversion of mammalian form. The dog is to be pitied for not being cat. It's to be disdained for its panting, slobbering canine flesh. It's to be scorned for its lack of sensitive whiskers and retractable claws. Neither cat nor human, it is simply a domestic servant. Unlike cats, dogs have no freedom. Purrl looks down on all that is not feline – all, that is, except me, and that's not just because she likes me. It's more than that. Underneath (and this is what Purrl has recognised in me) I have a feline soul. Whereas Zara is a dog, she's an animal thing, an *it*.

It's not just the fact that Zara is a dog that irritates me, it's more that she's stupid. Of course, theoretically I do believe all animals, including animals of the human variety, are equal. My head tells me that much, but my intuition doesn't quite fit. There's a hierarchy we don't yet know about. How can a level-headed animal lover who knows her Dawkins from her Darwin say that kind of thing? But there's this little voice inside that says dogs are not as equal as cats. I look at Zara. I look at the dog and it makes me feel ill. All that muscle, all that 'thereness', all that dog smell, those short brown hairs and that ever frantic wagging of the tail. That's dog for you. I feel sorry for her, of course. The dog can't help it that she is a dog.

Owrrr ... Owrrrr ... Owwwwwrrrr ... It starts howling again, comes thundering through to the front room and starts scrabbling on the floor. It's a big, brattish baby. Josh always spoilt it, always let it do whatever it wanted to do. And this is the result. It scrabbles and whines and jumps on the sofa, then heads for the armchair, where Purrl is sitting. It stops short. Purrl is staring at her. Purrl's gaze strikes her. For a moment the dog is still as a statue, motionless with uncertainty, maybe even with fear. Then the dog turns, runs back down the other end of the room and starts howling again.

'For Christ's sake, you daft oaf,' I say, and grab it by the collar, trying to haul it through into the bedroom. It's a huge weight to drag and unless it comes willingly you're stuck. Zara barely budges. I try a different tack. 'Come on, silly cow,' I say, sweetly and temptingly and with all the lightness and charm I can summon. 'Come on, you stupid bitch,' beckoning it through to the kitchen. 'Walkies.' Once in there, I slam the door and shut it

163

in. With all the intervening doors closed, we shouldn't hear the barking for a while.

It's all a bit of an anticlimax, the end of the movie, and before our screening is even over Purrl strolls on to the carpet, then languidly stretches her body across the floor like some resplendent queen. Breathtaking ... I love watching her. She's so sensual. *Miiiaaaaaouueeeehhhh,* she croons with delight. Standing on all fours, she reaches out with her front paws, lowers her head to the ground, brushing first one cheek then the other across the floor. Her buttocks rise provocatively into the air as if waiting for some pressure to slip between those hind legs, waiting for her tom to come. *Mhrnnnhhh.* I wonder if she might be on heat. She moans throatily, then collapses down and tumbles on to her back to reveal her soft white belly fur. I reach down to rub across her stomach, grasping a palm across her ribs and lightly pinching.

She's so gorgeous. I plunge in and tickle harder, attacking her legs with my right hand and flipping her from side to side. I push and I pull and I stroke and I tickle and I twirl and I twiddle and I twist and I rub and I roll and I grab ... It feels such fun and so good, makes me giggle, but then ... ah ... then it's all too much. With a squeal, she flips over and grabs my hands with claws, making me pull back, but not drawing blood. Purrl shakes herself together, splutters and wanders off to sit on the sofa.

Brrr ... Brr ... The sound of the front doorbell

164

wakes me from a sleep. Josh can never quite be bothered to get out his keys, so he always rings first, in the hope that I'll just open the door for him. My body vibrates into life. I fumble. How long have I been asleep? What's happening? Who's ringing the bell? Within seconds I'm beginning to orientate myself. I scramble to the front door, but Josh is already in the process of unlocking it.

He looks a little irritated. 'What's up with Zara?'

Suddenly I realise that the rasping noise in the back of my head is Zara whining and I'm in big trouble. I look around helplessly, trying to get my brain together before I say anything. *Collect your thoughts* ... Zars is still in the kitchen, she hasn't been walked and it's after eight and I'm in trouble.

'Did you take her for a walk?' he asks.

This is bad. This is very, very bad. 'No. She didn't seem to want to go out earlier,' I say, before I've managed to work out what I should be saying. This is the worst of all possible crimes. My sleep-clouded thoughts race to find an excuse. 'It was asleep.'

'*It* was asleep? What do you mean, *It was asleep?* Mills. She's been pacing around madly. I'd say she's obviously been wanting to go out for a while.'

'Sorry,' I murmur. 'I fell asleep.'

'Mills ... what's wrong with you?' he whines. 'All you had to do was take her out for ten minutes. If I'd known I would have come back earlier.'

'I dunno ... I was just asleep. I've been feeling sick.'

I don't seem to get a lot of sympathy for this.

'Sick?' he asks grouchily. 'You should have phoned me. What's been wrong?'

'A bit of a stomachache.' I moan, hoping to appeal to his paternal side. 'But I didn't want to bother my honey.'

Josh snorts quickly out through his nose. I can see he's not in the mood for this. 'Grow up, Mills,' he says, and though it's a throwaway remark, the words smack me right in the guts. All those times I've wanted to say, 'Grow up, Josh,' but was too happy to go along with the childishness of it all . . . All those times flash through my head.

'Why don't you just grow up?' he repeats.

'Babes,' I plead.

'*Ba-abes!*' Josh mimics in a wimpy voice.

He walks through to the kitchen and snatches the lead off its hook. 'Come on, Zars,' he says, and clicks his fingers, signalling to it to come. The dog jumps up and heads for the door. I don't follow. What's the point?

Lying in my bath . . . I've retreated here because I can't quite deal with Josh. I told him a good long soak might make me feel better. No sympathy. He's having a sulk and it's best to keep out of his way. He'll be better in the morning, I'm sure. Then I'll beg for forgiveness – well, not beg, but crawl a little. It's not that I don't realise that I've done wrong and that I've got stuff to make up for, but when Josh is in this kind of mood I'm battering up against a brick wall. Nothing I do will make him happy. I laze in the water, soaking up the bubble bath. It's just the way I like it, stingingly hot.

Normally I'd put the radio on, but the batteries are dead and it doesn't run off the mains, so I'm forced to day-dream. The room seems big and echoey, with the steady sound of water running and splashing filling the space. I'm left to listen to the vibrations of the house, to Josh in the room next door, and the distant noise of the telly in the living room. A few guitar chords ring through the emptiness. Josh, I hear, is strumming to himself, something which he always does when he's feeling down. He's a shoddy guitarist – knows about three chords and has been 'learning' for the last four years. His melancholic, off-key voice starts to sing out some half-made-up melody. It lulls me into a gentle daze. I hear him hum. I feel the water going cold, drawing up goosebumps on my skin, but I don't bother to move.

As I get out the bath, I hear Josh murmuring something and suspect he's probably speaking to Zara. It's near her feeding time and she kicks up a fuss when she's hungry, but there's something vaguely aggressive in his tone of voice and I wonder what Zars could possibly have done wrong. Wrapped in a towel, I quietly open the bathroom door.

There's a sudden clattering, the ping of a broken string. 'For fuck's sake!' In the background Purrl is crooning and mewing. I can hear her, high on hormones. She chirps and she prowls.

Waaooooooooouuuhhh. Then, suddenly, there's a *hisssss* and the sound of spitting. A small squeal. 'Shit, you bloody little cow . . . that hurt.' Sounds of swearing, muttered violence, Purrl mewing . . .

What's this I hear? Josh getting at my cat . . . I roll my hair up into a towel and wander into the kitchen.

'What's going on?' I ask.

Josh is cradling his hand protectively. 'That cat of yours bit me.'

'She bit you?' I echo. 'What did you do to her? She's never bitten anyone before.'

I can see a dribble of red blood running down his palm. It makes me retch slightly, Josh's blood, his clumsy body. It's such a pathetic wound. There's a gash in the fleshy part of his hand beneath his thumb, where she got her teeth in. Josh wanders over to the sink, cradling the injured palm in his other hand. He looks weak and I feel little sympathy.

'Hee . . . hee . . .' I giggle as I beckon to Purrl, who is now lurking in the corner. I reach out a hand towards her and she runs over. 'Has my little sunshine been a bit of a mischief?'

'Hey, *sunshine?*' Josh interrupts. 'Excuse me, but who's the one who deserves the sympathy here? Who's the one who's bleeding?'

'Tut, Josh. Don't be such a wimp!' I say, as I tickle Purrl under the chin. 'It's only a tiny nick. You'd think you'd had your hand bitten off. You probably deserved it anyway. You can't blame her – she's just on heat!'

'Just on heat? Mills. You think she's your little angel, your sweet little kitten. Well, she's not like that. She's not some cutesy little ball of fluff.' His voice is rising. 'I mean, *Jesus* – I never liked cats in the first place . . .'

'Shut up,' I shout. 'There's nothing wrong with her. She's a beautiful cat. And I can't understand why you just can't be nice to her. For Christ's sake, Josh, you sound like you come straight out of the Dark Ages – you're so ignorant. When a cat's on heat, you've got to be careful.'

'Right, I see,' he shouts. 'It doesn't matter that your cat has just bitten me for no reason whatso-ever, because she's on heat.' His voice is getting louder and louder, rising to some sort of crescendo of indignance. He glares at Purrl as he speaks. 'Well, that's nice to know.'

Purrl cowers up against me and I pick her up. I'm staring at Josh in disbelief. 'What's wrong with you, Josh?'

'There's nothing wrong with me.'

'Why are you shouting then?'

'I'm not shouting,' he shouts, then his voice lowers. 'It's just I think you're being a bit soft on that creature.'

'Maybe I am being a bit soft,' I say. 'But I'm a soft sort of girl. There are plenty of times I'm a bit soft on you.'

Josh never pays any attention to what I say any more. I can tell he gets bored and switches off within seconds or changes the subject and launches into one of his own monologues. This is all well and good, but how am I supposed to tell him about Mina if he never listens to me?

Not that I really care. I don't even want to have sex with him any more, he seems so phlegmy and unwieldy.

Angel, Babe, Brighteyes, Honeybunny, Buttercup, Muppet, Lollipop, Cookie, Cupcake, Beauty, Dreamboat, Charmer, Sweetpea, Princess, Honeysuckle, Gorgeous, Cherub, Applepie and Sexy. These are just some of the names that Josh calls me (the sickly lovetalk that I have to listen to every day).

Uglymug, Rat, Idiot, Schmuck, Slime, Prat, Prick and Moron. These are the names I have been calling that unmentionable one. Just for the last couple of days since that certain scumbody started acting like a complete and utter rat. We've both been muttering these names under our breath, Purrl and I.

'Would you like a cup of coffee . . . *prick brain*?'

'What was that?'

'Would you like a cup of coffee?'

I am convinced that Josh has done something to Purrl. Oh yes, he may stroke her in front of me, but I'm sure that behind my back it's quite a different matter. I can see it all in Purrl. She's wary of Josh and steers clear of him whenever possible, a fact which leads me to suspect that he has already threatened her in some way, though as yet I have no clear evidence.

170

Purrl sits there staring at him with those big pink eyes of hers. I can tell she's thinking the same as me. She's watching him sat there in his chair and thinking what a slob, what a lump of repulsive human flesh, what an obstinate, irritating *thing*. Her eyes slide haughtily over his limbs, over his clothes, over his creeping stubble. The look says it all: *'Men, they're so unrefined.'*

'Creep,' I whisper under my breath. But he doesn't hear, which is fine, because I don't want him to hear. I just want to share my thoughts with Purrl, who, I'm sure, knows what I'm saying. She's saying it too. She's been saying it since she arrived.

'So what's up with Purrl?' I ask. *'You little schmuck . . .'* This time I say it quite loudly, but he still doesn't hear it.

'Sorry, babes?' He's reading one of his stupid sci-fi novels. Funny how men do this: think they've got a perfect right to switch off whenever you're talking. It's like Josh has got this special aerial inside his head which stops picking up when it receives my wavelength. When he's reading he never pays any attention to me. I could say anything and he would nod or utter some meaningless noise just to signal to me he's listening, when in fact he's doing nothing of the sort. Half the time I feel I'm talking to a fifty-foot-wide brick wall.

'I was just wondering if you knew what was up with Purrl?'

He stops reading and listens for a second, eyes screwing up like he's trying to make out a memory

171

from the jumble his ears just heard. He frowns and runs his fingers through his hair and I notice he has something scrawled on the back of his hand. I move closer. 243-5649 – it's a phone number.

'Is there something wrong with her? I never realised,' he says absent-mindedly.

I stand there with my hands on my hips and sigh. 'Well, there is.' 243-5649. I rack my brains. I think about questioning him but can't quite be bothered. He'll only make something up.

'Wanna go out for a drink?' he asks, almost without thinking.

'No thanks,' I say. 'I'd prefer to stay in and watch television.' Anything rather than spend a couple of hours with Josh.

'Mind if *I* go out for a drink then?'

'Well, I'd prefer it if you stayed in with us,' I say, while thinking, *Do what you bloody well like!*

'You never go out, never do anything. Just staying in the house all the time.'

'I like staying in, and anyway you go out if you want.'

'Well, I did say I might meet Guy and the gang tonight.'

'Well, OK then.' *But don't expect me to wait up for you. Uh-uh . . .* Guy and the gang? I'll bet.

243-5649 turns out to be the number of a shoe-heeling service. A man answered the phone and I can't help wondering if Josh has been wrong-numbered by yet another girl.

*

172

Mother calls. She wants to come down and see me. She'd love to meet Josh, and she's feeling generally nosy.

'How's the cat work thingy, darling?' she asks.

'Not too busy,' I reply.

'You know, you really ought to get a proper job.'

'Mmm . . .'

'You are earning enough money, aren't you, darling? Because if you're not . . .'

'I don't need any more money.'

'You sound tired, love.'

'Mmmm . . .'

'Are you sure you're all right?'

'Fine.'

'How's Sophie?'

'Haven't seen her for a while.'

'You are getting out enough, aren't you? I mean, you're not getting into one of your funny moods, are you?'

'No, Mother, I'm fine.'

'Because you are a bit bad that way. I mean, you're not like Mina was. You can be a bit bad with people.'

She always says this and it always gets to me. I'm not bad with people, and Mina was never the real charmer that everyone goes on about. *Bad with people?* And even if I used to be, I've got past that stage now. I've got beyond the horrible shyness, the fear that would scrunch me up inside. I can deal with the world now and I'm not a little baby any more. I've grown up.

'I always used to say,' starts my mother, and I know what's coming, and although I hold the receiver out at arm's length, as far from my ear as possible, I know every word of it. 'It was clear even before you went to that little playgroup. Whenever the two of you were in company, she was always the one who would come out of herself. She would always speak for you both. She loved a crowd. But you're special in your own way Milla. You always liked making things. And you were so good with animals.'

And now she tries to compensate. But she's done the damage. Mina's there again – big and mighty in my mind. So perfect, so bloody right. *Dear Mina . . . lovely Mina . . .* If only we could have swapped places. If only I could have been her – the sunbeam Mina, not the Mina stuck in a chair with raspberry juice dribbling from her mouth and head lolling, the Mina who'll occasionally laugh at bad sitcoms and nothing else. Not that Mina. Not 'Not Mina'. Because then, I'm sure, she would have given all the world to be me. I could see it in her eyes. No one else could see it, but I could. And the funny thing is, more than ever, I still would have rather been in her shoes. All my plans never changed anything. I only ended up feeling more of a drip. Mina still had precisely what I longed for.

There's a silence as mother's voice stops. I slowly bring the receiver up to my ear again. 'Milla, are you all right?'

'Fine, Mother.'

'You in on your own, darling?'

'Mmmm . . . Josh went out for a drink with his friends.'

'I wouldn't be standing for that, honey. This going out while you stay in. It's not right. He could be up to all sorts of things. I wouldn't . . .'

'Mother,' I snap, 'if he wants to go out with his friends he can do that. It's not the Dark Ages, you know.'

'I just thought you might want to talk about it.'

'Well, I don't.'

'Listen, maybe I should come and see you, darling. You sound like you need a little visit from your mumsy.'

I try and put her off. I don't want her down here. Not right now, when Josh and I are rowing so much. The arrival of my mother would just drive us over the edge. I know what she's like. We've been through this before.

Besides, I still have to tell Josh about Mina.

I'm sleeping in the front room because I don't want to sleep with Josh. Hopefully when he comes back in he'll get the message. I won't actually have to ram it home to him that I can't stand the idea of his body near mine, that when he touches me I feel irritated and sick, that I want him to stay away, to leave me alone. Christ knows where he's been tonight. Out again with the boys? Really? Not that I care. He's a free man and he can do what he likes. It doesn't matter now. I've worked it all out. This perfect fit

175

we had has now gone wrong, misshapen and shrunken in all the most unexpected places. Somehow it seems we're not two people who want the same thing at the same time any more.

Purrl sleeps on my pillow. Something that Josh very rarely allows her to do. She nuzzles into the crook of my neck with her nose, hiding among my hair. I can hear her breathing as I fall asleep. It calms me, relaxes me. Contentment. With Purrl I feel at peace. Purrl and I are closer than Josh and I. It's only lying here in the half-dark that I can really feel it, that I can really understand what this means.

Something is kissing my neck. Something is trying to sing next to my ear. Some slobbering foghorn is creeping from my nape to my earlobe. It rattles and croaks. It moves slowly and surely like a warm slug. I can feel it through the half-drawn curtains of sleep. There's a warm wetness nibbling away at the skin beneath my ear. It drools. I am aware of the cushion of lip, the boniness of tooth, the wetness of tongue, creating a vortex against my skin. I shake my head as if to get this creature away.

The curtains part further and I become aware of weight moving over my legs, of shifting pounds across my chest. I start to become conscious of the person clambering on top of me.

'Milla,' this dark figure murmurs, 'what are you doing in here?'

'G'roff,' I drawl.

176

'Come through to the bedroom.'

'Mm-mmm.' I shake my head.

'Come on, hon.'

Purrl is still lying on my chest and I sense her getting squashed between our two bodies. She squeals and squeezes out of the way, her small form racing over the bed. 'Careful!' I groan.

He smells of lager and his words are slurred. His lips plant themselves on mine and I get that trapped feeling. A sense of suffocation rises inside me, as if his mouth stops my mouth from breathing. It feels hot and oppressive and I am irritated at being woken, clinging to the last threads of sleep, hoping to fall back and be left alone, but Josh persists. 'What's this all about, Mills?' he says. And he kisses me again, his tongue probing.

I push him forcefully away. 'Lemme alone,' I say, not bothering to explain and hoping he'll understand that sleep is more tempting than him. I just don't feel like it at the moment. I don't want him to touch me. I don't want to feel his skin against mine. I want space. I don't want to be hemmed in.

The slobber attacks again.

I recoil, but my body, weak with sleep, hardly seems to move as I ask it. I feel Purrl by my head, pacing the cushions and watching me anxiously.

'Get off, would you?' I mutter at Josh, and I push him back as hard as I can. He slips backwards, sliding off the sofa, but struggling to keep with me.

'OK, OK,' he says, fumbling backwards over the bed, reeling drunkenly. 'I get the message. You can stay in here on your own with your fucking cat.'

Then there's a squeal and it's Purrl crying out in pain.

'Shit,' says Josh, stumbling into the darkness. 'I didn't know she was there,' he groans. His breathing is now forced, sucking in quick desperate rhythm. 'Always . . . gets under your feet.'

Purrl runs towards me and I cradle her in my arms. How dare Josh hurt her?

'Sorry, I didn't . . .' He coughs and fumbles, but I don't want to hear. I block him out.

Josh deliberately kicked Purrl. I'm sure of it. It's not that I actually saw it, but all the evidence is there: Purrl squealing, Josh standing there looking sheepish, guilt written all over his face. What other explanation could there be?

I decided to bring it up again at breakfast this morning. Coming up for eight and I was sat there having my muesli and the little prick had just finished breakfast and was fiddling with the radio and trying to get the news, and I couldn't help myself. 'Stupid thing . . . I told you we need a bigger aerial,' he said. I shrugged my shoulders. Purrl was wandering round the kitchen, vying for some attention. I suppose I wanted to get it all out in the open.

'I don't think I know you, Josh,' I said calmly.

'What?'

'I don't think I know you. I've only just realised how cold you are. Kicking cats! That's the lowest of the low.'

178

'What are you talking about?'

'Don't try and pretend you don't know.'

'You mean last night? But I only tripped over her.'

'You kicked her. I saw you kick her.'

'You *did not* see me.'

'I did. And anyway, whether I saw you or not, you kicked her.'

'Did not.'

'Did.'

'Did not.'

'Did.'

'All right, believe I kicked the cat. Believe it if you want to. I also stuck pins into it, electrocuted Tibbsy, chopped the tail off the dog round the corner and disembowelled some random stray!'

'I wouldn't put it past you.'

'Mills,' he said, sighing. 'I don't need this. I don't want to have to deal with it. I'm just about to leave for work and you're accusing me of something I didn't do. I would never kick any animal. You should know that!'

'Well, I'm beginning to wonder. You're not the Josh I thought I was going out with.'

'Oh, come off it. Of course you know me. I wouldn't kick any creature.' Josh sighed and fastened his coat as if about to leave. 'I'm going to be late.'

'You know what I think? I think you're jealous. I think you're jealous of Purrl.'

Josh stared at me in disbelief. 'Me, jealous of that thing? As if I would ever get jealous of some puny, ugly stray. It's a cat. C-A-T! Why should I get

179

jealous? No, I think the person around here who's jealous is you.' He looked at his watch impatiently. 'This is ridiculous. I'm going. I'm not getting into this.' He grabbed his bag, clicked his fingers for Zara to follow and glared at me with the full force of his indignance. 'When are you going to give up on this Purrl stuff? You know what? I'm fed up with it. I think it's time you decided what you want out of life – me or the cat. Cause this flat ain't big enough for the both of us.'

'I think I've already decided.'

'And?'

I simply shrugged.

'I see.' He stared at me helplessly. Those eyes spoke a million words, but they didn't sway me. I was sure of myself. He strode towards the door. 'Well, don't try and stop me then,' he cried, walking out into the street with Zars at his heels.

And I didn't.

~

I haven't called Milla for a long time. I've been waiting for her to call. It's all to do with guilt – and this suspicion that she might be angry about the kitchen incident, that maybe she's annoyed that I stepped beyond those boundaries that have been built up over the years. Since the party I've been tormenting myself about it. The first few evenings I just sat and moped, mooning around my flat, thinking about what I'd done wrong, how I'd ruined a good friendship, wondering if she would call and hoping that she was thinking about me. Part of me hoped that maybe she liked it enough to realise Josh was wrong for her – and given that he was flirting with that other girl, there was a possibility . . . But she didn't call. And, anyway, maybe the opposite was true, that she had found my fumbling desires unappealing. All my excuses for doing it seem so pathetic. I won't even begin to go into them. The truth, I know, is straightforward enough. I wanted to. I'd thought about kissing her so many times that it was amazing I hadn't done it beforehand. Years and years of chemistry have to work their way out at some point. You can only go on for so long like that . . .

Milla has always told me I'm too much of a thinker, not enough of a doer . . .

But you'd have thought she would have called just to smooth it all over. A whole week and a half and still no word from her. Normally we would talk to each other at least once a week – Wednesday evenings, when Josh is out. It has to be a bad sign, and the worst of it is that I can't remember how that evening had ended, whether I said anything really bad.

~

Old sodface hasn't come back tonight. I sit here and wonder where he is. The usual thoughts cross my mind (he's been late before) – lying in a corner somewhere, beaten up by some savage fifteen-year-old, run over by some hit-and-run truck-driver, sat in a hospital bed without a note on him to say who to contact. Of course, I know all of these aren't true. My intuition tells me that much. I know he's probably gone to stay with one of his rich mates, maybe even Guy and Tams. Yet my imagination can't help dreaming up the most awful sights. It won't accept that I've simply been ditched. No, I'd rather the very worst. The hospital scenario won't leave me be. It runs round and round inside my head in vivid Technicolor detail – head sliced open, bones shattered, car crash victim on a life support machine. I almost think of phoning our local casualty, but decide not to. I'm just being stupid.

'You've just got to accept it, Mills,' I repeat to myself.

Once I've said it a few times, I actually don't feel so bad. *Who cares?* He's going to have to come back to get his stuff, after all. And I'm not even sure I want him to come back. The longer I think about it, the more I start to feel glad he's gone. I've made my choice. Everything in your life is about choices. Dog or cat? Gabriel or Josh? Human or not human? Purrl or Tibbs? Milla or Mina? Mina or Not Mina? It's all too much.

Of course, I don't wish him rib-cracked and concussed underneath a car, but I also don't want him to turn up tonight. I don't want to have to deal with his heartless selfishness. It might seem cold, but I don't feel as I would expect in this situation. I haven't got that desperate come-back-so-we-can-sort-out-our-lives type of feeling. No, my needs are simple.

I know why he's left. I'm not stupid. It's partly because of Tamara, but mainly because we argued and I took Purrl's side. I regret it a little, but not much. When you're in the right, you never regret fighting. You stick to your guns. My father told me that. And that's what I'm doing. I won't accept Josh until he reforms.

The phone rings.

I leave it. It rings again, keeps ringing for ages. I can't face answering it, in case it's him. *Give up uglymug.* I don't want to have another argument. In fact, I don't really want to know what he's decided to do . . . but still, the phone keeps going and going. 'Hard luck, Joshy babes, nobody in,' I mutter under my breath.

Suddenly the ringing stops and I feel hollow inside. I switch on the answerphone. No more talking. From now on I'm screening my calls. None of these hours wasted, no more Mother raving on about her latest toyboy, no more stupid whingeing clients and most important of all no more Josh.

Josh, after all, needs time to come to his senses. He needs to become frustrated and anxious at not being able to get through to me – and playing a little hard to get can only help persuade him. He needs to worry about me and want me and Purrl and everything that goes with me, more than anything else on the earth, because otherwise this relationship is just not worth going on with. *Learn, Josh . . . learn how to love me.*

At least this morning I didn't have to listen to that stupid yapping. I am glad the dog is gone. It always bugged me, always got under my skin, like some itchy-scratchy mite. I'm sure before long I would have ended up strangling that dog.

Some people say cats have ESP.

I'm not sure about the rest of the feline world, but I know that Purrl has a bit of a strange side. Not that I believe in all that paranormal psi-factor gunk. I hate it. I hate the fact that it's unexplainable by the laws of physics and all those real-world theories. And though I like to think I believe only in what can be explained or understood, Purrl is living evidence to the contrary, evidence of my petty superstitious instincts. Purrl defies all my expectations. She is uniquely incomprehensible and, so, utterly magnetic. Purrl is a little mystery and that's why I love her.

There's a faintly precognitive streak to my Purrl. A tendency almost to anticipate the very worst events, to be ahead of me in the ups and downs of our daily life together. Take last night. Only a couple of minutes before Josh rang, she suddenly halted in her tracks, ceased her regular rhythmical pacing of the carpet and stood stock still. She cocked her head to one side, as if listening, and then began a long, low moan, a laryngeal *wooooooooohhhhhhhhhhhhhhhrrrr* which vibrated through the room. Then she walked steadily into the corner with the telephone in, stared at it, again cocking her head from side to side, and, once more, *wooooooooooohhhhhhhhhhhhhhhhrrrr*, walked away again. Finally she made a quick dart to sanctuary on my knee. I stroked her gently and she moaned again, ever watching the telephone, ears

184

twitching and tail flicking. Then the phone rang.

Coincidence maybe, but a mighty potent coincidence.

Now I suppose you might call that ESP. What other explanation is there? It's not a freak event. There have been plenty of other occasions. Like the time that nasty Mrs Mingerston came round from number four and Purrl was up at the window crooning away long before she'd even left her own house. Purrl knew. Purrl always knows. She knows me inside-out. Purrl and I have a mutual sense for each other. It's a sense that, despite my long-run feline passions, I've never before been so consumed by. I am forced to acknowledge an intelligence, even possibly a superior intelligence, that I cannot, as yet, understand. We talk. Sometimes it's just a soft mew here and a little *wow* there. Just the smallest squeak. Other times I speak to her in human talk and other times again I am strangely aware that she's caught on to my feelings. It sets my nerves on edge. But it's also weirdly comforting.

The trouble with research so far into animal communication is that it fails to take account of the profound difference of their mode of living. I believe cats may have other senses beyond the five we humans have. Who knows what bodily cells are responsible for perceptions? Cats, after all, have their own antennae, their whiskers. Mightn't these whiskers have a further function which we have yet to understand? It may be foolish, but I believe some day Purrl and I will talk.

I stare out of the window. It's grey and cold, despite being summer. Purrl sits on the window-sill with me. Through the sun-stained net curtains we can look out on the world without it really looking at us. We both like to watch, but neither of us wants to go out there. Why go out when it's so safe and cosy in here? Why go out when the world is so difficult? I watch Mrs Mingerston out walking her dog and I think, *I'm glad I don't have to bump into her any more.* I watch the kid who keeps hanging round on the corner and think, *At least no more wolf whistles from that prick.* More than anything else, I watch Mrs Jarvis and think, *Thank Christ I won't be hearing about her bad hip again.*

People . . . they're such a drag. I don't think I ever liked them.

The phone rings twice and the answerphone clicks on.

'Hi!' my irritatingly adolescent voice comes crackling through. 'Josh and Milla aren't in at the moment. If you'd like to leave a message, then you know the routine.' I sound like a baby. There I go, lilting along and ending on a grating up-note. Time to re-record that message, with one big amendment: it's not Josh and Milla any more. It's just me – just me and my cat.

Sure enough, it's Josh. 'Mills, sorry I didn't come back last night. I just needed time to think . . . I think we both do.' He sounds distressed – almost nervous. 'We need to give each other a bit more space. We both know things haven't been quite the same over these past few weeks. I'll ring you tomorrow . . . Bye then.' He stays on the phone for an extra couple of seconds, just breathing. It's as if he hopes I'll finally come to my senses and pick it up, but I don't.

Fine. That's perfectly fine. That suits me. I didn't really want him back anyway. Though I do wonder where he's calling from and I do feel as if a vast hole has suddenly blown up like a big bang in my body. All that time together, wasted. I feel sucked out and drained, not liberated as I should feel, like I'd hoped I would feel. Maybe I did love him. Maybe this is the pang of love lost. What if he never calls back at all?

~

I was finding it difficult to concentrate on my work.

The trouble, when you've been waiting for a thing to happen for as long as I had, is you almost start to enjoy the chronic tension of not having it and yet almost having it. It adds a certain vibrancy to your life. Up until the dinner party I'd felt fairly happy. I'd been able to work and function well, without Milla taking over. I'd had her company but not her heart. That was good enough and in some ways as much as I could ever expect, although sometimes images would flare up in my imagination of Milla having sex, Milla giving Josh a blow job, Josh kissing Milla, Josh with his hands on her breasts, and however hard I'd try to repress them, they were there as a reminder. It was as if my libido was constantly telling me that I wanted more. The longer it went on, the more I tried not to indulge it and the more that internal projector of mine fought back, reeling out the flicks. I didn't like it. To be honest, I'd rather not be telling you all this, because I'm not proud of it. Milla was always meant to be a friend. Or at least that's what she felt.

But after that kiss, it was a different state of affairs. The chronic tension had broken, exploding into an acute nagging pain, and it seemed, as far as I could tell, that I could have neither Milla's heart nor her company. The lines between us had been severed and all I could do was sit around wondering if she would ever ring.

~

A salmon sliver slips out from between her lips and flicks along the edge of her jaw. The pink flange glistens, smooth on one face, rough like sandpaper on the other. It darts – this rosy worm – slipping from side to side. Purrl likes to be clean. She likes to be spotless, and she has her routine. Again it flicks out. Lips licked, she settles on the sofa, preparing for her beauty routine. Her slim white body strains attentively. Concentration on the job in hand: getting rid of all that filth. Not that she looks dirty. Purrl always looks snowy white.

She raises a delicate white paw to her face and out the tongue darts again. It strokes once along the side, pushing short white fur against its pile. Then it pulls back, and quickly and rhythmically repeats the movement. Again out and along and in and out and along. Wet and lithe, it pulls hairs together and dampens the fur. Out and along and in and out and along. She's devoutly focused, religiously applying saliva to paw.

Then she stops, happy. Quick movements of the paw coat the side of her face, rapidly wiping away dust that's so insignificant I can barely see it, coating the face in her scent, the odour that marks her as her. Like some unconscious reflex it goes on. Dampen the paw, wipe off the face. She jerks against her cheeks and her forehead. *Off . . . Off . . . whatever's there.* And again. For minutes this repeats. Purrl is meticulous. Each area of her body must be rendered immaculate before she moves on. I'm fascinated by her. I can only aspire to being as diligent as her.

Next . . . the right paw. Purrl's slippery tongue swipes out again along the edge of another foot. Stroke, stroke, stroke . . . and stop . . . her rhythm is interrupted as she discovers grime between claws, and attacks with full mouth, teeth and tongue to remove the criminal element. Then to her face again, with fast movements, almost like brushing, puffing at her fur and working away the dirt. Eye closed, she swipes over it. Then back further, behind the ear. This paw swabs relentlessly. Taintless . . . that is what Purrl needs to be.

She halts and stares at me with those unyielding pink eyes, then goes on again. I suspect she likes to be watched. I think she does it partly for me. Now the legs. She settles down further into the red cushions of the sofa and stretches a long, spindly white limb in front of her. Her pink, snake-like feeler slicks along the front of it, leaving a damp

189

trail of fur. Then again it goes and we start the rhythm. Each little bit must be done, from the claws to the toes to the thighs to the shoulders. Legs are laundered – both left and right – and minutes pass before she moves on to her sides, to those sleek, smooth flanks of her body. She stretches out, turning her head in on her ribs. Sinuous, she contorts herself. This is the bulk of the job and where she gets up to speed, her tongue flickering through the air, flesh against white, pummelling away at fur and skin. It pulls one way, then the other, coating skin in saliva. Then she cocks her head and looks up again, then goes on.

Purrl stalls. *Something in need of attention here.* Though her fur is short she still gets the odd small tangle, and here is one. She tugs at the offending knot. Her teeth nibble. In she digs to get rid of the speck that should never have troubled her. She licks and she pulls and she wriggles. Then . . . enough . . . She flips over and starts on the other side. All over again the routine is repeated, the licking and pulling, the pawing and the tugging. This is the reason why Purrl is such a beauty – because she is so vain.

This cat puts my hygiene to shame. Every time I watch her, observe the intricate details of the routine, the lip-licking, paw-wetting, face-brushing, side-swiping, tail-tidying inevitability of each step, I feel embarrassed. Recently I have come to appreciate the fact that this house I keep is in no way clean enough for Purrl. I can tell by the way she pads about so delicately. The carpet is too crumby, the lino too grimy, her plates too scummy, all the surfaces too dusty to be brushed upon by this princess's snowy fur. She seems to glide through the rooms without touching anything, as if she can't bear the contact. I am aware of every wipe of her tongue, every snatched grooming session, and also of her endless daily routine – her regular disinfection.

Of course, I've made my efforts to amend things. My house was not clean enough. It still is not clean enough, though I try. I try so hard. In just a week I have been enlightened, finally transforming myself from a slob into the picture of housewifely diligence. I have discovered that I like to clean. There's a pleasure in disinfecting, sterilising and purging, in ridding my environment of the ever encroaching grime. I have sterilised the floor, bleached the toilet, scrubbed out the corners and scraped out those hidden spots underneath cupboards and oven in the kitchen. No longer will Purrl have to deal with the dead skin, mites, hair and food particles that make up my dust. No longer will she be faced with my daily waste. This house is slowly becoming fit for my little queen. And the dirt must be controlled – otherwise it takes over your life.

As I watch Purrl grooming, I see it all, I become alive to her distaste. This room is still too dank, too grimy. I can almost taste the dust in the air. I can feel particles clogging my lungs, visualise them lodged in the crevices of my cells. I can see the sediment against my skin. I look at my hands and they are grey, not white. They are covered in some thin, almost invisible layer, but one that is definitely there. I must get rid of this. The rug . . . I look at the rug. That is the offending article. It must be washed. Shame, the shame. How can Purrl even bear to be with me, when I am so inferior to her? Cleanliness, they say, is next to godliness. Yet cats, who have no concept of God, know that better than men. They understand that perfection lies in the immaculate.

I must clean.

Phone calls round here are never really for me. They're always either for Josh or from Josh (or from my mother, who phones nearly every day, and the whingeing clients, who just don't count). It's as if I have no existence other than through *him*. Over the last few days this has really hit home. No one calls me. No one wants me. They all want Josh, Mr Popular, Mr Sociable, Mr Fake. Out of the five calls I had today, four of them were for Josh and one of them was for me (from Josh). Not that I'm hoping for any calls. I'm quite happy to be left in peace, but I wish these Josh people would just stop hassling me. Don't they realise he's left me? Why do they think his name's not on the message? Do I have to ram it home that Josh doesn't live here any more?

Each time the phone rings I want to kick the machine in and I'm surprised I haven't just yet. These last couple of days have been bad enough. There was up-his-own-backside Guy, asking if Josh wanted to go to some party thing. ('Uh . . . yeah . . . Josh, it's me, the Guyser. Just calling to see if you're up for going out on Friday. There's this drinks bash at my club. Would love to see you.') Then his mother checking up on whether he was going to be paying the parents a visit this summer. ('And do bring Milla.') There was Lucy, whom I've always been suspicious of – along with Tamara and all the rest. ('Haven't seen you for ages, lovie.') Finally there was Alan, his football mate, who addressed his phone call at both of us, but clearly has no interest in me whatsoever. I'm not his type. ('Gimme a buzz, mate.')

So what's wrong with me? Why is it always him, not me? What do they all love so much about that drip? I guess it was always this way, even before Josh left, but it seems more conspicuous now. I'm a social loser and he's a winner. He's a real schmoozer who sucks up to everyone he meets. Everybody loves Josh. They all adore him. Whereas me, I'm awkward and annoying and I prefer the company of cats to people. That's what suits me. I'd rather not have to speak to a single person. Not anybody. That's the way I like it.

Lemon sole for dinner tonight. Raw, of course, with a sprinkling of lemon juice on it and some freshly ground pepper. It's almost like sushi, but nicer.

Not that we'll be having this sort of feast much longer. This is the last of the fresh sole and the cupboard is almost bare. From looking through our stocks today, I'd say that things have taken a bad turn. Purrl doesn't eat much, but we're still running low. I've got a couple of pieces of frozen trout in the fridge, but once they're gone, we're at the end of the line. It'll be shop or drop. We'll have no other option. Of course, there are a few cans of baked beans, some tinned tuna, rice, half a loaf of mouldy bread (*must get rid of it now ... before the mould spreads*) and some onions. All are completely unappetising. None of these appeal to either Purrl or me. All those things that I used to eat make me nauseous. I'll eat only what Purrl eats. She's the guiding gourmet around here.

Despite my initial qualms, I think I may almost be able to venture into the culinary realms of raw meat. Of course, I would never eat chicken – the salmonella question worries me too much – but the idea of a sliver of raw pork is something I'm not averse to. Purrl after all eats it. Why shouldn't I?

Being with Purrl helps me see straight about many things. It's like being in a different country. Suddenly you start to realise how bizarre your own habits are, how unfounded they are in any reason. This time spent with Purrl has made me rethink my eating habits. For instance, surely it must be bad for us to eat near-boiling-hot food? Our bodies cannot be made to consume huge amounts of junk at a temperature way beyond what our skin will tolerate. Meat is not meant to be cooked. Why should it be? And when did we develop this strange ritual? Who knows, but I'm sure that, when carefully selected, raw meat is perfectly suitable for human consumption. The French have long had a taste for steak tartare.

I go through the cupboard throwing out stuff. Plum tomatoes – in the bin. Rice – out it goes. Mouldy bread – wrapped in several carrier bags and chucked. We don't want all this rubbish cluttering up our lives. Clean out and get in order. That's the way. The environment reflects the mind and all that. Out, out, out, out, out.

Get rid of it all. I wish I could be like Purrl. She survives on virtually nothing, barely eating at all. Her svelte body shows it too. I'm trying to train myself not to eat, so I can be tiny and delicate just like her. She's almost weightless and, while I'm not fat, I do carry a little flesh – a modest layer on the front of my tummy, a slight padding on the thighs and maybe at the back of my arms. These should go. Skin and bone is where I want to be. I shall have just the thinnest layer of fat, barely the thickness of skin, lying over muscle. I shall float through life like Purrl. Who needs to consume? If Purrl can get away with it so can I. The thought of chocolate bars and caramel cookies makes me feel sick. The idea of swallowing much more than the smallest slivers of fish makes me dizzy. There's no reason for me to bother with the dynamics of fuel and waste. Why should I work? Why should I eat? Why should I go out? Purrl and I can live on so little for so long.

Out, out, out, out, out, out, out.

When I've finished clearing there's nothing left

but our lemon sole (and the five trout in the deep freeze). I know the time is coming for Big Shop, but I'm staving it off. Big Shop means going outside again. It means dealing with all those people I never wanted to bump into again, those people who look me up and down like I'm only halfway there. Those outsiders. I hate the outside.

Purrl prefers inside to outside. She isn't like most cats. She doesn't seem to need that freedom. Of course it's there to be taken – she can slip through the cat flap whenever she likes – but she doesn't choose to. Or at least at the moment she doesn't. She's done her roaming, travelling like some lost waif from house to house in search of a haven. Finally, she's found it here. This is where she has stopped and ceased to long for the chase and the hunt. Yes, Purrl occasionally used to go for the odd wander. From time to time she used to come back with a mouse or a bird – a little gift for me and Josh. But no longer. These days she's a little homebody. There's no more of that wild-cat drive to succumb to her primitive instincts. Most cats lead a double life. They're cute kittens in the home and terrorising tigers on the streets. Purrl isn't like that. In her, outside never wins over inside. In some surprisingly human way, she prefers her own internal world.

She has her playground here. She needs no more. That's what I didn't realise when I first went to visit her at the Bensons'. I thought that she was hiding from something, but in fact all she needed was a few rooms and a person to dedicate herself to. Every scent, every nook and cranny of this flat, is known to her. Each day she reacquaints herself, as she pursues her endless rounds of the rooms. I know her route. It's always the same, and sometimes as I watch her I can imagine what it's like crouched down on all fours, scooting round the floors. I can imagine the whole thing from her point of view.

Here we go. Come with me and check out the territory! The hunt is on.

Down on all fours we hit the carpet. We're low now and the ceiling is high. Paws padding on short-pile carpet, we skim the level of the skirting boards. There's dust on them – she's not cleaned yet. Right now, we round the corner into the hallway, which is long, stretching a good five metres. You can get a good speed up here. Hind legs under, we make a dart for the end. We're chasing shadows, but we don't mind. This is our game. Turn now, crouch again and then leap. The corridor is dark because she never leaves the lights on, but we can see it all – the grime on the doormat, the hairs clinging to the carpet, the dirt. As yet we can't imagine the smells, because I haven't got that far yet, my senses can never be that acute. Dart again, past the book-shelves, past the boxes, past the coat-stand ... the full length back to the kitchen. And now we check out the kitchen, paw by paw, slowly strutting along the edge of the cabinets towards the sink. We hear the trickling buzz of a slightly running tap and,

197

gathering strength for the spring, we push off hind paws and leap into the air. We glide gently and land on the aluminium surface. It's cold on the paw-pads and slippy, but we balance around the edge, not wanting to actually stand on the bottom, and straddling the basin we bend forward to drink from the running stream. It's cold and wet as we lap away. *Lap, suck, gulp . . .* We stand there for several minutes. *Lap, suck, gulp . . .*

Enough of that then! We stare out of the window for a few seconds, surveying the back garden. What's that moving between the rose bush and the sapling? Too small – probably a bee. Our eyes follow the movement, nose tracing lines against the glass. The flutter of a leaf grabs our attention – but not for long. The territory has still to be checked and, our thirst quenched, we jump down from the sinktop, landing gently on all fours, tail streaming behind us, muscles contracting to take the impact.

Putta . . . putta . . . putta . . . putta . . . across the floor. This is our domain. We stop for a second next to the cooker. Was that a flicker of something in the darkness under there? Crouch for a second and watch, but maybe it was nothing. Cock a head to one side to listen out for the sound of a merest rustle – maybe a mouse. But there's nothing. Frustrated, we stick a paw under, reaching with long thin white limb and flailing. We hit blank space, just a few rotten pieces of courgette that had crept under there months ago. No luck here . . . is there ever? Fed up with waiting, we stand up and pace around the cooker. It's white and shiny and cold. Our fur brushes up against the surface. We push with our flanks, reflexing into action, spreading our scent. White hair pushes against white surface. We mark our territory, uttering short mewing noises.

Then, with the kitchen claimed, we move on, skipping through the hallway again, and turning left this time to enter the bathroom. The smell is potent here, though she barely realises it, and there's that patch in the right-hand corner beside the loo that stinks of Tibbsy. That was his spot, the place that he always sprayed. The aroma is strong and overpowering, but this is our house and we don't need to worry. We brush up against the bath. This is our bath. Tibbsy is dead. His smell may linger, but his presence is gone.

And out we go again, rounding the corner to enter the bedroom, which we love. It's the bed especially we're drawn to. We love that dark netherworld underneath. It's the place that we go to hide, our little den for when we don't want to see her, a place where we can crouch low. There's not much under there at the moment – just a couple of bags and a few shoes. She hoovered it out recently and got rid of all the junk. But it's still a little playground. We dive on a slipper, pushing it and rolling it over. A favourite game. It tumbles and we grab it and then we push it again and again and again. Roll it, push it, grab it . . . our little private fun. But the slipper doesn't do much and we tire and there's still much of the home to cover. We emerge from the bed into daylight. For a second we see it again. The bird – which turns out not to be a bird but a plant. Every time it happens though, instantly we remember what it is from the day before. We see this bird in the corner – maybe it's the way a leaf flutters in the smallest breeze – but for a second it really looks like one. It imprints itself on our brain and we see it so clearly our heart skips a beat. We gather to pounce. And then the eyes clear and we see it for what it is: just the leaves moving in the draught again. It all comes back. There's only leaves, only ever leaves . . . never any bird. Will it always happen, that haunted moment? Disillusioned we pad out of the bedroom and lollop round to the living room.

She's there, sitting in the corner with a book as always, her lumpy, graceless human body slouching down into the cushions. She raises her head and gestures for us to come over, but we don't – we're on a mission. The carpet is thick, heavy pile in here. Our feet dig in and we want to scratch, to pad away like a kitten, exercising our claws. The corner of the armchair is the favourite place and we shuffle up to it, preparing paws to extend claws. On the soft velvety surface, we dig. Then we release, then we dig again. We keep doing it until she tells us to stop and then we track across the floor, taking a quick roll over the rug. We stop for a second – listening, thinking, sniffing the air – then move on. We're ready to take our place, our niche, by the window, looking out . . .

*

From this corner, behind the curtain, I watch the street. There she is, hobbling up and down, 'Ida snoop', with her greying ginger hair, her raggedy raincoat, anklesocks over tights and plastic slipper-shoes. I can clock her darting head and eager shuffle from a distance. No one else snoops like Ida Little.

Ida bloody Little . . . I spy her. I know she's up to something. She can fake it all she likes, pretend that she's only doing her rounds, but I know what she's here for. She's here to see Purrl. Why else would she have trekked all the way over? It's quite a hike for her, several bus changes, and, as she hasn't got a car, it takes a considerable prize to draw her into Hermitage Road. She wouldn't be doing it just for the hell of it. Ida's not the type for some random jaunt.

I see her standing at the door of Mrs Flatface. Purrl watches with me. Flatface frowns a lot, habitually standing with her hands on her hips. She shakes her head, sniffs, contorting her skull-hugging nose. Ida nods. I almost imagine she gestures my way. Her hand movements wander loosely and it's difficult to be sure where she's pointing or what she's getting at. Seconds later, she grasps Flatface's arm and pats it affectionately before moving on again.

House hubby from number three comes out with his two-year-old daughter. He's looking typically worn and pale and I guess he's been spending too much time on his woodwork. He lingers half in, half out the door. He seems vaguely suspicious of Ida and not entirely happy to be disturbed, but they stand there chit-chatting for a while, and he gets quite animated. I see him point across the road towards the house next door – or was it us? Little Lisa is tugging at his arm. She wants him to come in and play, but Ida's got him now. The old biddy is such a nosy busybody – she won't let go till she's got what she wants.

The fact that she doesn't come straight here is what worries me. I know she just can't stay away. Why the delay? I've whetted her appetite with my phone calls and now she's metamorphosed into Private Eye Little. She's on the case, checking out the comings and goings of the cat world. Nothing slips through her net. Any cat you want found, any mangy-looking stray – she knows how to find them. Including Purrl.

Through the pocket of glass, I can see Ida coming up the front path. I hear her open the gate. What's she up to? What's she thinking as she strides up the path, her frizzy ginger hair sprouting in the wind? One thought: I've left the top window open and there's no doubt that Ida the sleuth will guess that I'm in. It's too late to close it without her seeing my hand up there by the curtain. I panic for a second. Shrinking back into the wall, I pray that she can't see me through the thin veil of net. But I know, of course, she can if she tries.

Go away, I think. *Just go away* . . . She stands by the door for a few seconds, humming under her breath.

What does she look like? Her eyebrows painted on in huge dark lines, her coat creased and stained at the back. 'Come on, Millsie, love,' she mutters to herself, then rings.

Ida doesn't give up easily. She presses again, staring aimlessly around her, then waits for another few seconds. Tired of that, she turns and wanders along to the window and I shrink further back into the shadows. I can still see that she's staring, slightly perplexed at the open window, and probably I lip-read, 'That's odd,' then she presses her nose up against the glass. Fortunately she looks past me and it's right now that I start to think that I really can't bear it any longer. I might as well just let her in. It can't do that much harm. She's as batty as a fruitcake and everyone else in the world knows it. No one's going to pay attention to her ramblings. All I'll have to do is offer her a cup of tea and listen to some weird cat stories and then shovel her out of the door again. I wait for her to look away.

She turns and then she starts to shriek, 'Millie. Ohh Millie, love. It's Ida!'

Someone has got to do something to shut her up. I march to the door, sending Purrl skedaddling on the way. 'Ida . . . i-is that you?' I say as I twitch the latch. 'I'm sorry . . . I was through the back having a nap.'

'Ah, Millie,' she says. 'I was beginning to wonder. I saw your window was open and . . .'

'Just napping, as I said.' I try to smile, but feel it

203

hanging around the corners of my mouth as a grimace. Then I beckon for her to come in.

'You're looking . . . very . . . different,' she says, casting an eye over my white T-shirt.

'Oh . . . just something I had at the back of my cupboard. It's wash day,' I say, as I lead her through to the living room.

'A bit on the pale side too,' she comments, squinting at me through her tortoiseshell-rimmed glasses. 'Are you sure you've been eating enough, dear?'

'Loads,' I say quickly. 'So, Ida –' I gesture to her to sit down in the armchair – 'what brings you up to this neck of the woods?'

'You know . . . the usual. I just happened to be in the neighbourhood and thought I might as well call by for a cuppa and a little chit-chat.'

'That's *lovely*, Ida . . . How would you like your tea?'

'The usual – white with one and leave the bag in.'

I wander through to the kitchen and switch the kettle on. Ida calls after me. 'Of course,' she says, 'I have been very much looking forward to meeting your little kitty. I've heard so much about her.'

'Well, she is a bit out of the ordinary,' I say. I'm disturbed by the sound of her rustling round in there, fumbling with something and pacing the floor, so I head back in to keep an eye on her. 'Kettle's boiling!'

Ida jumps guiltily as I walk into the room. 'She's not around at the moment, is she?'

'I don't know.'

I am staring at Ida's twin-set. I can't help noticing a couple of ginger hairs on her pale blue jumper: small, inch-long and fine, and they're not Ida's hair, they're cat hairs. As I walk a little closer, I notice that there are more and more of these floating stragglers clinging to her, all over. I want to reach out and brush them off. I can't stand the idea of ginger hair, ginger cat coming into my house. It makes me feel slightly sick. Thick, matted ginger hairs squirm across my eyes and all I can think of is how I want to get rid of them.

Ida looks at me, slightly bewildered. 'Is there something wrong, dear?' I reach forward and clutch a couple of these ginger hairs between two fingers, plucking them off the surface of the jumper.

'You've got a ginger cat?' I murmur.

'Yes – Muffy. Don't you remember Muffy?'

The name rings a bell, but I shake my head slowly. 'Matches your hair – two gingers together.'

'Oh well, Muffy's just a sweet cute little puss. I found him wandering about the streets just about six months ago,' Ida mutters. 'But you still haven't told me where your Purrl is.'

I frown absent-mindedly. For once I don't know where Purrl is, since I pushed her out of the way while heading for the door, and it seems, for now, that she's disappeared. 'She's probably lying on the bed,' I say, and take a quick look in the bedroom, but there's no sign. 'Nope, she's not there. I guess she must have gone out hunting.'

'Oh, that's a pity,' says Ida. 'I was so looking forward.'

The kettle has already boiled and I get a mug and tea-bag out. It's a long time since I had tea and the smell makes me retch. I pour the boiling water on to the bag and watch the dark swirls spread throughout the water, then pick out a bottle of milk that is lurking despondently at the back of the fridge. Huge cheesy lumps drop into the cup; a whiff of fermented protein hits my nose. I stare at the white chunks floating up to the top of the liquid. They smell salty and sweet.

This will do for Ida. I take out a fork and start whisking it around in the water. The pale yoghurty stuff begins to break up into smaller masses, until it forms a smooth top layer of very small white globules. She'll be able to drink that.

Ida is sitting there in the armchair looking meek and innocent, but I know she's up to something. 'Here you go, Ida,' I say, handing her the mug.

I watch her take an absent-minded first sip, grimace and stare down into the cup, nose wrinkling. Her mouth puckers up. 'Err . . . Millie, dear,' she whines. 'I think you'll find your milk . . .'

I sigh. 'Would you like it black?'

She stares at me for a couple of seconds, as if not quite sure of what to say. A frown splinters across her face. 'No, no. I'll just skip tea. Are you sure you're all right, dear?' she asks.

'Fine, yes, perfectly fine,' I say, and reach forward. 'I'll just take care of that.' I take the cup, walk through to the kitchen and throw it into the sink, flooding it with hot water. The milk swirls, leaving faint trails of globules on the stainless steel.

Ida follows me through. 'Don't worry about that, dear,' she says. 'I wasn't thirsty . . . You know, the strangest thing has happened recently. You must have heard. The thing about the cats around here . . .'

I shake my head.

'Most of them have gone. Plain disappeared.'

'No?' I say. 'I hadn't heard.'

'Well, you ought to listen out . . . And as you're a cat owner yourself, it affects you. I mean, you wouldn't want your Purrl disappearing, would you?'

I turn and look at her. This shabby old hag is getting at something and I don't think I'm going to like it. I know what she's going to say. She's going to say bad things about Purrl and none of it's true – not one word of it. Purrl is a darling and I love her. 'I can't imagine how it would affect me. Purrl is perfectly happy at home.'

'Well, you never know,' she says, then pauses. 'Millie, your neighbours have been saying things. I hate to say this, but they've been saying that some white cat has been around and it's been behaving very oddly . . .'

My ears muffle over. Her voice becomes a haze. I can't be bothered to listen to her nonsense. And besides I'm totally distracted. I am preoccupied. Not with Purrl, or with Ida's stories, or with any cat

207

thing, but with Ida's face. Ida has one big ginger hair sprouting from her chin. From the middle of the point of her jaw, it juts out distractingly, drawing my attention every time her mouth opens and closes. It makes me want to reach right out and pluck it. I've noticed it before, but never mentioned it. I sometimes wonder if she's aware of it, if she even lets it grow deliberately. Unlikely, I think. Ida is such a mess. Look at her, all covered in cat hairs, stinking of cat piss, her clothes all shabby and stained, grime on her shoes. I almost feel ill from looking at her. There she sits, polluting my nice clean house, scattering her dirt over my floor, breathing her germs into my air. Did she think about scrubbing the muck off her shoes before she came in? Not likely.

'Millie . . .' Her hand reaches out to touch my arm and breaks my fevered thoughts. 'What's wrong?'

'Nothing.' I shake my head.

'No, there is . . .'

'What . . .' I answer slowly. 'What could be wrong?'

'Well, I just thought you seemed . . .'

After all our afternoon-tea sessions I've come to know Ida very well. I've come to understand what's going on inside her tiny brain, what her problems are and what drives her to be such an unashamed snoop. Yes, I've thought about it a lot and I've come to the conclusion that Ida's nosiness is a genetic trait. The result of some melting-pot of dominants and recessives that have worked their way down through Ida's family. Ida talks of her Granny Little with great affection. Granny Little knew all the stories – yes, she knew every measly morsel of local gossip. Granny Little was a snoop and a busybody just like Ida. You could say that Ida's gran was her role model, but I think it was more than that. I think you would find there was a huge long line of snoops in Ida's family. In the genes. That's where this madness comes from. That's where she gets her great big nosy nose. She was always destined to have it.

For a second I imagine I'd like to bite the end right off that interfering conk. 'Well, don't just think! It's you. You're crazy,' I say. 'You're just like your granny, who ended up in an institution. What's inside your brain? You come round here, bringing all your dirt and your nonsense – and what do you do? You tell mad stories. You concoct weird nonsense and spread trouble wherever you go. It's you . . . don't you know?' I imagine blood dripping from the end of her nose, castrated, ineffectual. 'You're nothing but a snoop,' I say.

'Millie, I –'

'Your mind perverts everything, makes it all into some sort of mystery or conspiracy, but that's not what the world is. You don't have a clue. And if . . .'

I want to continue, but Ida is already picking up her handbag and heading straight for the door. Her wide eyes are smarting and she lifts a yellow-stained hankie to her nose. I've got her. It hurts but she's got to know it. All this snooping around is not good for a person. It screws them up. If she stops it now she might be saved. She might be rescued from her madness.

'You're the one with the problem,' I say.

The yellow flicker of Ida's raincoat disappears round the corner of the hallway and I hear the door slam.

~

Still no call and I'm thinking about her again.

Milla must feel she's better than me. Well, it's true, she is better-looking and maybe Josh is more on her level, but I can't help thinking we're a match. It's as if both our essences really work together. The things Milla does might seem odd to some people, but that's just because she needs a bit of a wide track to run on. Without sounding patronising, she has a good heart, she does good things – at least some good things. When Jemima Spall was dying, she visited her in hospital every day for the last month or so of her life – and she looked after her house, her cats, everything. And my dad really liked her, which is a rarity. Dad hated Melanie and said he knew from the start that we weren't meant for each other. But he thought the world of Milla. Even though I kept telling him we were only friends and she wasn't interested, he kept asking if we were going to get married and when he could expect his first grandchild – ridiculous really, given that Milla was only twenty-four and hardly thinking about that sort of thing at all. I wasn't either. I'm still not.

If Milla's so kind, why doesn't she call? She has cut off

210

before. She's very good at that, disconnecting herself from part of her life – and she just does it. Almost without thinking. The good thing, though, is that Milla always comes back round again. Always.

~

Finally someone for me . . . Two calls in one day, one from Sophie, the other from my dad, and it seems I'm almost popular. I don't pick up on Dad, though it's good to hear his voice on the speaker, telling me that he hopes things are OK and he's thinking of coming over soon. With Sophie I can't resist. She sounds so warm and, though I know it might irritate Purrl, I pick up.

'Hey, sexy,' she says. 'Guess who?'

'Hello gorgeous. What's up?'

'Nothing much . . . just thought I'd give you a quick ring – my lunch break. I went to that yoga class last night that we were talking about. It was really good. You've got to come sometime. Mmm . . . I'm just drinking some tea, sorry –' *Gulp.* 'I've got so much to tell you. But really the thing I was calling about is I've got a day off next Tuesday and wondered if you wanted to do lunch or an afternoon drink or something – if you haven't got a job on?'

'Yeah, OK,' I say. 'When? Where?'

'Three-ish at that pub by the river. You know, the one where you can sit outside, the one we went to that time with Paul.'

'Oh, yeah, good. I know the one.'

'Have you seen any more of those idiots from your dinner party?'

'No. I'm hoping I won't.'

'And how's Josh?'

'Oh, fine,' I say. 'To be honest, I'm getting a bit bored with him.'

'Look, I've got to dash, otherwise my class will be like a war-zone by the time I arrive. But let's talk on Tuesday.'

Josh called, saying he might come round tomorrow.

He left a message on the answerphone, which I heard and ignored, according to my policy at the moment. Not that it worked this time. His voice wheedled its way into my inner ear and got set on continual replay in my head. 'Mills ... I know you're there ... Come on ... Answer ... I really think we ought to sort things out. I'm coming over at about seven tomorrow. Hope you'll be around, sweets. Give me a ring if you want to make it another time.' Effortful and self-consciously cheery, he was pretending nothing had happened.

Several seconds later and I'm already in a huge panic ... What am I going to do? There's no way I'm phoning the slimy prick back, but he can't come round, *he just can't*. There's no way I'm having him in this house, not after what he's said. But what to do ... what to do ... what to do? My mind races with ways of keeping him out. Options ... It seems that several options lie open to me. At this point I could (a) just put the chain on the door, or (b) get the locks changed. With a wimp like Josh, the chain would probably be enough – but I need to be certain. I need something stronger. I fumble for the *Yellow Pages* and scramble through looking for numbers. I've got to find a locksmith quick. Which one?

I put a circle round three cheap-looking ads and frantically phone to see what they can do for me at short notice. 'Sorry, dear, but if you want it done on call-out today, it's gonna cost you seventy quid and more depending on what locks you got,' says one. Another: 'Sixty pounds is the cheapest we do it for, and basic locks at that . . .'

It looks like it's going to cost an arm and a leg to call them out at short notice. But what else can I do? Physical barriers could be one solution. I test it out by dragging the chest of drawers into the hallway and slamming it up against the door. The idea of Josh standing outside, pushing fruitlessly, is very funny. I giggle to myself as I edge it across the ground. But if I can move it, then so can he. Josh might not have bulging biceps, but I can tell he could knock it flying. It looks like I'm going to have to splash out. I call Through the Keyhole and order a lock change for late this afternoon.

That's the last morsel of trout gone.

Looks like it's shop or drop now. Starvation, added to the lock problem, is sending me into a tizzy. I've been meaning to go to the supermarket for days now, but Purrl doesn't want me to go

213

without her. I can tell by the way she squeals every time I go near the door. Just entering the hallway can cause her to let out a long, low, warning wail. I'm so weak-willed. I give in to her almost immediately. I've already gone against all my best cat-behavioural advice by caving in to her too many times. But now we have reached a crisis point. There can be no delay to my shopping mission – our hunger just won't bear it – and so I shut her in the kitchen and block my ears to her cries. I ignore the sound of scratching on the other side of the door. She's only play-acting. There's no need for concern and I have it all planned: Milla's big day out in the urban jungle. It's going to be my last one for a while and I'm going to really stock up. I've written the list, planned out our menu for the next few weeks and I think I can really make it work. It's like stocking up for a nuclear winter.

Ready.

Miiaaaouuuu . . . Purrl persists.

Don't listen to her . . .

All set then, though I pause by the door and momentarily find my energy ebb away from me. The fear gets to me. It grips me like a muscular spasm: the fear that I'm not going to be able to deal with all those people, that someone might come up to me and say something that I will not be able to reply to, that I will be humiliated, that they will stare at me, that they will snigger behind my back. My hand rises to open the latch, but stays irresistibly suspended in mid-air.

214

I take a deep breath and open the door.

Outside it seems so light it almost blinds me. I'd forgotten what the whiteness of daylight was like. It plays on my eyes like something too sweet, leaving a sickly ache. I look from left to right and check that Flatface and Mingerston aren't around. The coast is clear and I hurry along the pavement towards my car. As I slip the key in the car door, my heart skips a beat. A thought occurs to me. *Maybe I haven't locked the flat door . . .* I try to clamp down on it, but the image of an unlocked door is expanding thickly inside my head. I try to remember locking it . . . There's no picture there, no memory of key entering hole – or if there is it could be a memory from weeks ago. I have to turn back and check it.

When I get back it turns out to be locked.

I get in the car and it feels like I haven't driven for weeks. My limbs just don't seem to coordinate quite properly and it's a jerky ride along the street, braking at the junction for a car that needs some extra space to turn into. *Oh, yeah, and who do you think you are, sticking your fingers up at me, mister?* It surprises me that there are so many aggressive drivers on the road. They're all out today. First there's Mr Smoothie, who eyes me up at the traffic lights – I half-smile back but stop myself – and then there's the prick in the sports car, who starts honking his horn at me because I didn't pull out on to the roundabout. He glares angrily, then sticks his fingers up. I glare back and hiss.

*

I walk in, head down, past the security guard at the entrance to the supermarket, trying to avoid his gaze. I notice it says no dogs on the door, so I guess that means no cats too. But then, maybe it doesn't – maybe it means dogs are the only animals that can't go into a place like this. Maybe it means dogs are the enemy.

As I roll out one of the large trolleys I begin to relax. The rows and rows of brightly coloured tins and boxes calm me. Abstract names and abstract shapes glowing in the fluorescent lights. My fears from earlier seem ridiculous and, as I glide across the tiles, I begin to wonder what in the world I'd been worried about. Shopping's routine. It's a cinch. You don't even have to speak to anyone, and all the other shoppers keep themselves to themselves. I throw in a few packets of frozen trout, then seek out the fresh fish counter and pile my trolley high with tuna, sole and salmon – imagining how Purrl and I will salivate over it. Now I'm really feeling hungry. The monkfish catches my eye.

Then, between the yoghurt and the butter in the dairy products aisle, it happens. The one thing I'd never really expected but secretly must have been scared of. My heart skips a beat. Ahead of me I see a scraggy-haired figure in a checked shirt and jeans. His hair is dark, just like Josh's. He's over six feet tall, just like Josh, and he's got skinny, bandy legs, just like him. I freeze. It must be him. My stomach turns and I teeter back a few steps. This guy lifts up a tub of margarine and inspects its lid, still turned away from me. My mind whirls . . . Is it Josh? Is it him? Is it? I'm practically reeling.

The man turns towards me . . . Slowly his head lifts in my direction. My breath is in my stomach. But it isn't him. No, it isn't him. He doesn't look at all like Josh: the lines of his face, his nose and cheek-bones, totally different. He smiles at me because I'm staring at him and possibly he thinks I must be an acquaintance that he just doesn't recognise, and I smile back, but feel a bit of an idiot because it must look as if I've just been standing eyeing him up. I turn away embarrassed and move on to the next aisle. I'm a fool.

Flushed with embarrassment, I quickly absorb myself in cleaning products. Staring constantly at the shelves for fear of accidentally making eye contact with the man again, I try and imagine what Purrl would have wanted me to get. Fish, yes . . . Purrl would have gone for fish and we already have plenty of fish . . . but bleach and toilet roll and washing-up liquid would be important too. A strong bleach. I begin to panic. I can't make the choice between multi-purpose, eco-friendly, new-action fancy stuff and the supermarket's own. Which would Purrl choose? Lemon-scented? Heavy-duty? Special bathroom stuff? I feel my breath quicken and my head swim. My thoughts go out to Purrl, all alone at home. I shouldn't have done it. I shouldn't have left her and I know that I should just grab one of these bottles and leave now. I grasp hold of a pale pink bottle of bleach and thrust it into my trolley, then start heading down the aisle.

At the counter, the queue is long and I become irritated and impatient. The girl on the till seems to be working in slow motion. As I stare at the magazines, I become aware of the fat, lecherous bloke behind me. He's sweating and stubbly and revealing a two-inch stretch of belly. He has only a couple of items in his basket, and he could move to the express till, but he doesn't. He just stands there with his hands in his pockets, breathing heavily, his belly virtually touching my back. I move a little further forward and he does too. He barely looks at me, but I know what he's thinking. I can almost smell him.

It makes me feel sick and I move on to the next counter. Here things move faster and soon the till-boy is whisking through carrier bags of fish. He grins at me flirtily. 'Starting an aquarium?'

'What?' I say, not sure what he's getting at, and trying to work out if he's really staring at me. I wonder what he must make of my mismatched shirt and skirt. Is he really thinking he fancies me? 'Oh, err . . . no. Just hungry.'

'Savings card?' he asks.

'Sorry?'

'Got a customer savings card?' He's watching and waiting, impatiently running my credit card through his hands.

'Wha . . . err . . .' I panic and scramble around in my pocket for a few seconds but am unable to find it. 'I . . .' I'm flustered and aware of him still staring at me and smiling, almost laughing at me. For a moment I am overwhelmed by one of those waves of intense shyness and feel my body tense up like a clenched, immovable fist. This is the kind of moment when I wish I was in a movie. I wish I could just pull out a gun and do a runner.

But I don't. 'No ... no card. I'm crap. I don't believe in them. Sorry.'

Sleep.

I could never be an insomniac. None of that late nights, cups of coffee, padding around the house till four in the morning stuff. I love to sleep. It's the most comforting thing in my petty existence. Sleep soothes, it seduces, it takes you away. I have no problem sleeping ten, eleven, twelve, sometimes thirteen hours a day. Though it's only really recently that I've started going for these big sleep days – days which are more about sleep than waking. Lately, it's true, I have got worse. I can sleep like a cat. Every time I sit down, or lie on my bed, to read a book or to write a note or two to myself, I feel it pulling me again. I wake up groggy and unable to function, so I go to sleep again.

Even coming back in the car today I start to feel the heavy tug of sleep. My eyes droop and I have trouble concentrating. I stick an extra-strong mint in my mouth from the pack that's been on the dashboard for months and months. The sharp, cooling sting brings my senses back to life. It keeps me going till I pull up outside the front door. Wearied by the stress of the outside, I lug the carrier bags full of food inside. Purrl follows, clinging to my heels, brushing her body up against my legs.

Not bothering to put all the stuff away, I collapse in an armchair and switch the telly on. A perky jingle assaults me and I hit the mute and watch some wide-eyed brunette mouthing away on screen. Already I feel the longing to go to sleep. Eyes shut . . . Offbeat but tangible thoughts cross my mind. I'm thinking about Josh, about what Josh will think when he comes round, about how I will deal with him. Josh has featured in my dreams a lot lately. Though I've almost erased him entirely from my waking life, my subconscious can't get rid of him. My dreams are so vivid.

Somewhere in the darkness I find Mina. She's sat at the table in Granny's house. Only this time it isn't a young Mina, it's her in her late teens, as she never would have been. It's Mina with that characteristic Purrlishness about her. We're waiting for ice cream. Granny has promised us ice cream if we eat all our lettuce and cucumber salad and we've both shovelled it down like pigs, unable to wait for mint choc chip, which is our favourite. Our yellow plates sit there empty with anticipation on the Formica kitchen table. This is where we, the kids, always eat. Only at Christmas do we ever get to eat in the dining room, which is really for grown-ups and way too tidy ever to let the kids loose in. Granny has gone to the front door to answer the bell. Mina sits there and stares at me moodily. Her thin lips pout at me. She's wearing a red T-shirt, from which her pale arms protrude like sticks, skinny and brittle from lack of use, like they've been for so long now. Her hair is longer than it ever was as a kid. She gurns at me, as if to say, 'What you lookin' at?' and I kick her underneath the table. No reaction. Mina just looks away and stares. She often swings like this. She is by turns devoted and distant. And when she's distant she really is. She's the kind of girl who gets under your skin just by doing nothing. She's always playing a little hard to get.

Mina stares down at the table. She's watching a spider crawl across the mat from the pepper pot to the salt shaker. She seems totally absorbed. I watch the spider too. It's a small one, fawn-coloured with an egg-shaped abdomen. With fast little twitches of each leg, it moves across the surface. Its line is direct and it runs without hesitation. Mina puts a finger down in front of it, cutting it off. The spider turns away, but her fingers are too fast, quickly another one arrives in its path. She holds it there, still and motionless. The spider hesitates, then proceeds in its path. It touches the pink cushion of Mina's index finger and begins to climb, crawling cautiously over the top. But Mina doesn't move her hand as expected. Instead she just lets it clamber all the way over on to the mat. She smiles as the confused arachnid starts to run, faster and faster. 'Cute spider,' she says. Her hand comes down with a heavy thump on the table. Her white fingers crash on to the mat, descending quickly over the spider

221

like an ominous shadow from nowhere. No way out. It's flattened – table-kill. 'Huh! Dead spider.'

I wake up to find Purrl licking my ear. It's dawn and she wants me to get up.

At about six o'clock in the evening Purrl starts to whine. She lets out long, low throaty cries and begins pacing the floor, running her check of the territory, from room to room to room to room. I know what she's saying. She's saying Josh is on his way. *Watch out . . . he's coming back . . .* But it's all right. I'm happy. No worries. Eddie Wright from Through the Keyhole has been round and I've got the toughest locks on the planet. Boy, is Josh gonna get a shock when he comes round and tries to stick his dud old keys in the front door. Yup, Eddie's done a good job. At a bargain rate ('specially for a real flower') he fitted me with a fortress-like two Chubbs and one Yale. I liked Eddie. He was pretty cute – though a bit strange. He kept making weird croaky noises under his breath as he worked – short, sharp grunting whines. He also liked Purrl, and that's a rarity. He even said he'd like to take her home with him, but his mum wouldn't like it.

'It'll take a master burglar to get in here now,' he said as he left.

'Perfect,' I replied, and gave him a Mina smile. I found him so easy. He's the first person I've been able to speak to for a long time.

I shift the armchair round to the window and take

up my post. I'm almost excited. *Hee . . . hee . . .* This could be fun. Purrl is restless. First she sits on my shoulder. Then she moves up to the top shelf of the bookcase for a better view. I sense her eagle eyes monitoring things from on high. Not only is she watching out for Josh, she's also watching me. She's keeping check on her mistress. I pull back the curtain a bit further and peer through. *Come on, JoJo . . . let's see you get through this one . . .*

He's taking an age. Maybe Purrl was wrong for once . . .

Within two minutes I'm bored and I get up, go to the bathroom and start flossing my teeth. I can't even entertain the thought of Josh being around without flossing. I suddenly find myself dentally obsessed, preoccupied with the state of my incisors, gaps and gum edges. Then, just as I'm stringing up, I hear Purrl. She goes wild, suddenly screeching like a mad creature. I freeze, yanking my floss so hard I draw blood. *This is it. This must be it.* Then, on tiptoe, I return to my watching post. *Finally, he's back.*

I watch him open the front gate. He's still tall and handsome, a bit stubbly around the chin, but the green shirt suits him and those worn grey cords are sexy in a battered sort of way. My heart leaps at his combined strangeness and familiarity. Though it's not been long, I'd almost forgotten what he looks like. For a second I'm so scared I almost think I fancy him again. But what does that mean? What does this chemical kick stand for against the huge gulf that separates us?

The bell rings.

From this angle all I can see is the edge of his back, leaning towards the doorbell, but I already know this is going to be good. This is my moment. This is where Josh really gets to see who's in charge. I quietly pad round to the front door.

'Helloo-oo.' I hear his muffled voice. 'Mills . . .'

There's the jangle of keys and coins as he tries to get them out of his pocket. As yet, he doesn't seem to have noticed that the locks have changed. Metal clinks against metal. I peer through the fish-eye. There he is with his head down and body contorted by the glass. There's my Josh. His nose is large, Pinocchio-like, body descending into short skinny legs.

Then I hear something: a long sigh, followed by a short, 'Shit.' Now it's dawned on him. He's got my game and he's looking at the lock and he's realised. 'What the hell is this, Mills?' he mutters, but he persists. Not daunted, he still tries to fit his Yale key into the one Yale lock. The key goes a little way into the lock but no further. I hear him pulling it from side to side. I press my eye up hard against the glass, straining to see what he's doing.

He halts, puffing, then tries again. No luck. The doorbell rings again and I hold still, breathing slowly to calm myself. If I make even the smallest noise I might give myself away. 'Milla! I know you're there. For Christ's sake, open the door,' he shouts. The blood is pounding like a metronome inside my chest. I breathe in, making a short sharp hiccuping sound. Did he hear that?

'What the hell is up?' he calls, low and abstracted. 'Come on, Mills!' He's so close. He sounds so sweet. His voice catches hold of something inside me and I find myself thinking, *Poor Josh, have I been unfair to him?* His face pushes up to the peep-hole, looming large and distorted but almost kissable. Closer, closer it moves, until the panorama goes dark and I'm aware that his eye must be pressed right against the glass. I don't move. If I don't move he won't see me. I breathe as quietly as possible.

'Silly cow . . . come on,' he mutters, his voice lowered to a whisper. 'I know you're in there! Come on, Mills! The joke's over.'

He can't know it . . . I'm sure he can't see me. He's only guessing.

'Oh, for fuck's sake, you awkward cow. Open the door, would you?' he booms.

Metal clanks against the wood and I realise that he's fumbling with the letter box. With only the barest rush of a sound, I move out of the way, pressing up against the wall to my right.

Three pink bulbs of flesh emerge through the slot, like noses trying to sniff me out. These rounded fingertips with immaculately manicured nails. They slither around. Blind creatures. I almost feel like bending down and biting the ends off.

'Uh . . .' he breathes. 'Hmmphhh . . .' he exerts. His nails glide along the edge of the brushes and then dart in again and the flap bangs shut.

225

There's a silence. I don't move. Twenty seconds pass. Twenty breaths as I wait . . . In and out and in and out and in and out. *Twenty times.*

The silence continues and curiosity gets the better of me. I put my eye to the glass again. Still silence . . . I can see the back of his head and he's not moving. His little tufts of sticking-up hair give him that early-morning look he has when he's slept on hair still damp. They're not even fluttering in the breeze. My breathing is shallow and quiet. My body strains under anticipation. I'm a patient spy – but so is he. He doesn't move. He just slouches there, leaning up against the door hopelessly.

Minutes pass – and I realise I'm so bored I'm biting my nails.

It's Josh who breaks the silence, and with a bang. His elbow rams against the surface of the door. It thuds, making me almost jump up in the air. Then another thud – a punch from his left hand. And again and again. Harder this time, and louder, as he kicks at the bottom of the door. The rhythm, starting slowly, builds up, and I find myself teetering back from the wooden surface. Bang . . . Bang . . . It shakes, it trembles each time, and I wonder if it might give way. Now, I'm scared. Fear gets the better of me and I feel my centre whoosh from my stomach to my mouth as I begin to tremble. Bang . . . Bang . . . Again he kicks and again – but still I don't respond.

'Mills, if you don't let me in I'm going to call the police.'

Fine, you do that! I'm thinking. *This is my home.*

His fist whacks out again, and I can feel the pain of its contact against wood. I know it must have hurt. 'I will do it, Milla.' There's another sigh and he turns away. I hear his sullen footsteps traipsing up the tiny gravel path. He's leaving. Finally, he's given up . . . and I want a last glimpse. I run round to the living-room window and look out. The gate squeaks as it closes behind him. There's anger straining in his posture, in his jutting-out chin and clenched shoulders. Sticking his hands in his pockets, he turns to walk away, kicking a can absent-mindedly with his foot.

So long, sucker . . .

Am I unreasonable?

'Mills! I just thought I'd give you a ring.'

It's only an hour after he left the house and already Josh is on the phone. He sounds falsely cheery as he swings into his speech. 'I just thought I'd give you a ring because I called round today – but I guess you were out. Anyway, I discovered the locks had been changed . . . Is this to keep your insurance happy? I'm assuming you still live there, because, well . . . I just am. Give me a call, please!'

'Look . . .' Fifteen minutes later and it's him again. 'There's no point pretending. I get the message. You don't want me to come round. You don't want to see me right now. You've made it fairly clear. But if you could just give me a ring. All I want to do is come and get my stuff. Really . . . I'm talking minimum contact.'

'Mills! Oh, Mills! Will you fucking pick up?' Silence . . . 'I said would you pick up? What are you on? What the fuck makes you do this? I've had it. I know it was bad of me to run off the other week, but you have to admit it's not all my fault. You were being a bit of a cow. Pick up . . . pick up . . . pick up! All I wanted to do was come round and speak to you and maybe pick up a few things. But no. You have to make things difficult. I mean, what kind of nutter goes to all the bother of getting the locks changed just because she's had a row with her boyfriend . . . or was it just another one of your stupid jokes? Oh, hell! What's the point? If you don't want to talk to me, we won't talk. Let's just forget everything then. Let's just say we're finished. That's obviously what you want. I'm hanging up now . . .' Another silence. 'If you don't answer I'm going to hang up after the count of three . . . One . . . two . . . three . . . OK, fine, I'm hanging up . . . Now.'

'Milla!' Josh again, forced and businesslike. 'I'm not putting any pressure on you or anything, but I need my address book. My whole social life is collapsing without it. Give me a ring!'

Next he's whimpering. 'Mills . . . Come on . . . Why? I mean, just a month ago I thought we had it so good.

228

Why this? I don't understand. I mean, I love you . . . loved you, well, whatever.' He hangs up again.

No, no, no . . . That kind of speech leaves me totally cold. Josh has said, 'I love you,' so many times to me before that one half-hearted, cut-off attempt means nothing in the great accumulated scheme of things. Maybe the real reason we're over is because we've already said our love quota and there's nothing else left to fill the gaps.

Before I even have time to mull things over the phone rings again. 'Oh, fucking hell, Mills, forget what I just said. Just forget it all. Forget everything. I can get the phone numbers and addresses off other people. Forget it.'

The final call comes an hour later. This time it's a reasonable, slightly slushy and almost wimpy Josh. 'Milla, I don't want to think I didn't do my best to make this work out. I know I must seem a bit of an idiot calling you back again and again. But . . . it's no skin off my nose. I have to do it for both of us. You see, I did think we were the works. You know . . . the big one. Stupid, I know. So, all I want to say is . . . I'm sorry. I'm sorry for whatever you feel I should be sorry for. I'm sorry I didn't try to get on with your cat. The truth is, you convinced me. Cats are pretty amazing creatures . . .'

There's something in the tone of his voice that makes me crawl towards the phone. Impulsively I move a couple of steps. 'Sorry' takes me a few more, and by the time we get to 'amazing creatures' my ear is practically pressed against the speaker. Momentarily I want him right here, want lip-to-lip contact, to forget the past.

'Josh . . .'

'Milla . . .'

My stomach flips. My head churns. Within seconds I feel I'm doing the wrong thing but I can't put the phone down. There's a long, long silence.

'Milla . . . Was I hearing things or is it you?'

I can't answer. I don't want to answer. It's so long since I last talked to him – *Or is it? How long is it?* – that I can't think how I ever did. I wonder how we used to spend those hours.

'Milla . . . I can tell you're there. I can hear your breathing.'

I can hear his breathing too. It intoxicates me. It's all too much. It makes me feel faint. Josh pauses. He's waiting, all that questioning hanging in the air.

I try to hold my breath, hoping he will think he's made a mistake.

The tension is excruciating. I can think of nothing to fill it up and so I put down the phone.

Purrl looks at me in disgust. Her tail twitches from side to side in annoyance while her body holds rigid. Her solid, unwavering gaze sends a rippling chill through me. She stuns me. She paralyses me. She drains the moisture out of my mouth. For a second she looks so colossal, so like a big cat. Her eyes strike a faint ring of terror in my guts. The

230

pose, the gaze, the slow angry breathing all say it. Purrl is accusing me of something, and I know I'm guilty. I let her down. I spoke to Josh. Just one word to him and now she feels betrayed. *Spleurritttchattt . . . sss . . .* She splutters at me with disdain. Then, like a whirlwind, she scuttles out of the room.

'Purrl, sweets!' I call after her. But she's gone . . . and I feel a wave of guilt seep through me. My head seizes with pain and pressure. Purrl's a drifter. If I don't entertain her whims, she will eventually go. I can't keep her for ever.

~

I wonder if I've always been fooling myself. Those occasional strained silences in which we would glance at each other, look away, glance again, never knowing what to say, suddenly awkward: did they mean as much to Milla as they meant to me? Did they mean anything at all?

~

I hang around by the phone but it's not Josh who calls. No, I guess even he would never crawl that much. Instead, the next call is another one from my mother – just a message. 'Milla . . . Helloo-ooo!' She thinks I should go and visit Mina. But I won't. I've done my share of visiting Mina and now I've left all that behind.

The cover has a skull, grinning from edge to edge with a dentibrite set of sparkling teeth. This skull is attached to a dark set of shoulders, arms and well-

231

manicured hands. From its scalp flow waves of blond locks. Between the set of red-painted fingernails balances a gun. This is the paperback cover of *A Cure for Cancer* and it's going straight in the bin liner that sits at my feet. This is Josh's book and I'm getting rid of it – just like I'm getting rid of all the other crap that's cluttering up my shelves.

Crash in the bin, *The Men Inside* in the bin, *The Book of Skulls* in the bin, *The Dispossessed* in the bin . . .

Josh is such an anorak. Despite his good looks there's a really nerdy streak to him. You wouldn't believe that such a down-to-earth kid could have his head so cluttered up with starship dimensions. I should have known things wouldn't work out as soon as I found him glued to the set and babbling about William Shatner.

Fahrenheit 451 by Ray Bradbury, *The Man in the High Castle* by Philip K. Dick, *Starship Troopers* by Robert Heinlein, *Voyage of the Space Beagle* by E. van Vogts. All in the bin. The names seem so familiar to me now. I've heard them too many times through too many long, tedious monologues from Josh. I've heard all the arguments in favour of sci-fi and I still don't get it. I still don't get why I should read Asimov or Arthur C. Clarke or whoever else to get a trip on what the future means for us. I just don't see the point. Who cares about the future? Human existence will never get any better than this. Probably it will only get worse – more lonely, more disconnected, more pointless.

What bewilders me is the intangibility, the

irrationality of it all. Everything is suddenly disconnected. Josh, who had been like part of my own body, is now a stranger to me. Maybe this is the way all things end. Bit by bit, the baggage of our relationship slips away. Bit by bit, I gain Purrl's approval.

I walk down the hall, into the living room, across the carpet, to the bookcase and back again.

The TV screen sits dead. Silence, deep and hollow, hovers in the air, like someone switched the world's mute button. This booming noiselessness is so strange. It makes the walls inert and unfriendly.

It's funny how the house seems so empty all of a sudden. There's a big, gaping nothingness echoing through the rooms that scares me. Purrl, who almost never leaves, has gone out and I doubt she will be back for a while. It's her way of saying she's not happy. She's demanding more devotion. And I'm willing to give it. *If she would just come back.* I swear I would do anything in the world for Purrl. I don't know why, but I would – maybe just because of the hope she gives me . . .

But I'm not falling to pieces. I'm not that type. Instead I'm cleaning. I'm scrubbing and swabbing that dirt away. Every little tiny odour of Zara or of Tibbs or of Josh is going. Every particle, every tiny little hair, will be erased. Then Purrl will be happy.

I scramble around in the cupboard and assemble the Hoover – a cranky old model Jemima used to have. When I switch it on, it roars like an animal.

The noise reverberates through the flat and fills up the emptiness. It's like a beast. Sometimes it splutters, sometimes it chugs, sometimes it hisses, sometimes it whirrs like it's going to explode, and with its great long nozzle it sucks up and eats any little bits that don't belong.

I apply myself to the area around the chair where Ida sat the other day. Every scrap of dirt that she brought in must be erased. Not a single molecule of Ida must be left. I run the nozzle backwards and forwards, watching as the specks of dust disappear. Backwards and forwards, again, I run over it. I flow with the regular rhythm of the vacuum pump as it ebbs and revives. Backwards and forwards . . . And again, backwards and forwards, like a dance. Getting rid of it. Getting rid of Ida. Getting rid of every last cell of her presence. Backwards and forwards . . . I feel the buzz of the Hoover vibrating up through me.

That's when I hear it. A long, descending wail. *Miiiiiiiiiioooooouuuu* . . . Purrl not just mewing but howling. I halt for a second in my movement. The scream vibrates across my eardrums. Purrl calling. Purrl warning. Purrl caterwauling. She comes hurtling into the room like a wild animal, scrabbling up the bookcase on to her watching spot. Then she turns and she sits there on high, as if ready to pounce. And I have no doubt – I now know there's something wrong.

I freeze on the spot, gripped by a spasm of fear.

234

I'm trying to listen for a sound, any sound, above the puttering of the vacuum engine, but I barely make out anything. Cocking my head to one side, I attend for several seconds. *And yes, I hear it.* In an instant it dawns on me what's happened, but it's too late. I'm a fool, an idiot, an incompetent. I should have thought things out, but I didn't and now, yes, I'm sure of it . . . Beneath the hum of the Hoover I can almost hear footsteps: a shuffle, then the clatter of something falling against the garden wall. Looking straight up into Purrl's warning eyes, I can see that it really is true. *He's here.*

I quietly put down the hose and walk towards the door almost on tiptoe. Moving slowly and cautiously, I brace myself for fear that someone might just jump out. I'm scared, jittery. Every nerve in my body feels exposed and as I push my head round the doorframe into the hall, I am aware of a solid lump expanding in my throat. I realise it's all too late. The face shadowing the doorway gives it away. A silhouette that is heart-stoppingly familiar. Yes, it's *him*, by the unlocked back door. I press my face up against the wall, feeling my heart pumping against my ribcage. I need to push on the plaster for support as my knees sink from beneath me. I'd never thought. I'd never imagined he would come this way – not via the back entrance – invading my territory like this. Not here, not now, getting the upper hand, playing me at my own game. *Not here, not now . . . Why didn't I prepare for this?* Josh is too wise to me. Why didn't I think to get Eddie to change the back lock too? It hadn't crossed my mind . . . or maybe I was repressing . . . I forget. And who would have imagined he'd climb all those fences? There's a string of them to be negotiated between here and the road in this row of gardens backing up together. But Josh is determined and now he's here. He's wheedled his way through my defences. He wants this ground back again.

I feel myself retreating, teetering towards the living room. *Stay away*, I whisper. *Stay away*. The blood is pulsing through my veins, my heart pumping like a mad thing. This is it. This is when I really have to face him. *If only there were a place to hide*. But there's nowhere. I can hear Purrl uttering long, low throaty miaows, which blend in with the buzzing Hoover to form an ominous chorus. I teeter back and back, reaching a hand out to balance myself against the wall. The only place I can see is behind the door, now held open by a wedge, and I edge myself inside. With a bit of luck, he'll just quickly look into the room, then go away again. He won't spot me. I pray he won't spot me.

I hear the back door creak open. 'Milla!' he calls out, at first quietly. His footsteps are slow and cautious. 'Milla! Are you in! It's only me, Josh.' Only *him*. Only the one man I can't deal with seeing and never want to see again. I lean heavily against the door, wishing this were all a trick of my imagination and he'd just disappear. I feel so sick.

'Milla! Oh, Milla! Where are you?' His voice is half-hearted and nervous. I can feel his slow steps

236

cautiously edging towards me and I know where he's heading. I know this will be the first room he looks in. There's no way out, but at least I'm with Purrl – Purrl, who crouches up there, eyes glistening with hostility.

'Come on, Mills!' His breath is just the other side of the door from me, its soft rasping wheeze so familiar, and I feel his presence seeping into the room. I think I can smell him. *Just go . . . Please . . . please go . . .* That fleshy odour is so strong.

Before I have time to think, he strides across the floor, glancing quickly around, but still not seeing me. Then he turns my way, and that's it. 'Mills?' He catches sight of me in the corner, his eyes hitting mine. Those eyes have a dominant gleam, making me want to turn my back and crouch away in fear, but there's nowhere to go and all I can do is shrink further into the corner, pushing my eyes into the wall. 'What's up, Mills?' he asks. His voice is distant and muffled, almost as if under water. It barely competes with the roar of the Hoover.

He coughs.

I knot my eyes into the carpet. I don't want to look at him.

There's a long silence, throughout which I feel him staring. My nerve-ends prickle. I am aware of his eyes boring into me for so long it almost makes me want to scream, but I don't, I just refuse to look up. Then Josh breaks the stillness.

'Christ, Milla! You look awful – really pale, really rough – like you could do with a good few weeks on a beach.' He's looking me up and down, checking me out, like he always used to. I can't bear it. I curl my body inwards and close my eyes in the hope that when I open them he'll be gone, thinking that maybe if I just pretend he's not there, he'll go away.

'I've come to get my stuff,' he says.

'Mmmm . . .' I glance quickly up at him and then look away. I don't want to deal with his ugly, manly form. I don't want to face that expectation. People don't have a right to demand that sort of thing.

'I couldn't get in through the front door because the locks were changed and it can only have been you that did that and I don't understand why. It was just a little tiff. I know I left . . .'

He's off, and he's droning once again. Blab, blab, blab. I can barely tell what he's saying. I just find myself watching his lips moving, entranced by his tongue and his teeth as he talks and talks and talks and talks and talks to me, and while he talks I'm suddenly aware that the talk is moving forward and getting closer and closer and I try and move back but I can't. That dark hole behind his teeth draws me in. The talk is in my face.

It's a horrible, warm, sweaty hand that touches my arm, sending alarm messages pulsing up my nerves, and I shrink away, stumbling out of the corner and backing my way towards Purrl, whom I see as my protector, who will help me deal with Josh. *Get off!* I think, or maybe I say it . . . I'm not quite sure which. Nothing seems to reach my mouth. I feel like I'm suspended in a thick, immovable gel.

'Mills ... Come on! Let's talk about it!' He's moving in again. This time, he's more persuasive. This time I don't move away. This time I almost want him to try it on, to break the cold anaesthesia with a shock. I remember what it's like to be touched. *I missed you*, I murmur, eyes focused on the buttons of his checked shirt.

'I mean, we could have sorted things.'

I said I missed you. My gaze climbs up his chest, searching for his face, for his eyes, but he doesn't seem to respond, doesn't seem to even hear me.

'I really didn't have a problem ...'

This time I try it louder, pushing the words out from my stomach. *I missed you*.

He hesitates for a second, seemingly disorientated, frowning and shaking his head. 'I don't get it, Mills! You've been up to some pretty weird shit. I don't know why, what it is about you. I must be stupid to be saying this ... Well, can't we make this thing work?'

Silence.

'So, tell me ... what's up?'

I shrug. 'Nothing.'

'There must be.'

'It's not worth it ...'

'Oh, come on, Milla ...'

'Not worth bothering ...'

'You expect too much. I know you, Mills. I know that's it.'

'Too much? Maybe ...'

'Aren't you going to ...'

239

I shake my head.

He moves forwards and presses a foot on the off switch of the vacuum cleaner. It putters to a stop. 'That's better.'

A hand reaches out towards me, a clean, familiar, friendly hand. For a second I almost feel like touching it, rubbing my cheek against it, scenting it, making it mine, but only for a second.

Then . . .

Miaaaooooouuwwwwwww . . .

Before I can move, I'm frozen by the sight of a white blur rushing past my eyes. Purrl is hurtling through the air, white limbs splaying, claws landing on Josh's head. She grips him, parasitically enveloping his face, her chest pressed up against his nose, tail curling around his neck like a fifth leg. Her white form clings to his hair, teetering on his nose and forehead. *Miwoouuuwwwwwww*. She squeals, she hisses.

All motion stops. Josh howls, a long excruciating shriek. His hands float up in the air, and I watch as they draw inwards on the white blur and try to throw Purrl off. His head swings from side to side in agony. Pain. A claw lashes out and catches him in the corner of the eye, ripping through the flesh at the edge of the bottom lid, causing him to reel backwards, only just maintaining his balance and puffing with the pain. Another hand flails out. This time it catches Purrl, throwing her off balance and hurtling her towards the wall.

Thwack! There's a thud as white fur smacks up against plaster. Purrl's body bangs and falls to the ground, as she lets out a loud piercing squeal. It rings through my ears, echoing in my skull. I watch as stunned, she lies for a few seconds barely moving, then struggles to some small movement.

I am petrified. I cannot move. There, in front of me, Josh stands swaying and clutching a hand to his eye, which is starting to release a slow, tiny trickle of blood. He lets out a short, sharp sobbing noise. 'That fucking cat . . .'

'That fucking cat . . . That fucking cat . . .' This is no *fucking cat* you fool. *This is more than that.* Mina and Purrl and me – our voices whirl round inside my brain. *'That fucking cat . . .'* Reeling round, I sweep up the handle of the vacuum hose and swing the leg recklessly at him. It sails through the air with all my strength behind it and I hold my breath, waiting for the thwack of contact. In slow motion I watch it rise, hover, aim and then dent into the corner of his head, metal clashing with skin and bone.

Josh shudders, his eyes open wide, blood collecting on the rim of the left lid and dribbling down his cheek. His mouth stretches into a grimace. His head twists away from me, whiplashing back against the blow. Then he sways and overbalances, collapsing to the ground. 'Mi-ills?'

His breath is hoarse and strained, chest heaving. I stand over him as he edges back from me. I watch him crawl. Now it's my turn to glare, to make him feel small. I see his eyes questioning – but it makes

241

no difference as in the back of my head I still hear Purrl. Josh shuffles further across the floor. His arms push up against the carpet, but collapse under him. He always was a wimp. He pulls up from his stomach, moaning and reaching another hand out to lever, then gathers himself again.

Suddenly he looks really angry.

Shit . . . Within seconds he's back on his feet again, but I'm still so stunned I haven't moved, and before I know it he's grabbed hold of my hand and I feel the firm clench of his fingers around my wrist, digging in hard and painfully, and I let out a sharp breath of hurt, then find myself pulled, his arm wrenching me forward, dragging me over the top of the Hoover, so that I almost trip, stumbling, and lose my balance for a second, but he keeps pulling.

'You're coming with me,' he splutters punishingly, lugging me along hard behind him.

I pull back, but it's fruitless. Even when I lean my full weight against his momentum, when I try to drop to the floor, he still hauls me and I find myself teetering along on my knees, collapsing forward and desperately scrambling to get back up again. I feel my shins bruising against the hard floor, my wrist grazing between his fingernails.

'Come on!' he yells as he swings through the living-room door.

A soft, inarticulate whine is all I can vocalise. My head swims. What is he up to? The pain. Why is he doing this? I scratch, digging my own claws in hard to his arm, hissing with anger as I press them deep into his skin. He winces momentarily, but holds his grip hard. *Hssssss* . . . I breathe. 'Purrl . . .' But I can't even turn around to see what she's doing. All I have is a vision of her lying there on the floor stunned, helpless.

Josh turns left towards the front door and halts, realising he has no keys. Then he yanks me round to the right towards the back exit. With my free arm, I flail out to grasp hold of the doorframe, my fingers scratching over it, and for a second I pull back against the force of his body levering against me. I dig in hard to the flaking white paintwork, bringing him up short, causing him to halt, but he yanks again, flinging me forwards with greater force.

'I'm not letting you do this,' he says, as I'm pulled stumbling through the kitchen, banging arms and legs against walls and furniture, wincing and squealing and shuddering with pain, falling back against the cooker. Then, I lunge at him, throwing my face at his arm and sinking my teeth in.

His skin tastes salty. I feel the pressure of my teeth against flesh, trying to slice through tissue, waiting for the pop of enamel puncturing skin, but I'm not used to this and, though Josh squeals with pain, some conditioning from inside won't let me really dig in and I don't draw blood. One arm lets go, but the other holds. 'Fuck, you fuck,' he yells, as I try to shake free, but the other hand comes round again and he grabs me by the upper arm, and, in a haze, I find myself propelled out of the back doorway, stumbling on to the garden patio, tripping and falling and scraping my knees, then being flung up again.

We're outside. Breathless and panicking, I let my legs sink to the ground again. 'Stop, stop, stop, Josh.'

'Don't do that,' he yells, pulling me up with both arms underneath mine and thrusting me against the wall. My stomach somersaults. His face comes into line with mine, dripping with sweat and blood, his arms pinning me up against the bricks. His chest is warm against mine and I feel my guts sink to my soles.

'Ouch,' I mutter pathetically. I am weakened by the familiar smell of his fresh sweat.

'Milla, what is this?' he asks – for a second not so harsh. 'I don't care about us any more, but this is ridiculous. I mean . . . a cat . . .'

A drop of blood drips from his forehead on to my face, and I look up into his eyes and I remember. For a split second I remember some feeling from long ago and try to grasp on to it, try to look through the sweat and the stubble and the red smears for something. Just for a moment. Yes, for that moment I see his face as I always used to see it, up close and kissable, and I feel the tingling of saliva in the back of my throat, like I want to thrust my tongue down his throat, feel the clash of teeth against teeth, or dig my teeth deep into that smooth soft flesh on his neck until blood comes.

'JoJo,' I sigh.

Everything collapses back into memory. Bliss,

play-fights, giggling sex, long breakfasts, dentist's chairs ... every second of our happiness. It's all there, all in one lingering sigh of contentment. So sweet. So happy. But not for long – as his brow furrows, his teeth grit and it occurs to me he's just about to attack me. I strain to let out a scream. But the face in front of me creases up. Nails dig into my arms. His body strains closer. It's that dark space of his mouth again.

His lips open further and it's him who screams like a wild animal. Turning his head down, he looks away.

I look down too, and there she is, *my baby*, Purrl, her snowy-white jaws wrapped round his ankle. Teeth digging into flesh and blood spurting. Her claws wrench into the skin between jeans and plimsoles. Her mouth holds and his foot jerks sideways.

'Bitch!' he yells.

'Queen, actually.'

He tries to shake her off and loosens his grip on my arms. Barely thinking and with all my might, I push him away, push him back from me, trying to get free from the panic that's racing through me. I throw myself at him. From nowhere comes strength. I push hard, harder, so hard ... and he falls. Under my weight, which is pushing, but also straining to stay steady, he collapses back. He tumbles to the ground, hand grabbing out at my wrist to try and steady himself, pulling me forwards with him.

245

It's all so quick. In barely an instant his shoulders hit the stone patio. His head flicks back and thuds against the paving, his grasp loosening as he hits ground. And I reach out a hand to break my fall, planting it dead centre of his chest, only just preventing myself from landing right on top of him.

Kerrack! I hear the crack of bone against concrete.

Josh's head bounces in front of me. Mouth wide and still mid-howl, I can see down his throat, I can see the red fleshy wetness inside, the saliva, the fillings, the sliding tongue. Then his jaw shuts tight, teeth banging together. From his throat comes a low grunt. His hair falls back from his face and his eyes flicker, closed then open. I'm so close, it all seems a blur.

I hold myself above him for a second, then stumble to my feet. He does not move, though he's still breathing. He groans and his throat makes small croaking noises, and I teeter backwards towards the wall, not quite sure what's going on, or what to do next. I've got to get rid of him, get rid of this nagging in my chest. I catch sight of the garden tools propped beneath the kitchen window and back towards them, all the while keeping a check on my prey. Once there, I grasp a large metal fork from behind. It's hard and heavy and stubborn in my hands, and it feels like it could stop even the toughest of assailants. I weigh it up and stare at Josh. His face is wet and bloodied and I swing the fork in my hands and watch as he twitches slightly but does not get up, and, anyway, I'm not letting him get up. Not after this. Metal handle in hand, I stand over his body. He tries to pull up and shuffle back.

I breathe in deeply, gritting my teeth and feeling the blood pumping through my head. He struggles to cry out again, and for a second he looks so sweet, making me want to reach out to him even now, because it's not as if the feeling's gone.

'I do love you, JoJo,' I say.

I thrust the fork up underneath his chin, where the skin is all soft and kissable and vulnerable. Placing the prongs on his tanned, roughly shaven neck, I test the strong elasticity of his skin. How much weight to puncture that? How much tension before skin will give? Two spikes straddle his Adam's apple, two teeth digging into his jugular veins, and I push a little but nothing happens, then a little more. 'Love you,' I murmur, eyes blurred with wetness, but still nothing gives. This skin is tough and I'm resistant to the idea of pushing too hard. Even just this moderate pressure makes my stomach turn. Josh moans, his eyes look up at me, gazing straight into my face, but it's all gone too far. *Do it . . . Do it now . . .*

With a hefty yank, I kick down on top of the fork bridge, in a sharp, earth-shovelling action. The rusted prongs burst through the skin, popping it open, splitting through the layers, easing into the flesh and thrusting down towards the ground, and he tries to let out a final scream, but the pain seizes him around the throat. Red pools ooze out. Blood spurts and flesh tears. I'm hit by a splash of warm, sticky wetness. A damp, glottal noise croaks from the throat. His body spasms and more blood erupts and floods around his head in a large puddle.

I let go of the fork, which is heavy, and the metal handle falls back a little, swinging like a catapult and levering Josh's head up a couple of centimetres. It sways there for a second and, though it's only the smallest fraction of a movement, Josh almost seems to be pulling up his face to look at me. The prongs scrape along the stone underneath and yes, I can tell, Josh is definitely seeing me. For the last time.

I stand there, not moving at all, taking in every detail of his last moments – the slight jerking of his feet, the straining of back against patio, the fluttering of eyelids, the phlegmy bubbling of saliva at his tonsils – and I don't feel a thing. I feel nothing at all. As I watch the blood still spurting in small jets from his neck, I just marvel at the force of the heart pumping through his body.

One last twitch and it's over. I'm breathing hard and tired and my blood's still racing and I stumble back against the wall, panting, exhausted. I try and work it out. I feel dizzy and disorientated and find myself pushing on the surface to support me as I just stand there, my feet by his feet, staring, not sure it's all really happened. I see the blood, I see the wreckage, I see his body twitch in a final isolated spasm. I see everything. I take it in. I let my eyes lap it up, not quite sure what to make of it all. I still don't understand. *How did I get from the living room to here? How did it happen?* Josh's limp, contorted body blurs before my eyes. *How?* Maybe I didn't really do it . . .

He's still handsome, though messy and blood-sodden.

I look around. Purrl is playing with his left thumb, wafting a paw at it, as if to encourage some prey back to life. She licks it, nibbles at it. The edges of her mouth are coated in fresh red blood from when she attacked his ankle. She looks wild, like a lioness with her kill.

I go into the kitchen and fetch a piece of kitchen roll to wipe it away. I spit on it and smear off the blood, which is wet and thick and clings to her whiskers. Purrl looks the proper meat-eater now. Her canines are fierce and dangerous, and, as she opens her mouth into a huge demonstrative yawn, I observe those killer teeth. I wipe again. *There, all clean* – apart from the vaguely pinkish tinge, which I suppose I can probably remove if I wash her properly. Water!

Wandering over to the sink to get a proper dishcloth, I stare out of the window absent-mindedly as I walk. It's a beautiful day and the sun is shining through the purple flowers outside, making them shimmer bright violet. A blue, cloud-less sky hangs cloyingly over everything – a Techni-color stillness – and then it strikes me. Has anyone seen me? It suddenly dawns on me that if anyone happened to be out, then they would surely have heard our fight, and if you stand up on tiptoes you can almost see over the intervening fences. I glance in one direction – to the teacher's side, and then in the other, to Mrs Mingerston's. Nobody there. No one's about, but if I'm not careful they might appear. They might see Josh's body.

I step forward and grasp hold of the fork handle. With a sharp wrench, I try to pull it out of Josh's still blood-oozing neck. It doesn't come. I pull harder and feel the prongs slipping and sliding against wet flesh and blood. The fork is almost moving, and small bubbles of blood fill up around the prong entrances. I feel nauseous. The sounds of bone splintering makes me retch. I pull again. *Ugh!* This time it comes up, lifting his head with it, and instead of pulling it out, I find I'm just pulling him up. I'm forced to place my foot in the centre of his chest to stop the body from rising. The toe of my trainer rests in the puddle of blood on his neck, below the bottom of the fork's teeth. I push down with it as I pull up, swallowing down the wave of sickness that envelops me and wrenching again. This time it pulls away so quickly that I almost fall backwards, slipping against the body and only just maintaining my balance.

I glance around again. Still nobody.

Time to shift my Josh, to get him out of sight. It's not that I want to dispose of him, just hide him. I want to keep him. I'm happy with him this way. This way he's under control. Now he's inert and ineffectual, I'm reminded of blissful mornings snuggling up to a quiet, sleeping body. Just the way I loved him. Those were the best times: the times when he was too sleepy to cause trouble, when I could do whatever I wanted with him. And now he's going to be like that at all the time – a perfect relationship.

I step over him and slip my hands under his arms, hooking beneath his armpits with my arms and trying to haul him up against my legs. Blood soaks up into the arms of my white blouse, staining it scarlet and splattering over my front. His head lolls against my stomach as I hitch him up against my chest. *Come on, honey . . . Time for bed.* He's heavier than I expected and it's a strain to drag him even a few inches. But I persist and, with his legs still weighted on the ground, I circle the axis of his pelvis, turning him round to pull him backwards through the door.

I stagger a couple of steps and then stop for a rest. My blouse is damp and warm and sticky and I can smell the strong salty odour of fresh blood. I breathe in and haul again. Just another few steps. *Then, my JoJo, we'll have you in bed. Then, we can have a rest.* I'm exhausted and would ideally like to leave it, but I know I need to hide him. That deaf old bat Mingerston has been waiting for this sort of thing for years.

Josh's legs bounce along the paving stones of the patio. I breathe in heavily, straining as I fight weariness. At the step into the house I make an extra haul. His head falls forward again, blood dribbling out on to my hands, his weight tearing at the muscles of my shoulders.

Inside, it's much easier. He slides along the carpet, leaving a trail of blood against the beige tufts. I pull harder and hear an involuntary grunt escape as I force up our momentum. My feet stutter quickly over the floor in small, short steps. Round the corner, through the hallway, faster, I staccato through . . . into the bedroom. There I stop, propping him up against the bed-end, and I look at him again, turning his face to examine it. More blood collects at the corner of his mouth, trickling down his cheek, and I catch it with a finger, wiping it away, cleaning his pale, damp skin. I step out of the way and his head flops back against the bed-end with a small, echoing thud. I get out my hankie and clean the red dribble from his face. *That's better now, baby . . .*

Josh needs clean sheets. I quickly change the pale yellow bedlinen for some white stuff, though I find I leave small crimson smudges on the edges of the bleach-white fabric from my soaked white shirt, which is now practically red. There's not much I can do about the shirt and I'll have to throw it away. I feel so hot and sticky, I decide to quickly change, slipping on that little black T-shirt I haven't worn for ages, but which won't show the blood.

I attend to Josh again. Now, the final haul, and the most difficult bit – getting him into bed. Again, I hook through his armpits, dragging him round to

252

the side of the bed. I'm already panting. I perch on the edge and pull him up on top of me, so that when I shift from under him, he's almost half there. His still-warm weight leans on top of me, spreading into me, and I linger for a moment, feeling that oneness inside, feeling his heaviness overwhelm me. Then I struggle out from under and, from a crouching position on the bed, edge him up a little further. He really is a dead weight and hard to shift, but I throw all my strength into it, hauling and edging him over gradually until there's just the legs to move. Grabbing hold of his feet, with one last wrench of effort I flip him over on to the mattress.

There we have it. All comfortable now. I ease Josh's head over. It has now twisted round ninety degrees on his loosely hung neck. Underneath, I see blood sopping into the sheet, but there's nothing I can do to stop it. His hair spreads out in sticky curls on the pillow. His eyes seem to be following me.

With two index fingers, I draw the lids over the surface of each. *That's better now.* He looks so at peace, like he's sleeping, and there's only one thing more to complete the picture. I have to get him out of these scruffy, bloodied clothes. I begin to undress him, surprised that actually I don't find it erotic, unbuttoning his shirt, unzipping his trousers, feeling the soft limp flesh beneath his underpants, dragging my hands across his damp, sweaty skin, pulling his jeans down over his hair-speckled legs, easing off his sticky, reddened shirt and smelling his chest and armpits. Not erotic at all. I consider dressing him in pyjamas, but it seems too much effort and I just cover him with a sheet.

Purrl stands on the patio mewing gently. She looks lost and uncertain, though I can feel her message to me is that we've got some covering up to do. Out here is a huge pool of blood, a huge reservoir of evidence.

There it is, a glistening crimson puddle in the middle of our patio – and I almost imagine that it's spreading. I connect the hosepipe up to the hot tap in the kitchen. *I've got to get rid of this mess.* With the power-jet attachment on, the water spurts out in a concentrated stream, jetting across the paving stones, collecting the blood on its way. I feel the splash of warmth against my feet and let the water stream over my red-stained trainers. The heat seeps inside. It reminds me of times back in the milking parlour at Al's farm, washing the floor down, spraying away the milk, muck and slop. I almost imagine I hear the sound of the old tape-recorder playing in the background. I start to hum as I watch the bloody swirls run down into the drain. The pool washes away, disappearing, leaving only the lingering pinkish stains of blood clinging to the stones. *Mmm . . . mmm . . . mmm.* I hum as I force the jet down on to them, desperately trying to purge them. Looking down, I see my arms are still covered in it and I apply a couple of quick slooshes of the hose, leaving my arms warm and wet and clean. *Soon . . . mmm . . . mmm*

254

'What are you doing?'

I jump, swirling round and sending water spraying up into the air.

It's Mingy Mangy Mingerston, out with her squinting eagle eyes and her purple housecoat. She's got up on her stepladder and is leaning over the wall, like she usually does when she's nosing.

I stare at her as she peers over the top of the wall. 'What?' I shout, because she can't hear me otherwise.

'I said, how are you, dear?'

I pause for a moment in silence, feeling my frown as I try to decide which of her two diverging eyes to focus on. 'Yeah . . . fine . . . just cleaning.'

'Mmmm – really. That young man of yours, I saw you kill him.'

My heart skips a beat. 'What? What do you mean?' *She's on to me. She must have seen me.*

'Where is that young man of yours. I want a word with him. Tell him I want a word.' Her long spindly, wrinkled finger wavers in front of me and I wonder if I just imagined her say that. *Kill him?*

I'm panicking. What is she trying to do? This must be some little Mingerston trick. Not sure whether to run inside, confess all or take her on, I walk over to the wall. 'Well, he's not living with me any more,' I answer.

Mingerston's pale brow wrinkles up with infuriation. 'Well, that's very odd. I could have sworn I heard his voice earlier. I could have sworn it. Anyway, if he's hiding in there, tell him I've had enough of him pinching my geraniums. One or two was all fine and good, but there's hardly any of them left now.' Her voice runs on like a train, words tumbling over each other, as it gradually dawns on me that this is either a very clever ruse or she didn't see me, didn't see me with the fork. 'And that's not all. Those blackberries of yours are growing into my garden, right over the wall there.' She taps the wall with a stick. 'I don't see why an old lady like myself should have to be cutting back that kind of thing, with all the prickles and everything, it's a devil, and it's you that let it go. And another thing . . . you should see your lawn. Well you can't miss it. It's a jungle. You may think that's fine – who cares! But there's all kinds of weeds in there that are spreading over into my garden. If you could just control it, it would make all our lives a bit easier . . .' Whinge, whinge . . . 'Mind standing there, hosing down the patio! I'll tell you, I'll be sending our Billie round if we have any . . .' Whinge, whinge . . . She pauses for breath.

I look over at the lawn and see that it's verging on about three inches high. 'I was going to cut the grass later,' I lie.

'Not that it's any of my business anyhow, but . . .' she says.

'No, it isn't really.'

She stares at me, then shrugs her shoulders. 'Well, it's your problem. You have to deal with it. You try and give your neighbours a word of advice and what do you get? It just gets thrown back in your face. I was going to say you could get my little nephew who's staying to cut it for a few pounds. But if you want to be like that.'

'I like it long . . . I like the grass long. I like the wildness.'

'Mmmmph.'

I watch her turn away and go back to her own gardening. *Stupid cow.* Suddenly I feel a sharp tingle in the back corners of my mouth and imagine chopping her nagging tongue out. That would shut her up.

While I'm cleaning in the bathroom, Sophie calls by. She's a little angry with me and I don't like the way she's going on, so I decide not to let her in.

Mother rings. It was her birthday last week and not only did I forget to send anything, but Dad did too. A double whammy for Mum.

I apologise but not convincingly.

'I don't ask much,' she says, 'but to forget your own mother's birthday. I mean, that's a slap in the face. All my care and I'm repaid by this. Tell me you have a good excuse, darling. Tell me you have?'

'Oh, Mum. I'm so sorry,' I say. 'Things have been so busy with work lately.'

'Well, I suppose that's a good thing, darling, but I'm seeing so little of you at the moment. What's happened? We used to be seeing each other nearly every other week. I suppose my little girl's grown up now and thinks she's too much of an adult to need her poor old mummy.'

I cringe.

'Milla, honey, you forget. You're all I've got now. What with the Mina thing, and then your dad. You could spare me a thought.'

I know what's coming now. This is just what I always get. She says everything to me that she wants to say to my father. Ever since he left her, she's treated me like a surrogate husband. Because he won't pick up the phone, won't even listen to a word she says, won't open her letters, I'm the easy target. And what makes it worse is, as everyone says, I am so much like my dad. I'm my father through and through, and every time Mother hears my voice, she hears him. It's funny that . . . two twins . . . they look exactly alike, every single physical detail of them, right down to a mole on their left shoulder makes them indistinguishable, and yet people could see the difference. Though our appearance was almost exactly genetically midway between our parents, I was like Dad and Mina was like Mum. *She's just like her father*, they always used to say.

That's why she doesn't like me so much. I look like Dad. That's why she constantly reminds me that I was unexpected, that they thought they were going to have only one twin, that I popped out like an afterthought, a word that escaped before the mouth was closed, one word too many. It's probably also why I'm left feeling like the bad twin, even though I know I was no better or worse than Mina. The truth is there was no good or bad twin. No ultimate truth, just different versions. That's what we both were, different versions of the truth, and now there's only one truth . . . me. Just me.

'How can you just forget me – just like that?'

'Mum,' I say, sighing, 'I don't forget you. It's not me that forgets you. It's him. Don't blame me.'

'Didn't even think to call. Never does,' she moans, in a soft, throaty, half-sobbing voice. 'Too wrapped up with that Tom and Hilde.'

She's trying to pull on my heartstrings now by reminding me that my father has a new set of children, a new couple of teenagers who absorb him much more than me – that my dad has moved on from both of us.

'You've got to move on,' I say. 'It's years now. You can't just sit there hanging around for him to call. And what happened to that gym instructor you were seeing?'

'Too demanding. And, anyway, he was spending all his time surrounded by these young girls. I couldn't stand it.'

I can't stand it either and I hang up.

Miaouhhh. Miou . . . Miu . . . Miu . . . Miu . . . Miao . . . Miao . . . Miao . . . Miaouwww . . . Miaouuhhhhhhhhhh . . . Miaouwwwwwwwwwwwwhhhhh . . . Wioaouhhhhh . . . Wiouww . . . Wee-aouw . . . Wee-aouu . . . Weeiii . . . Weeii . . . Wiaou . . . Miu . . . Miuu . . . Mhhhrnnhhh . . . Mhhhrnnhh.

259

And again, I whine at her. *Miu . . . Miuu . . .*

Maybe its the way she stretches with delight, maybe it's the way she flicks her tail like a paintbrush through the air, but somehow I imagine I'm getting through. I'm plunging through that barrier between the human and the feline. *Purututututututututut . . . Purututut . . .* She purrs and then croons back, *Miaouu . . .*

Down on all fours I face her. I clear my throat, then release a little voice from the back. *Miouuu . . .* It squeals from my tonsils as my tongue closes up on my oesophagus. It rolls. There, I *fee-eel* it. This little voice inside me that is a cat. *Iiayahhhh . . .* It's as if there were some invisible creature down there throwing its voice outwards every time I speak. Passing the air over the top of my tongue, I whine. Then I breathe in again. I can feel the sound up inside my head, whistling through my nose. Unlike human speech, it's almost effortless. With ease, it rises in the throat and then trails away. I try to enunciate as clearly as possible. I call out to her. She picks it up. Contact. It's tenuous but it's there. I can see it in her eyes.

Purrl stares at me inquisitively. She cocks her head to one side, moving her ears as if she's listening intently. Have I got it right? Perhaps. I can see some look of recognition on her face as she calls back to me: *Iiayahhhh . . .*

What next? I let my voice work intuitively, like I'm playing the piano. I try it throaty: a Tibbs cry,

260

the cry he used to make when he was on the prowl. Pressing the bottom of my mouth downwards, I hollow out like one big bell. My tongue slides back and my larynx sinks, as the call comes from lower. *Wiaoouuuuwwwwwww* . . . And again. *Wiaouuwwwwww* . . .

She rolls over and purrs, her dainty limbs dancing in the air. My Purrl squirms with delight. She looks so content. *Eeayahhhh* . . . *Eeayahhh*, she says. And I know I have contact. Somehow I know she understands. In the thick vibration of her purr is a note that says, 'We're there.' It fills my heart with pleasure. Yes, Purrl and I have a very special relationship, a relationship which no cat and human I know have ever had. We really can communicate. We understand each other's every call, every murmur, every action, every look. We understand each other better than a husband understands his wife. Our communication goes beyond talk. These calls are just the superficial echoings of our communion.

For years, as you know, I've been struggling with a very basic form of communication – an odd, feeble, half-baked mewing sound here, a faint growl there. It's all been so primitive. I've tried to get through. I tried it with Tibbs. I tried it with Mopsy. I tried it with virtually every cat I had in childhood. But no other cat was as open as Purrl. We two can converse because we are both so close and sensitive. In the past I have never understood the fundamentals of cat communication. Now I know it works on such a different level from human speech and though I find it hard, almost impossible to explain its mechanics, I know I'm getting there. It's so much more than the mimicking of cries and the recognition of behavioural signs – *so much more* – and it's only by becoming completely subsumed in catness that I have reached out any further. I've thought about it a lot. Being with a cat day in, day out just helps you get on its mental wavelength. It stops you getting wound up in the science and semiology of communication, which is where most people go wrong. We're talking about a different species here, a whole new mode of language, and it's necessary to be this intuitive.

I trail a hand across her body, all the while staring into her eyes. I tickle behind her ears. I run a finger along the side of her cheek. I let out a long, low *miaow*.

Her: 'Purrl . . .'
Me: 'Purrl . . .'
Her 'Miaouuuu . . .'
Me: 'Eeeeyahh . . . Eeeeeyah.'
Her: 'Wiaowww . . .'
Me: 'Purrl.'
Her: 'Miaouuu . . . Miaou.'

And so it goes on, turn by turn. *Miaouhhh. Miou . . . Miu . . . Miu . . . Miu . . . Miao . . . Miao . . . Miao . . . Miaouwww . . . Miaouuhhhhhhhhhhh . . . Miaouwwwwwwwwwwhhhhh . . . Wioaouhhhhh . . . Wiouww . . . Wee-aouw . . . Wee-aouu . . . Weeiii . . .*

262

*Weeii ... Wiaou ... Miu ... Miuu ... Mhhrnhhh
.. .Mhhhrnnhhh.*

Our conversation flows like music.

~

*Finally the calm comes back. For a short while the cool,
blank cleanness of my life had slipped away, but suddenly
I was on line again. I could think straight. I was ready to
call Milla and I had the confidence that I could face her
without feeling remotely embarrassed. In the end it was
simple – I just left a message on her answerphone.*

*In doing so I noticed something odd. Habitually it had
become Josh who had left their recorded message, so I was
surprised to hear her voice on the other end of the line, so
unfamiliar as she mechanically lumbered through saying,
'Hello, Milla Hall speaking. You can leave a message.' It
was strange too that there was no mention of Josh –
though I took that as a positive sign.*

*'What's new, pussycat?' I said, hanging on a short
pause to see if she was actually in. 'Gabriel here, just
checking up. I note Josh has been bumped off the message.
I take it that means something's up on the romantic front.
Does that mean there's room for an old friend in your
life? Give me a ring if you need a shoulder to cry on.'*

~

Purrl doesn't really mind me going through to see
Josh. She says it's OK for me to sit there with him,
though obviously sleeping with him would be quite
a different matter. Sordid stuff like that is strictly off
limits and likely to result in sulking and rejection for

hours and hours – or at least, so she warns. Sex has always been something that Purrl has not been able to deal with, particularly between me and Josh. The idea of the two of us lying there together, flesh upon, below, alongside, against and inside flesh, makes her almost ill. There's no danger of that though. I wouldn't want to do anything. Not now.

I *might* be interested if it weren't for the sheets.

They're glued to the mattress with caked-on blood that's wet and sticky and almost sopping through to the floor and I can't face getting into bed with him. So I just sit there and look at him. I stare at him, minute after long minute, and while I'm there maybe I read a book in the chair next to the bed, or switch on the radio for extra company. It makes me feel everything's all right.

Sometimes, when she's bored and has nothing better to do, Purrl even comes through. Quietly she skirts his body, checking it out for movement, though now she clearly knows the coast is well and truly clear, and sometimes she even leaps up on to the bed and sidles up to his head, sniffs it curiously and starts licking the blood off his neck, cleaning him for me, washing away the last smudges of my violence. She says she almost quite likes him now – now that he's so quiet and uninterfering. Well, she would do, wouldn't she? She's won. I can see that much. She's flushed with victory. That's why she struts so proudly – like she's some newly crowned queen of a kingdom. She knows Josh has lost and now she can afford to be charitable, offering faint, limp apologies. In her pathetic whine she says she's sorry she pushed it quite this far. Not that she needs to. It's not as if I hold it against her. This was where it was meant to go. It's only now that the three of us can all exist happily within these four walls.

And we are happy.

Josh even looks a little happy. His face is so empty and still it almost looks like it's smiling. Freed of all expression, his muscles have melted down into a liquid, flowing, floating, streaming across his skull. I could drift in that face as if it were my own. Often I do, and I start to think that in the blankness I see the tiniest movements, the faintest quiverings, small groups of molecules vibrating with an energy that even if it isn't life is still something. He lives in the fogginess of my retina – in the fading evening light when things take on a different form. They blur. They move. Sometimes I even imagine his eyes might suddenly open, like Mina's did.

Mina's eyes ... Yes, my sister's eyes were the weirdest thing about her.

When Mina finally came round she looked like a completely different person. Though her features were all there – the same dusty-blue irises, the same long, fine nose, the same thin, upturned lips – they came together in a different expression. A look of constant surprise transformed her, fixed in her eyelids and the corners of her mouth. It clung to her skin. I found it odd because Mina had always been so unfazable, so unsurprisable. She was a rock.

265

Whatever else had stayed the same about her, that look was what warned me that she was no longer there. She was a stranger and no amount of persuasion by my parents would convince my otherwise. I could tell. I knew that face better than I knew my own. I remembered every detail of it. Beforehand she'd had the most piercing of eyes, eyes that could knock you flying with a single flash, eyes that could strip you bare, eyes that threw all the mystifying strength of her character out at you.

Yes, my sister's eyes were special – so why weren't mine too?

There are times when I'm sat there and I feel Purrl's gaze boring into me.

'Not starting to regret things, are you?' she asks.

'No.' I shake my head.

'Yes, you are.'

'No. Not regret. I'm just worried. What if someone finds us?'

'They won't. Why should they?'

And her logic convinces me. After all, no one knows. There would be no reason for the police suddenly to arrive at our house – not unless old Mingy Mingerston started blabbing, and even then probably no one would believe her.

'Of course, I can almost see why you fell in love,' she comments, as she strolls along the side of the bed studying him. 'He was quite beautiful.'

'Mmmm . . . He was.'

I gaze at his face, now paler and pastier, scanning

over the angular line of his jaw and the erupting growth of stubble. I remember how his rich olive skin used to shine and his cheeks would go all flushed after sex. Lying there, he still looks so strong. I almost feel like reaching forward and just slipping a hand under the sheets and gliding fingers over that smooth, taut skin, caressing, fondling, tweaking at his chest hairs and toying with his nipples. I find my hand creeping over the covers, slowly edging its way. Almost there . . . But then I stop. I feel Purrl's eyes throwing daggers at me. *Time to go*, she's saying. *Visiting hour is over.*

Purrl's very careful that I don't spend too long in the bedroom. She rations out the time and she's as bad as my sister (full of approvals and disapprovals), telling me it's not good for me to sit gazing at a corpse for hours, and besides, there's plenty of cleaning to do, plenty of sleeping and plenty of TV to watch, though we're a little tired of that now and the flickering screen sends us to sleep. Now we prefer just to sit and look out of the front window, watching the people go by.

Our road vigil has become almost obsessive and I've begun to view the world in a way I never used to. Every creature out there, every small movement, every flutter of the wind, every insect catches my eye. This morning it was the postman, dressed in his fluorescent waistcoat and carrying his large tatty shoulder bag. He lingered on the opposite side of the road, delivering one of Flatface's home-packaging parcels. Emma Flatface stood there in a fluffy dressing-gown shaking her head and blabbing, while he kept edging away, trying to escape her chit-chat. He is hardly your matey Postman Pat type and he doesn't like the pleasantries. He's in his mid-thirties, fat, grumpy and a man of few words. All he wants to do is stuff in the letters and get on his way.

Several minutes later, he was at the front door. I'd been momentarily distracted by the skinny kid from next door passing by my window, then I heard the clatter of an envelope slipping through the box and thudding down on top of the huge pile of post that's already stacked up. I imagined it was from Gabriel or my mother, but I couldn't even be bothered to go through and look. I'm not opening any of my post. It's all crap anyway – all crap waiting to be thrown away – though I do occasionally hold an interesting-looking letter up to the light just to test it and try and guess what's inside. I can easily tell there are several from my mum, one from Gabriel and one from Josh's mother, plus a couple of letters from the bank, and several Reader's Digest draws telling me I'm on the way to winning thousands of pounds. But who needs money? Only people.

This evening there's a sparrow perched on the overhead wires across the road. Purrl and I sit, lined up, staring at it. For once, it's me that catches sight of it first and she's a little slow on the uptake. But there it is, the sparrow. It sits there for a while and I become hypnotised by the tiny jerky movements of its head, as it flicks from side to side. Twitchy and abrupt, it fascinates me. *Come closer, little bird, closer, closer.* Almost on cue, it flies down to perch on the fence. *Yes, little bird, that's it . . .* Now it's so close I almost imagine I could lash out with an arm and catch it, if there weren't this glass between us. The sight of those fine, pale breast feathers raises the juices at the back of my mouth. Purrl flicks a paw at the window. It's almost as if she does believe she can touch it, and, although I know we can't, I can't help reaching out myself. Purrl crouches as if ready to pounce, her slim legs straining, gathering strength. She'll be the first to it. She'll have it. *Come on, come on, if we could just get you . . . if we could just catch you between our teeth . . .* The sparrow swoops down on to the concrete in front of us, brown wings fluttering through the air, briefly, before it looks at me, straight in the face, with its dark shiny eyes. It's wise and clever. It knows it's safe, isn't even willing to play the game of make-believe, of hunter and hunted, isn't willing even to pretend that the glass is gone. It turns away and starts pecking at the ground, its pale beak darting forwards. I sniff the air and catch nothing. Though I know I could open the window and really give it a scare, it somehow seems like too much effort and I just sit there with Purrl, watching and waiting and pretending to be a fierce huntress. *Here, here . . . my bird . . .* On and on we go, till it flies away.

*

'I'm fed up,' I moan. 'I'm tired.'

Purrl stops and turns and looks at me. 'Well, look at you. You're a mess. You should clean up,' she says.

'Am not,' I say.

'Oh yes? Your hair hasn't been washed in days. And you've put on weight and lost muscle tone. You've got bags under your eyes too. You're a mess.'

'So are you,' I answer, observing the reddish-brown streak of blood that has again appeared on her chest. I take a hankie out of my pocket, lick it and lean forward to clean the streak from her. It's dark and it looks like it's been dried on for a while. *That's better* . . . I bring my head up close to her as I slowly rub it off. It takes a while. Despite my scrubbing, a faint pinkish trace still remains and I spit on the hankie again and wipe again. Once that's gone I apply myself to the area around her mouth. The dirt comes away more easily there, damp and still fresh. I stroke the length of her back with the fabric, gently trailing my fingers over her fur. This makes her croon with delight and she starts clawing her paws into the fabric of the armchair. Cleaner, cleaner, cleaner. I want to make her dazzling white, and my movements become faster and more punishing. She purrs and she mews, as if the harder it gets the better it gets, and she turns to me and starts licking my hand. It's her turn to do it for me now.

I feel the papillated surface of her tongue dragging across my skin, roughly tickling me. As she washes over my fingers, the dirt begins to lift and I feel her tongue catching on my hairs, making my nerves tingle and setting my skin shuddering. Purrl works quickly. She keeps going despite my discomfort – and once I've stopped feeling edgy and ticklish, I start to relax and enjoy. She moves up my arm, carefully attending to every square centimetre of surface. For a small tongue it's a big job.

She's scenting me. The smell of Purrl is faint, but I can still identify it. I can even feel her leaving her odour, her trail of chemicals, her layer of Purrlness on my skin. Purrl's saliva is covering me, making me hers, and surprisingly I like it. After coating both my arms, she then mounts her paws on my chest and comes up to clean my face. Her cold nose meets mine. Out comes her tongue, wiping rhythmically. I close my eyes and let go. I surrender to the moment, quash all revulsion to being licked. After all, I'm perfectly willing to be kissed by a person and this is only a form of cat kissing. Her tingly tongue traces over the surface of my eyelids, traces along my eyebrows, rises up to my brow, then descends over my cheeks. Thoroughly cleaning, thoroughly washing. I am so hypnotised by this massage that I barely hear the phone ringing and the answerphone switches through.

It's Gabriel again.

~

Hearing about Milla had a disconnected quality. It didn't feel in tune with the normal ways of the world. Sophie's

271

a bit of a second-hand friend and we wouldn't normally phone or get together, unless it was mediated by Milla, but there was something that sufficiently alarmed Sophie to give me a call. It was like some bizarre report back from the front line.

I really wasn't in the mood for hearing about Milla at the time, but Sophie sounded very hyped up when she rang, gossiping for a while about all her regular stuff, self-help therapies and gardening, before she cautiously asked if Milla was OK. I said I didn't know – couldn't really be bothered. Milla can take care of herself. I've done enough fussing over her in my time, enough shouldering her problems. If she wants to come to me, then I'll be there, but I'm not going rushing to her at the merest sign of a problem. So on and so on . . . Actually I'd tried to put all thoughts of Milla to the back of my mind. Fortunately I'd been busy – plenty of work, exams for that radiology certificate coming up. One of the nurses had even made a pass at me – though that just depressed me more, wishing it were Milla. We both know Milla, I said. She has these funny moments but she can look after herself. Then Sophie kept repeating that I had to talk to her. That I was the one she listened to. I couldn't help thinking she was making a fuss over nothing.

'Milla can be so bad about arrangements, I know,' she said. 'But she normally does turn up – even if it is half an hour late. Well, not this time.' Apparently they'd arranged to meet for a drink in the centre of town. Thinking that it was all sorted, Sophie arrived at the pub and waited for several hours – but no Milla. 'I would have just left and gone home, but something worried me. There was something about the way that Milla had been talking about Josh, and besides I had this necklace I'd bought for her in Wales – late birthday present – that I wanted to give her. So I thought I'd call by at her place.'

When Sophie arrived, Milla didn't answer the door for four or five minutes. 'But I knew she was there because there was music playing really loudly.' Sophie was just about to give up and try to force the present through the letter box, when Milla arrived, clutching Purrl in her arms. Something about her disturbed Sophie. Partly it was the way Milla was holding the cat like a shield, as if using it as a protection against the world. She looked at her really blankly, as if barely registering who her visitor was. 'You would think she was on something. I mean, you don't expect your best friend to behave like that, least of all Milla.'

Milla had just stood in the doorway, blocking the entrance and not even letting Sophie step inside. Then she said simply, 'What do you want?' To which Sophie, slightly disconcerted, had replied that she'd thought they'd had a date. Milla told her she didn't remember setting up any date, swearing that she hadn't even talked to her on the phone the previous week. Eventually, after an awkward silence, Sophie asked if she could come in and Milla, it seems, simply cocked her head to one side, as if listening to something, then made a faint noise that Sophie couldn't make out, and shut the door in her face. That was it.

'The cat's a spooky little thing,' she said. 'Do you think it's a problem?'

'No,' I said, unable to believe that some skinny cat

273

could really be the cause of anything much other than a few vet bills. Still, I could tell what Sophie was suggesting – that there was something out of the ordinary going on and that as Milla's closest friend I ought to find out more. Before long, however, she returned to her usual gossipings, making several comments about 'things that go on in kitchens'.

It made me feel depressed.

~

Gabriel left a message on the answerphone this morning. The boy's almost as persistent as Josh. 'Milla, my love,' he says. 'Just calling 'cause I was really hoping you'd get in touch with me. I sent you a letter – hope you got it. Well, anyway, just thought you might be interested in something I heard about your cat. Also, wondered if you fancied a bit of wining and dining. Give me a ring! Same number as always.' His warm voice lifts me and, as the sun glances through the curtains on to the floor and over my face, I smile. I lean back, running my fingers up and down my legs, till my percussion finds a rhythm. I'm feeling good. Even though Purrl's gone out, I'm feeling rinky, tinky, slinky. This is a corker of a wonderful day and I'm feeling fine and feline. In fact, I'm in a dancing, swinging mood.

Mmmm . . . Can't get the song out of my head.

Everybody wants to be a cat . . . And it's a smart little puss who cuts herself loose . . . Everybody's shimmying in a cat-like style ... 'Cause that's the groove that brings a smile. And I squirm on the rug and I stretch out my limbs with a foxy flick ... *A rinky tinky dinky!* Then I scratch with my back and I flip to my side and I itch some more ... Finally I'm kicking up some feline heat. I have found my beat. *Mmm* ... I can claw with my paws, I can shift to all fours and stomp round the floor ... *Cat dancing gets me swinging!* I can leap, I can loaf, I can spring, I can romp, I can whoop out loud ...

Ow! Now I try a new song ... With this drive I'm caught up in, I throw myself around the room from wall to wall and push off the shelf and the table and then down on the chair, where I lounge for a while, clicking my fingers and humming under my breath, till I get up and dance again. As I sing to myself, I twirl so fast that the room seems to swirl, and my movement's so rapid that the world seems to fall apart. A shifting blur by the shelves makes me almost imagine I see something move in the corner and I freeze, hanging for a while in a state of suspense, suspecting I've seen something there, but not certain, cocking my head to one side, before launching myself up like a runner. I wave my hand through the air – nothing there. I check from left to right, scan round the room – nothing at all. I was wrong. Disappointed, I sit down. *Mmmm* ... *Everybody wants to be a* ...

For a few seconds I rest, but I'm still feeling fired by a strange desire. So I rise to my feet and on a swaying jazz beat I shimmy to the door. This rhythm's got me revved up. And pacing the floor I arrive at the door and do a quick skip-feet. Then I turn to the left, think of Josh in his bed and find myself blasting a song out loud.

I'm comin', JoJo, baby . . . I'm treading on the floor so quietly, trying to keep silent. Though Purrl isn't around, I'm scared she might know that I'm tempted to go and lie next to him. Even the blood on the bed doesn't put me off. I want to be close and, skip, shuffle, skip, skip, shuffle, I end up by his bed. With morning light on his hair, propped up by pillows, he looks cold and pale, but still I find myself irresistibly drawn, strangely attracted. Without thinking, I run a hand over his hard, fixed face. I want him, yes, I want him – and I lean down and place my tongue on his cheek, just the tip hitting skin, breaking the spell. I can do it. I can lick. A quiver runs up through my lips to the pit of my stomach. Saliva wells up in the corners of my mouth and I swallow. I lick. I lick and I lick again. My tongue traces the line from his chin to his ear with one deft stroke, running over bone into soft, fleshy furrow. The flavour's strange and salty. Stroke. Again. I want more. Do it again, I feel, and let my tongue wash over his eyelid and down over his cheek. Wipe, slaver, wipe. I want to know more. It tastes so good just to lick, lick, lick . . . and though his face doesn't move, eyes remaining still, unreacting, unexcited, I feel I could gobble it all up. I could eat him. I pull down the sheets and lower myself down on top of his naked body. Then

276

with my tongue I attack his neck, swirling and twirling and sucking up dried blood, licking up stale sweat. Devouring it all. And once the neck's clean I go down to his chest and I lick, lick, lick. Playing with his hairs and toying with his nipples, though they feel so cold. A coil is winding up inside me. With one large stroke I trace down his sternum to the pit of his stomach, ending in his tummy button, washing and sloshing about in there, kneading away, massaging with my tongue. But it's not enough. Further, further, I want to go down, as my tongue traces lower on to his groin. It still smells all right. It seems so soft and unthreatening. I lick, lick, lick at his testicles. I lick, lick, lick at his thighs. I lick, lick, lick between his legs. And down I go, down towards the feet. Lick, lick . . . lick, lick . . . Down the legs, finishing the job. Lick, lick on the top of the foot. Suck, suck on the toes. Faster, faster. Lick, lick . . . I stop and I sit down, exhausted.

And then I freeze with fear. Was that a shadow I saw in the doorway? In my imagination I see the slender silhouette of Purrl, large against the light of the hallway. Was it her?

I want to run to the toilet and throw up.

I notice that Purrl has chewed off the end of Josh's left thumb. The thick yellow skin has been torn and ripped, leaving an encrusted red crater and I can see the thin layer of fat, peeling away underneath the leathery, line-marked surface. I almost imagine I can see tooth marks, though I can't be sure, but I do, however, know that a thumb-pad can't peel away to the bone by itself. Any amount of decay can't lead to this. Purrl must have been there. Is this revenge? Is it because I haven't been feeding her? Is it because we've run out of food again?

Lounging on the sofa by myself, I try and pinpoint where it all went wrong. I guess that must have happened when the egg split in two. Of course, it took years to really germinate . . . years for all my planning to get under way – and believe me I planned. Summers on Uncle Al's farm were full of accident ideas, brimming with opportunities. Little did Mina know how often my mind was on other things. Little did she know that all those warnings Al used to give us about where not to go, what not to do, were simply food for my imagination. She had no idea what was going on inside my head.

Al's crackling *Safety on the Farm* cinefilm planted the first seed. He'd got it from the Agricultural Training Board and screened it to us as a warning when Auntie Mo found us jumping off the back of a tractor trailer moving at speed. Our mother and father would never have forgiven them if we'd had an accident, they said, and I remember first watching the ominous film flickering on the wall of the farmhouse living room. Blood splurting tomato ketchup across the screen, amputated limbs, bodies writhing in actorly agony. I pretended to be bored but I wasn't. The flickering men squashed by

278

tractors, drowning in slurry or poisoned by weed-killer were the stuff my nightmares were made of.

After that the slurry pit was never quite the same again. I remember so many times daring Mina to walk along the wooden ledge, tempting her to fall in. I imagined her slipping, tumbling, landing in the pool of brown, overpowering liquid. In my mind I saw her arms thrashing about. I saw her sink and I saw the tiny bubbles of the last gasps of her life rise to the surface. Of course, in the end it wasn't her who walked that plank, but me. Just as it always was.

'You've been dancing,' says Purrl.

'What's wrong with that?' I ask.

'I think you know what's wrong . . .'

A blank silence floats in the air and I wonder if she really knows. I turn on the offensive. 'Where do you go to during the day?'

'You're changing the subject,' she says.

'But who do you see?'

'None of your business – betrayer,' her voice hisses angrily across the room. 'You've no right to know.'

'Fine . . . I see. I'm not allowed to go through and see Josh. I've got to devote all my life to you. But you're allowed to go off and do whatever you like. I hardly think that's fair.' I feel an edge of hysteria rising in my throat. I try and clamp down on it, keep calm. *Don't row, Millsie. Don't start it*, I repeat over to myself. I know it will only all go sour.

And it does. Purrl turns on her tail. Within a couple of seconds, she has whisked out of the house.

As I sit around in this empty shell of a home, watching the hours tick by, I long to be able to turn the clock back. It's been two days now since I betrayed Purrl and the silent treatment she's punishing me with is driving me mad.

So, will I be forgiven or not? Hard to say . . . I mean, she's not left me yet, which is one good sign. Though I have to admit there's been no let up in my Coventry. I get that look of point-blank refusal every time I even try to touch her. She goes out a lot too and stays away longer each time, making me wonder each time if this time she's gone away for good.

Come on, Purrl, honey, I sigh, as I see her wandering into the room. *Let me off the hook . . .* I can't stand these long silences and without real contact with her, there's nothing in the world for me, apart from the odd answerphone message from Josh's work, who are wondering where the hell he is and on the verge of sacking him, or his mum, asking when he's going to take Zara off her hands again, or my mum, or Gabriel.

I figure if I crawl Purrl will forgive me. I've already promised her I won't go through and sit with Josh. I don't even want to. He looks so ghastly and bluey-yellowish and pallid and decaying, and the idea of having touched him makes my flesh crawl. Besides, the flies are starting to take over the room and it could be bad for my health. And then there's the stench, the foul stink that's beginning to pervade the entire house. At first I thought it was Josh – that he'd simply reached that stage of decay where it all starts to go very rotten. I shut the door on him, tried to seal it off, but no, this odour isn't him. It's got a sharp ammoniacal edge that sets my nose tingling. It's more nauseating than Josh's smell. When I go into his room I catch the rich, warm whiff of meat left out in the sun too long, and, though it's almost overpowering, I strangely enjoy it. I'm almost attracted to its menstruality. Soon, it may change to a rotting rat fetidness, but for now I can breathe it in, gagging but swooning.

This other smell is different. I sniff the air and almost imagine I catch the stench of rotting fish, particularly strong here in the kitchen, making me retch as I run a glass of water. Purrl, whose olfactory powers are more acute than mine, lingers by the doorway, watching from a distance. She struts disdainfully past the door, refusing to enter, and not just because I, scum of the earth, am in here. No, she sniffs the air and she raises her nose in an expression that clearly shows disgust. I sniff again. *Fish market on a bad day. Ick . . .* The smell is heady and repellent and makes me feel slightly nauseous, and if I use my nose like a radar somehow I can tell that it's coming from the region of the cooker.

In an instant it all clicks into place and I realise what an idiot I've been. I see the evidence. There's a supermarket carrier bag underneath the chair between the fridge and the cooker, from our shopping trip ... I'd been tired afterwards ... I wandered through to the kitchen and put some of the shopping away ... but not all, as I was distracted. Maybe it was a call on the answerphone or maybe it was the TV, but I never went back. I never packed away the rest of the fish. *What an idiot!* But how come I never noticed beforehand? Though the smell had got stronger and stronger, in all this time I never guessed. It shows how little cleaning I'd done recently – since the body arrived.

I bend down, pick up the carrier bag and cautiously peer inside. The stink overwhelms me and I pull backwards abruptly, almost straining my neck. Four festering trout. They are the reason we have no food. They are the reason we're now on rations, with only a tiny sliver of fish a day. They're why it suddenly seems I'm going to have to go on yet another shopping trip – and all too soon. If only I hadn't been so lazy.

Of course I'm not going to go out there. However hungry we might be, I can't go outside. Still Purrl, despite her haughtiness, doesn't want me to leave without her. She squeals and paces across the hall if I head for the door. 'Don't do it, Milla. Don't go outside!' It's the only time she reacts to me. But she needn't worry – actually I'm terrified of going out there, of dealing with all those people. At the thought of entering a huge supermarket, I feel overwhelmed by a wave of acute shyness. Even the idea of meeting one of the neighbours in the street

282

makes me clam up inside. And anyway, there's no point eating any more. I can barely stand the thought of it. I want to be skinny like Purrl, long in the leg and slim in the neck, with needle-thin bones and sculpted muscles. Svelte and sophisticated.

It's such a hot day and stuffy throughout the whole flat, particularly in Josh's room, I feel I have to go and sit out in the garden. I lie there on the grass, soaking up the sun, staring at the pale blue sky.

'E-mer-gen-cy.' A slow, clear voice drifts across the fence.

Someone's talking in the garden to the right where the two teachers live, and I strain my ears to make out what's being said. It's that skinny teenager who's been staying with them for the last few weeks. I've watched the kid a number of times and felt there was something odd about him, or is it her? I can't tell whether he/she is a boy or a girl, because he/she's so thin.

'I wont to speak to the poleese,' he/she says clearly, and it catches me by surprise, sending a twinge of fear puncturing through my lungs. I wonder if he/she knows, has seen me.

I freeze on the spot, straining further, and then I crawl towards the fence, where I can hear better. Putting my eye up to a small hole in one of the wood slats, I strive to see past some obstructing leaves. There's my teenager, sitting on a folding chair, body as thin and gangly as I remembered. *Funny* . . . Purrl, who is already obsessed with watching her, has always said she is a girl and maybe she's right. She's definitely in her early teens and I suspect it's precisely her androgyny that excites me. She wears a short, white T-shirt that hangs loosely over her flat chest, with long, lanky legs jutting out from loose cotton shorts. She's actually incredibly beautiful and I find myself staring at her rich red lips and fine bone structure. With her head clamped in earphones, she's listening to a Walkman and her short dark hair flops over her face. Her skin is lightly tanned but naturally pale and she's a little freckled.

'I wa-ant to riport a crime.' She enunciates every syllable carefully, measuring it out and frowning thoughtfully. *She must know! Surely she does . . .* The more she says, the more weird it seems. She reaches down to a can of beer at her feet, takes a sip, slooshes it around in her mouth and then swallows.

'I nid to see a doctor.' Her expression is pained, like she's acting out every sentence, and I can't quite work out what she's up to. It's as if she's talking to herself but not quite. 'I nid an ambalance.' There's something in the lines of concentration on her face and I suddenly realise what she's doing. It's simple. She's learning English. Her voice is harsh and Slavic and I imagine she must come from some Eastern European country. There's a drop of chocolate sauce or ice cream on her T-shirt. 'I hev a toothache.' Her lips make such exaggerated, animalistic forms that it's almost quite beautiful. She sighs, seeming fed up, takes her headphones off and leans forward again for another sip of beer.

It's now very quiet and I sit as still as possible, worried that she can hear, that she might know I'm watching her, as she leans forward and lights a cigarette. She breathes deeply and I pull back, not wanting to watch any longer.

I think we are safe.

I could swear I saw old Mingerston's face at the kitchen window this morning. Her hand shaded her features, but her big squinty eyes were plain to see, and her interfering conk was pressed up hard against the glass. For only a split second, I caught sight of her. It caught me unawares as I was wandering down the hallway and I halted and turned back. When I stopped to look again she was gone, but there was a faint banging, like someone trying to climb over the fence, and though it sounds unreasonable that an old lady would bother, it remains the only explanation. It's a good job I keep the curtains closed in Josh's room or Christ knows what would have happened. Then there would have been trouble. I can't help thinking she may have already called the police. I know she's been watching me. I can feel it. She has to be suspicious – what else would make her climb a fence like that? I wouldn't have thought the old biddy could have managed it. But she's a determined old cow.

I open the kitchen cupboard and stare at the single tin of baked beans lurking in the left back corner that I guess I neglected to throw away in my clear-out. The once squeaking voice of hunger in my stomach has now turned into a raging scream. I must have food. I must have fish. I must fill my body. I feel weak with lack of nourishment and so dizzy I have to lean on the bench-top, counting for several seconds and holding my focus on the lines of the tiles, until I regain some strength. There's nothing for it. The tin of beans feels heavy in my hand and I weigh it up there for a few seconds. I hunt through the drawer for a tin opener, all the while trying to deafen myself to the riot in my abdomen. Having found one, I lock it on to the tin and wind it round, observing the sharp knife-like edge I'm forming. Small bubbles of orange liquid appear at the edges and I catch that familiar, unpalatable whiff of tomatoes. I prise the lid off and examine the small pale sauce-covered nodules inside. Can I eat this? I reach for a spoon and take a scoopful, cold from the tin. It slides into my mouth, all slimy and sweet and salty, and I wrinkle up my nose, remembering that I had never really liked baked beans. They're gooey and unpleasant and the pulses themselves feel like tiny eggs. I can barely take having the things there, never mind swallowing them. I dive over to the sink and spit them out.

In a haze of faintness I stumble through to the living room and fall asleep.

Purrl wakes me up with a soft kiss on the lips. She's warm and comforting, her body sprawled languidly alongside mine. I put my arm around her and draw her in closer. All's forgotten, I sense. This is kiss and make up, and I smile as the buzzing vibration of her purr transmits through me. *Mmm* . . . I raise my hand and stroke her head, letting my fingers drift through her silky fur. Forgiveness is sweet.

'Friends,' she says, digging an affectionate claw into my arm. 'Let's put that all behind us.' Then she purrs like a little kitten. Her body slides across my stomach, tickling and massaging me.

'I'm forgiven?'

'Mmm . . . Just don't do it again. It hurts me when you go off with other people – even dead ones,' she pleads.

'But you know I adore you, Purrl. I don't see why . . .'

Purrl halts me with a paw on the lips. 'Don't you want there to be only you and me in all the world?'

Of course . . . of course I do, I respond. But her question suddenly flicks a switch, triggers some kind of well-trodden synaptic route in my brain, and before I've even said the words, I recoil. 'Don't give me any of that nonsense,' I snap, as I find myself hitting up hard against a memory.

For a second I'm back there with Nathan at school.

Nathan . . . freckle-faced, snub-nosed Nathan . . . He was different from all the other kids: a couple of years older than the rest of us and brought up by travelling types not interested in the three Rs, but he was clever in his own way, and very wise. He'd seen a lot and he had this weird sense of humour nobody else could put a finger on, but that would lead him to suddenly bursting into paroxysms of giggles for seemingly no reason.

I liked Nathan because he was one of the few kids who singled me out, chose me as the person to be interested in, and not my sister. I remember that day as clearly as if it were now . . . We were in the playground at break-time, messing around as usual, loads of us shouting and yelling and running across the slate-grey yard. Mina was in her element, wrapped up in organising a skipping game, and I guess she probably thought I was still stood behind her, like I always was. Rhymes rattled off, puncturing the air. The skipping rope sliced through the wind. Girls skipped and boys played football, but Nathan did neither. Across the frenetic crowd, I saw him standing over by the mobiles, his hand waving impatiently through the air.

Absent-mindedly, and without consulting Mina, I wandered away from the queue. The chant pounded abstractly in my head. 'I'm a little bumper car number 58. I drive round the co-orner!' Nathan's smile had won me over. As I approached, I noticed he was clutching a raggedy white packet, his cheeks puffing and hollowing as he sucked on something. 'Want a cola bottle?'

I nodded cautiously, then took one. Already I could tell he'd bought them specially because I liked them. Nathan noticed these things. He smiled nervously. 'I don't like playing their games.'

'Me neither.' I was aware of the blur of a skipping rope whirring away in the background.

'I know better games. Do you want to play?'

'Mina too?' I asked.

'No, just us . . .'

'Maybe,' I replied, slightly unsure.

'You can have the rest of the packet.' He was holding out the sweets towards me, as a temptation. Standing closely, he fidgeted nervously.

'Well, OK . . .' I smiled nervously. 'Yeah . . . Yeah . . . I'll play.' The thought of doing something without Mina gave me an illicit thrill. It felt like a rebellion, particularly as I knew she didn't like Nathan.

'These are the rules . . .' he began. But I never got to find them out.

Mina's voice came bolting across the yard. She must have got to the end of the game and realised that I was not there. 'What's going on here?' she asked. 'Are you two having your own game of kissy-catchy. Nathan handing out his sweeties? Don't you want to share those with all of us, Nathan?' She grabbed hold of the packet and threw the sweets into the air. Tiny little sugar-covered bottles scattered over the ground and Nathan flushed bright red but said nothing, just shrugged his shoulders and looked at me as if to say, 'It's up to you!'

I said nothing. I did nothing, stood glued to the ground like a dummy. I knew what Mina wanted me to do. I knew my duty and I turned away from Nathan, just like I always did whenever Mina asked.

Ever nonchalant, Nathan shrugged his shoulders again and walked away. He didn't care. It had probably always been a game to him anyway. He almost seemed to be laughing to himself. Mina wasn't laughing, though. She took me aside later and pleaded with me. I don't remember much of what she said (it was all the usual stuff) but I do remember one thing. *'Don't you want there to be only you and me in all the world?'* That was it.

'Don't say that,' I say to Purrl.

'Say what?' she asks, her face looming above me. 'All I'm thinking is that Josh shouldn't come between us.'

I sigh. I do, of course, adore Purrl. I crave her more than I ever craved Mina. 'That's fine,' I say, 'but all this you and me business, I don't like that.'

'Why not?'

I take a while to answer. 'I don't know, I just don't.'

Purrl stares at me for a few moments, looks away, then grumpily concedes, 'OK.'

'I do love you, though.'

'No more of this Josh stuff, then – if, as you say you do, you love me,' she whispers as her little nose nudges up by my ear. 'We have to get rid of him. Get rid of him or I'm going to go.'

'I can't,' I say. 'He stinks and I can't bear to go near him. It was different the other day, but now every time I touch him it's like a piece of his skin comes off or something. Can't we just wall him up or . . . I dunno . . . I dunno. I don't want to touch him.'

Purrl sits there silently, not purring, not moving for a few minutes, her face staring down at mine as she thinks things over, then she speaks again. 'OK. Leave him there. Leave him, if you want, but let's lock that door for good. Let's put him behind us.'

She stands up, placing her paws on my sternum, stretching her back and yawning. 'Time to get up,' and she jumps down on to the floor.

I stretch out my arms and heave myself up. Bliss – I feel it coursing through my body. *Purrl has forgiven me.* It runs through my mind, again and again, *Purrl has forgiven me.* I watch her as she wanders across the carpet seductively, with her tail held high. She crouches down and rolls on the carpet as if she's trying to rid herself of a restless itch. I crouch down on the floor and follow her. My claws dig into the carpet. My fur bristles in the air. I feel like a cat. I move like a cat. My limbs are slender and silky-haired, whiskers hover about my mouth. I can mew, I can squeal and I can let out one great big caterwaul. *Weeeeeeouuuuuuuwwieeeeeeeeee* . . . Purrl nods with approval, and I try it again. *Weeeeouuuwwwwweeee.* It feels better than ever before, coming naturally from my throat, effortlessly emerging, not straining but almost by reflex crying out from my brain. It's so easy.

291

Am I a cat or am I human? Like wave-particle duality, maybe I'm both at the same time, only solidifying under observation. Maybe the trick is to stop thinking, stop examining and let yourself run.

'Come on,' Purrl whispers. 'Let's check out the territory.'

The hunt is on. I feel my head lift, the heaviness falling away. My body seems to take on its own will. The fight between limbs eases and my senses come alive. I'm hearing, smelling, feeling more than I ever have before. The environment sets my fur bristling. I am one with it. It's also part of me. I have paws, I have whiskers, I have a tail. This is what it's like.

Down on all fours. I'm low and the ceiling is high. Paws padding on short pile, I skim the level of the skirting boards. There's dust on them – she's not cleaned them yet. Right now, we round the corner into the hallway – me first, followed by her. It's long, stretching a good five metres, so you can get a good speed up here. Hind legs under, I make a dart for the end. We're chasing shadows, but we don't mind. This is our game. Turn now, crouch again and then leap. The corridor is dark because she never leaves the lights on, but I can see it all – the grime on the doormat, the hairs clinging to the carpet, the dirt. As yet I can't imagine the smells, because I haven't got that far yet, my senses can never be that fine. Dart again, past the bookshelves, past the boxes, past the coat-stand ... the full length back to the kitchen. And now we check out the kitchen. Paw by paw, I slowly strut along the edge of the cabinets towards the sink. I hear the pitter-patter of a dripping tap. Gathering strength for the spring, I push off hind paws and leap into the air. I glide gently and land on the aluminium surface. It's cold on the paw-pads and slippy, but I balance around the edge, not wanting to actually stand on the bottom, and straddling the basin I bend forward to catch the drops. Unsatisfied, I push at the tap with a paw, as she sticks her head under the steady stream. It's cold and wet as we lap away. *Lap, suck, gulp . . .* We stand there for several minutes. *Lap, suck, gulp . . .*

Enough of that then! We stare out of the window for a few seconds, surveying the back garden. What's that moving between the rose bush and the little tree? Too small – probably a bee. My eyes follow the movement, nose tracing lines against the glass. The flutter of a leaf grabs our attention – but not for long. The territory has still to be checked and, our thirst quenched, we jump down from the sinktop, landing gently on all fours, tail streaming behind us, muscles contracting to take the impact.

Putta . . . putta . . . putta . . . putta . . . across the floor. This is our domain. We stop for a second next to the cooker. It still stinks of rotten fish, from that supermarket bag left under the chair for weeks. It's foul. Was that a flicker of something in the darkness under there? Crouch for a second and watch, but maybe it was nothing. Cock a head to one side to listen out for the sound of a merest rustle – maybe a mouse. But there's nothing. Frustrated, I stick a paw under, reaching with long thin white limb and flailing. I hit something slimy, just a few tiny slivers of fish, which I gobble up hungrily. I stand up and pace around the cooker. It's white and shiny and cold. My fur brushes up against the surface and I push with my flanks, reflexing into action, spreading our scent. White hair pushes against white surface. We mark out the territory, uttering short mewing noises.

Then, with the kitchen claimed, we move on, skipping through the hallway again, and turning left this time to enter the bathroom. The smell is potent here and we sniff out a patch in the right-hand corner beside the loo that stinks of Tibbsy. That was his spot, the place that he always sprayed, his point of belonging. The aroma is strong and overpowering, but this is our house now. We brush up against the bath. This is our bath. Tibbsy is dead. His smell may linger, but his presence is gone.

And out we go again, rounding the corner to enter the bedroom, but stop dead. The door's shut and anyway there's no way we're going in there. Purrl mews, disapproving, and reminds me that we're going to have to wall up that entrance. Disillusioned, we pad down the hallway and lollop round to the living room.

The carpet is a thick, heavy pile in here. Our paws dig in and we want to scratch, to pad away like a kitten, exercising our fingers. The corner of the armchair is the favourite place and I shuffle up to it, preparing paws to push out claws. On the soft

velvety surface, I dig. Then release, then I dig
again. I keep doing it until I'm bored and then we
track across the floor, taking a quick roll over the
rug. We stop for a second – listening, thinking,
sniffing the air – then move on. We're ready to take
our place, our little niche, by the window, looking
out. We watch for a while and then Purrl and I
dash and prance about till it gets dark and we fall
asleep.

Then I wake up again.

The nights are the strangest time now. They drive
me mad. Because I sleep at all sorts of hours, during
the afternoon, morning or night, whenever I feel
like it, I often find myself waking up at two or three
in the morning. The lights are off and though Purrl
is sitting near I am suddenly gripped by a wild
panic. A thought seizes my mind. I imagine I see
someone there at the window, imagine I hear
fingers running over the pane, a knocking at the
door, footsteps outside. It's like Josh is out there. It
makes me tremble. I go to the door and check it's
locked. It's always the same. It's just as it has been
for a while now. I go there. I check the bottom lock.
I check the top one. They are both turned, both
locked. And then I go back into the living room, but
there's something nagging me, something bothering me, and the fear rises inside me again. What
if I inadvertently unlocked the door when I was
checking it? For a few seconds I quash the feeling,
but it won't go away. I have to go back and check it

again. Both keys turned, both locks locked. I go back to the living room and the whole cycle begins again. Have I or haven't I? Was it or wasn't it? What if some madman tries to get in? What if it's Josh back from the dead? What if he's seen me in my night-gown through the net curtains? And what was that rippling sound of fingers against glass, or that crunching of gravel by the window? I check it one more time, only this time I haul my filing cabinet in front of the door. It's hard work and it almost strains my back, but you've got to be sure, haven't you?

Even after that, I can barely sleep. I imagine the madman smashing through the window. I think I see faces against the pane. I jump at every noise and I end in waking Purrl up. But it makes no difference. It simply leaves us both sitting there in fear, until we eventually fall asleep once more.

In the morning I'm still weak, but I think I've got past my real hunger. I'm working under Purrl's orders now. She's in charge and I've got to wall up the bedroom or else. Is this because she wants to keep me out or him in? It's a bit of a problem, as bricking it up is really out of the question. I'd have to go out and get all the bricks and mortar and stuff. Instead, I imagine just a couple of pieces of wood nailing the door in place will do, but there's no wood lying around in the house and I have to go out and ease a couple of pieces off the fence outside. I scrabble around in the cupboard under the sink, looking for a hammer and some nails. There's a couple of big ones there, and I guess they'll do, though I'm no Mrs DIY (Josh used to do all those things) and I have a feeling it's not going to be quite as easy as it looks.

Before I start, though, I decide I should go and take one last glance at Josh – a farewell to a lost love. I check around to see if Purrl's up and about. I call out her name, but she doesn't come. It's safe. Unless she's playing with me.

And then I slowly press down on the door handle, edging it open just a fraction. *Ugh!* The smell stuns me immediately. It catches me in the back of the throat and makes me want to gag, and I almost involuntarily pull the door shut again. But there's no escape. The stench lingers in the hallway and I run to the kitchen and get a dry dishcloth, which I put over my nose. Then I try again. My face muffled by the rag, I push the door open again – this time a little further. I can still smell it, but I can just about deal with it. A large fly hovers above my head as I stumble in. And there he is . . . For the final time, my Josh. I can see that parts of his flesh are starting to go black and a couple of flies buzz around the holes in his neck where I stabbed him first. A few more emerge from his mouth and, as I get close, I begin to retch, because, crawling out of there, emerging from his wounds and his mouth, are small white maggots. This is not my Josh. This isn't him any more. This mass of rotting flesh is a long way off what I remember. I totter backwards, almost tripping over a pile of books that I'd left on the floor, stumbling and overwhelmed by the odour, the potent smell of decay.

I stagger out of the door, letting it slam shut behind me. I feel weak and nauseous. I begin to wish I hadn't gone in for that last glimpse of him. Now the image of Josh that will linger with me is a foul, festering mass of something that is not a person, that has no connection with the Josh of months ago. I am unable to remember his face. What did he look like? I struggle to form an image of him in my mind, but come up only with the blurry ghost of a photograph I took of him. That was not the real Josh. Years of my life and he's forgotten – obliterated by a single moment, a single gruesome sight.

In a manic frenzy, I grab the planks of wood, the hammer, the nails, and begin to board the door up. I have to block it out. The corpse has to be boarded up for ever. Bam! I wallop the hammer up against the nail, almost thudding it into my own finger as I throw it. Bam! Again, and this time the point goes through the soft, thin wood of the fence. Then again, I hurl the hammer, as the nailpoint seems to enter the plaster. *Ouch!* I actually hit myself this time and my finger starts to bleed. *There has to be an easier way to do this . . .* I mutter under my breath. But I keep on going. Bam and again bam! I attack the next corner. *If only I had Josh here to do this.* And I keep on thumping away, whacking the nails in with my hammer, until all the wood is pinned.

I stand back and it looks like a two-year-old's been messing about with their dad's toolkit. A botch job. A mess. Hardly fitting for your true love. It all seems so desperately undignified.

~

I'm not sure how completely I'm treating this as a joke. If it is a joke, then it's in fairly poor taste – but then, if I become too serious about it, I have to question a lot of my beliefs about the world, which I am loath to do. I'll also look pretty dumb in front of Milla. Occasionally, just very occasionally, you do something that you think might expose you as being incredibly stupid. You know it all the while you're doing it, and yet you are still compelled to do it. Some little voice drives you on. Sending this stuff to Milla is a little like that. I suspect I might end up looking like some kind of hysterical New Ager, believing in ghosts and spirits and supernatural phenomena, everything we'd both always scoffed at. But, what the hell, I'll do it anyway. And what if . . . Yes, what if . . . that's always the question.

Something odd is happening, whatever way you look at it, even if it is just that Milla has entered some reclusive phase. Something very odd . . . I decide I'll end the letter with some puncturing funny line so she realises it's all tongue in cheek . . . Of course, it was Ida who started the whole thing off. She called in at the surgery on one of her weekly visits, some stray she was trying to fix up on the cheap. She'd been concerned about Milla. More than that, she was worried about the cat. About Purrl. She'd been hearing certain stories from other people with cats in Milla's neighbourhood and she'd remembered a newspaper story she'd come across in her files. (Ida kept a dusty cardboard box full of random cuttings on cats from newspapers.)

'Darlin', I know you're going to think I'm a mad old biddy, but it makes me nervous,' she said to me and handed over a small, yellowed piece of paper. 'It makes me very nervous. There's not much an old lady like me can do, but I know you'll look after Milla. You two . . . you're such a lovely couple.'

Naturally, I read it.

Last Wednesday afternoon Mrs Peggy Christmas was found dead in her living room, aged 91. She is believed to have been lying there for several weeks.

Mrs Christmas, known to have been a great cat lover, died surrounded by a litter of her pet albino cats. Only two of the seven trapped kittens survived.

Neighbours Bill and Iris Banks discovered the body. 'We thought we smelt something and called the police,' said Mrs Banks. 'We couldn't believe what we saw. The two cats appeared to have been gnawing at Peggy. It's a terrible thing to have happened.'

To say that it was a spooky or creepy story is to play down its sheer horribleness. Peggy Christmas is a real person, after all. I have to admit I laughed at the time because I didn't know what else to do, and this was Milla's cat that Ida was connecting it with and that was absurd, because I like to think I know how things work. But Ida was deadly serious. She persuaded me. I'm sending it, though I'm not really sure why. Maybe it's

simply because I feel I owe it to Ida. Reading the cutting
again, I can't believe I'm taking it seriously. I imagine
Milla's throaty laugh, her shaking her head at my idiocy.
But the compulsion is there and I seal it, post it, commit.

'I was only doing what's best for you,' says Purrl.

'What's best for you more like.' *Do we have to go*
through this again?

'For us both.'

'But I'm the one who loses the boyfriend and gets
thrown in the slammer.'

'Yes.' She flicks her tail from side to side smugly.
'I suppose so.'

'You're an accomplice,' I remind her.

'I'm not. I'm just a cat. Cats don't get put on trial,
do they? It's your problem. After all, you're the one
who killed him.'

'Am not.'

'Yes, you are. If you didn't, who did?'

'If it wasn't for you, I would never have done it.
I'm not the one who wanted him dead. You're the
one who wanted that.'

'And quite rightly too.'

'So you admit it?'

'Yes. He didn't deserve you.'

'He was a wonderful man and I loved him.
Women love men . . .' I stop sharply, already aware
of the dark resentment brewing in the air. Already
aware of what I've implied, that cat souls can't be as
compatible as boy souls and girl souls. I've said it.
It's been uttered.

301

'Oh, did you now? I see . . . Well, you should have thought before you stuck that fork right through his neck, shouldn't you?' She stalks off, her head raised high in the air.

'I was only defending myself,' I call after her.

'So you claim. But what did he do? All he did was pull you through to the back garden. It's not like he was going to hurt you. I think you can hardly claim self-defence.'

Are you a particular person only because other people recognise you as that? For instance, what if I wasn't really Milla at all and I'd always been Mina? As I lie here staring at the carpet I start to wonder. Some people look the same and are very different, we know that much. But there are also people, things, animals, that are the same but look very different. Perhaps that's how it is with me and Purrl. Maybe we're the same – we only look different.

Purrl is out. I don't know where she's gone. I take up my morning watch without her, and within several minutes wish I hadn't because I see *her* again: Mingy Mingerston. It makes me feel sick. As soon as her small, hunched silhouette enters my view, my heart skips a beat and I shrink back from the window. *Does she know? Is she keeping an eye on us?* There she goes, hauling her stupid shopping trolley along the street, probably going to fetch her pension. Even from this far back in the room I can see her clamped-set hair and neatly buttoned summer coat. Even from here I can tell that she's watching my window out of the corner of her eye. Just outside our house, she pauses for a moment and frowns. Her hand rises to her mouth and she looks as if she's about to turn back again, then she searches in her bag, but I know it's a ploy. She's faking a lost key or lost cheque or something in order to get a good look in. Her body turns towards me and she looks up from her bag, glancing over in my direction. I freeze, my eyes still locked on her. Has she seen me? *She knows. She suspects something.* Her gaze lingers on me and I'm suddenly aware of the bizarre, lascivious hunger in my eyes. I'm suddenly aware that it gives me away, that she can see me. I try to smile, but feel a grimace forming. Mingerston closes her bag, frowns a 'What do you think you're looking at, you scum?' sort of frown and walks on. Her eyes say she knows. They accuse me of murder.

I shrink away, embarrassed and scared. Staggering back on to the sofa, I feel like hiding. The humiliation. *Mingerston is going to have to die.* The awfulness of people, of the world out there. Lying there, I run that moment over in my mind again and again. I see those eyes glaring at me, I see the frown. It makes me sick with shame. *Shame on you, Milla! What did you think you were doing? Why weren't you more careful?* I toss and turn on the cushions. I stare at the ceiling. I stare at the velvet flock wallpaper. I stare at the tiny crack that seems to be gradually creeping from the light to the doorway, and I think that I am vile, I am scum, I am slime, I am not worth

303

the body I live in. I disgust even myself. *Yes, Mingerston will have to die.*

The phone rings.

I hear Gabriel's faint voice crackle through. 'Hello, Milla. Thought you might have called me by now, but if you don't want to, you don't want to. I just wondered if you had got that letter I sent you, kind of relating to Purrl. I thought it might tickle your fancy. Give me a ring!'

He hangs up.

That Gabriel . . . always interfering, always sticking his nose into everybody else's business, always concocting stupid stories. If Purrl finds out about this message she won't be happy.

Gabriel's envelope sits on my lap for half an hour before I open it, carefully and guiltily folding out the contents. Inside is a letter and a small, yellowed clipping, taken from a local newspaper. It's faded and dusty and I weigh it up in my fingers, trying to resist reading it, but I can't help myself.

As the words penetrate, I begin to feel slightly sick. Each line runs numbly past my eyes, only just penetrating after I've read it several times. I can't believe it. My Purrl? She's much finer than that. And yet . . .

Next to the story is a picture of two cats, a dark, blotchy print taken with a cheap flash camera. It's like criminal evidence – a mug shot. Two small white kittens stare out, eyes gleaming in the spotlight, caught as they must have been found in the Christmas flat. They look trapped and scared, and it's difficult to tell, but if I squint and try to allow the picture to form from the dots, I almost imagine I see the faintest blood-like traces around their mouths. Beneath the photo is the caption 'Petrified: two kitten survivors are being homed by the RSPCA.'

It could be Purrl. It could easily be Purrl, just a little younger and even skinnier, but then, it could easily be any number of other cats. I stare at the print for ages, hoping that she won't walk in on me. After a while I find I can't make anything out. Maybe it doesn't look so much like her. *It couldn't be Purrl. No, it couldn't.* I see her face coated in blood, hovering before my eyes. I imagine her licking, digging her teeth into the old woman. I see her jaws wrapped around Josh's thumb. I see her tearing at human skin.

All sorts of thoughts ravage my mind and, feeling weak and hungry again, I lie down and drift.

Has the electricity gone? I wake up and there's no light. I reach for the light switch – nothing. The fucking electricity has been cut off. I stumble through the darkened hallway towards the toilet. I can't see the walls. I can't see the floor. I can't see the ceiling. Are they far away or up close? It's like I'm entering one dark, absorbing womb. I'm stretching out in nothingness. The whole flat seems to be giving way in the night. Where's the wall? I fumble

305

and find a surface. The bathroom seems such a long way. And I have to make it across the space from one wall to another. Holding this surface, I wave my hand around in search of another. Ouch! I bang up against it. There's the door. There's the handle. Now I can see a little, from the light outside the window. I find the toilet and sit down. Then let it all go in one great big warm flow.

When it's over I stumble up again. I strain to see through the heavy darkness, pushing outwards with my eyes. I try and strip away the night with all my mental force. And then suddenly it happens – the flat opens up. My eyes are shot with a pale dusky light and the space enlarges around me, growing bigger and bigger and bluer and bluer. I sink lower into the ground. There is light and there is space – a huge pale misty light that seems almost heavenly to me.

Through the dusky haze of sleep, I feel a faint tickling at my feet. There's a strange scratching at my big toe, which at first I half dream is a spider, but then it becomes a gnawing and the spider's big jaws seem to clench the fleshy part of my toe, digging deep into it. I try to shake it off, but it keeps hold. This is no longer a tickle. It's an intense pain and I feel myself dragged quickly into wakefulness. I lie there, not daring to move. I am seized by the thought that what I am feeling is not a spider, it is Purrl. My throat contracts and saliva collects at the back of my mouth. Even without opening my eyes,

I feel I can see her there, nibbling away. Feeding from me. I want to scream, but can't. I'm so weak and tired, I can barely move.

'Purrl,' I whisper. In the half-silence, I think I can just make out a faint licking noise, the sound of tongue against flesh. I see teeth digging into skin. 'Purrl,' I murmur again.

And the gnawing stops.

For a few long seconds, or maybe even minutes, nothing happens. I am still weighed down by this sense of weakness. The hunger has now gone. I just want her to be there, to calm my fears.

I open my eyes and she is standing above me, her nose practically pressed up against mine. Her mouth is maybe slightly flecked with red. I don't know. I can't tell.

'Don't you worry,' she says. 'I know you're tired, but come with me. We'll go hunting for mice. Just jump up!'

I spring up on to my four feet, feel the carpet against my pads, the air-cushioning hair all around me, whiskers sensing the tiniest vibration. A voice at the back of my head keeps saying get a grip, but another says go. It's Purrl, saying to go with the feeling.

'Let's go!' I call. 'Let's hit the tiles.'

I've got to get out. I've got to get away from her. Purrl . . . she's crazy. Her power is too irresistible. I can't hold back from her. And yes, Gabriel is right . . . there's something strange, something horrible in her. I'm infected, and as I lie here, my skin itching and crawling all over, stranded and paralysed, I begin to suspect the Christmas story is true. *Rescue me, Gabriel . . . Come and rescue me . . . Someone.*

Purrl?

You're back again . . .

Being human again, lying all stretched out, all cumbersome and fleshy, is no fun. It makes me feel like a slug. It confuses my make-up, makes me unsure of which should rule, this day-dream imagination or this irritative body. I've always wanted to be one or the other: a purely physical being, or dispense with the body and be left to think and dream, without worrying about varicose veins, choked arteries and cellulite. Being a cat rids me of those problems. I want to be like Purrl – even though she sends a chill through me.

Like now, as she paces her way towards me, making my heart freeze and causing me to fret. Which little bit does she want now?

'I've been thinking,' says Purrl, angling her face with feigned wisdom. 'We're probably going to have to get rid of that Gabriel.'

'Get rid of Gabriel?' I ask in disbelief. 'Why?'

'To protect me . . . And you do want to protect me, don't you, Milla?'

'But get rid of Gabriel . . . isn't that going a bit too far? Isn't one dead body enough?'

'You do love me, don't you, Milla?' she asks.

'Of course I do, but . . .'

'I'm not sure you do. I'm not sure you know what love means.'

'I do. Yes, I do.'

'If you really loved me, you would stop at nothing. That's what real love is – taking things to their limits. Not Josh's soppy domesticity. Real love is more . . .' And Purrl's pale eyes gaze straight at mine. They demand that I listen. 'Love is the total obliteration of yourself in your beloved. It's making big statements, big sacrifices. Love thrives on those. Without it, it dies. It is the ever increasing focus of all your energies on one being. Every day expects a little more from you. And if you can't face that, Milla, maybe we should stop here. Maybe I should find someone else.'

'I'm up to it, Purrl, but Gabriel . . . I mean he's such a sweet, innocent kind of person.'

'Milla . . .' She casts me a glare that says her will is final. It must be done.

'But how?'

'Well,' she says, 'I thought we could have some fun. When I'm hunting a mouse, I always tempt them and invite them, play with them first. Then I launch my attack. Why don't you invite Gabriel round for tea?'

I feel like I'm being suffocated. The room is so hot that I can barely breathe, each intake of air seeming to drown me. Even though I take off my nightdress and kick back the covers and lie there, arms wide open to gain as much free surface area as possible,

309

I cannot cool off. Everything my skin contacts feels warm. The sheets, the sofa, even the air – too stifling. I am sticky with sweat. The back of my neck is clammy. I flip from side to side, trying to find fresh, colder positions to sprawl in, but only begin to feel more flustered. In the bluish moonlight, I suspect I can see faint pale globules on my white arms, a smooth sheen running over my thighs. My skin is so white against the dark sheets. But worst of all is this feeling that there is no air, only heat. Nothing to breathe, I stumble round, opening all the doors, but find it makes no difference and I have to open the window to let this pressure out.

~

Standing here, outside the flat, I can't help finding this situation absurd. What compelled me to come here? Pressure by some crazy old woman who's so insane she even works for a cat detective agency? I'm nervous. I feel nervous, not because I'm scared or believe there is really anything to this cat story, but because the last time I saw Milla I kissed her and I think she might just hate me for it. But everything's going to be fine, I tell myself. I'll just breeze in. Milla will make me tea like she always does and hand me a stale wheatmeal biscuit, laughing and apologising, and we'll be just as normal. All will be forgotten. But as I approach the door I can't help thinking that maybe there is something out of the ordinary. The white-glossed surface of the wood is patterned with a splintered crack where it looks as if someone has kicked in

310

the bottom of the wood. There's a strange smell in the air
too – a smell that seems familiar, but maybe it isn't. I
hover for a few seconds, not sure whether to press the
doorbell, and then do it. If she has hammered the door
shut, as I suspect, then there's no way she's going to be
opening it. It's not worth even starting to think about
what this all means. I ring the bell. Shout. Ring the bell.
Shout again. Still no answer, and I look along towards
the window and notice that it has actually been hitched
up by a couple of inches. You have to understand that I'm
an opportunist.

~

The next time I wake up, it's to Gabriel's distant
voice filtering through my sleep. 'Milla . . . Oh,
Milla!' The front doorbell rings. *What's he doing here?*
I imagine it must be a dream. But the voice keeps
coming. 'Come on . . . Milla, get up! It's me!'
Another ring.

I lie there, wrapped in a sheet and unable to
persuade my body to move, and watch as his
silhouette passes in front of the half-open window.
His face presses up to it, squidging his nose to the
glass so that the end goes white and his cheeks splay
out in all directions. But I don't remember inviting
him. *I mean, who asked him to come?* Maybe, in some
strange feline ESP way, it was Purrl. Nothing is
beyond her.

'Come on, Milla,' he repeats. 'I can see you in
there. Get off your backside, you lazy old cow. It's a
gorgeous day. Fucking GORGEOUS!'

311

He waits a few seconds – and I don't react. I figure if I don't move, maybe eventually he'll go away. He won't linger any longer, won't come barging in like a lamb to the slaughter. I will him to leave, will him not to tempt me, not to put himself up against the desires of Purrl. But he doesn't know. He just keeps calling obstinately.

'It's one of those days that makes me feel great to be alive!' he bellows.

I sink lower into the sofa, grasping my night-dress and, with the slowest, smallest movements, trying to pull it over my head. I hope he won't notice me.

Gabriel sighs. 'Don't be silly, Milla. I mean, I'm not up to anything. I just thought you might like to talk, what with Josh gone and all that. Thought you might like to go out for the day!' He has arrived, as if summoned, but of his own accord. I see his fingers grip under the window and wonder what it's doing open. Why is there that ten-centimetre gap between the frame and the pane? Then I remember – last night. I remember thinking, *Too hot in here. We need some air. It's all getting so heavy and sweaty.*

Gabriel heaves it up.

A leg hooks over the wall, scruffy-looking brown leather shoe landing precariously on a pile of books on the bench beneath the window. The books slip slightly, tumbling on to the ground, causing the leg to straighten, with nothing to push against, and ramming the knee up against the wall. 'Ouch!' he mutters, as his whole body comes tumbling through the window, landing with a thump on the ground. 'Uh!' He gets up and starts rubbing his leg pathetically.

I giggle.

'I suppose you think that's funny.'

'Mmmm.'

'Ha bloody ha.'

'Pisshead,' I mumble, though actually he looks surprisingly coordinated. Finally, after two whole years, he must be getting over Melanie.

He hops around for a few seconds and then stops to look at me. 'Haven't in ages, I'll have you know, but I don't suppose you're interested . . .' He stares through the darkness. 'Hell, Milla,' he says. 'What's been going on? You're in a bit of a sad state.'

I stare back at him, not sure of what to say, and whether I really can say it. 'Mmmmm . . .'

'It stinks in here. Like a cesspit.' His body is a giant silhouette looming up against the light of morning. He steps forward a few more paces and now I can see him properly. 'What's up?' he asks. 'You look sick. Really sick.' And he stands there awkwardly as if not sure of what to do. '*Are* you?'

My gaze doesn't waver, and for what seems like an eternity my lips refuse to utter a word . . . then they do. 'A bit.'

'Well, you look awful. How long have you been like this?'

He comes in towards me and kneels on the carpet next to the sofa. Gabriel never knows what to say when it comes to these difficult situations and, nervously, he examines me, with his head held back, as if taking in a painting or some other aesthetic object, just as he does when he first looks at an animal. Taking in the whole thing.

'Well . . .' he says, finally summoning up the courage to put a hand on my shoulder. 'Well . . . haven't you been to the doctor?'

'Uh-uh.' I haul myself up to sitting position. 'Just a bit of flu,' I say.

'I'll get you some water,' says Gabriel, ever practical.

I nod my head, then watch him disappearing out of the doorway.

'Christ, it stinks!' I hear him mutter as he heads down the hall.

~

I'd like to be able to say that in this drained, flu-ridden state I don't find Milla attractive, but I do. Even the pale, glistening, sweat-globulated skin, the hair plastered to the side of her face and smell of feverish sweat still arouse in me a faint palpitation, a quivering of the heart. I feel nervous. It's just not that I feel sorry for her and want to look after her in some fatherly way, but her lips seem just as alluring as ever and I'd love to put my arms around her. It's an effort of will to take on this formal doctorly bedside manner.

I'm so shocked at the mess, I can barely think. I've never seen her this ill before. All around her is disorder, sheets strewn, dirty plates, the stink of rotting fish. The place even smells like she might have wet herself or at

314

least thrown up. Though I know flus can be bad, it seems that she has really sunk into this one. If I hadn't come along, who knows what would have happened?

~

Purrl emerges from the shadows by the armchair. She must have been there all the time, watching me, studying my actions. My hidden examiner is back to guide me.

'You must do it, Milla,' she murmurs. 'It's time to do it.'

'I can't,' I whisper.

'You can.' She smiles at me, suffusing me with her soft confidence. 'Of course you can. You know you can.'

'I don't know . . . I mean, yes, maybe I can . . . But how?'

'Don't ask *me*! However humans normally murder other humans. You've done it before.'

I look round the room. 'I could hit him with something . . .'

'Mmm . . . Like what?'

'A chair? A bottle?'

'A bottle . . . Yes, maybe . . . maybe something heavier.'

'Something heavier?' I look around at the floor and the shelves and the furniture and the magazine rack, and find my eyes resting on a two-foot-tall china faience cat that Jemima bought at some auction. Intricately painted in blue and gold it smirks at me from beneath its jewelled eyes. I ges-

315

ture towards the smiling figure. It would certainly be heavy. 'Will that do?'

'Perfect . . .'

'Yes, perfect,' I repeat, though I feel a little distracted as I run my fingers over the slippery glaze and wonder what the reason is, the explanation for why I'm now standing here thinking of killing Gabriel. It's absurd and yet somehow it still seems right. There seems no good reason not to do it – nothing I could explain to Purrl anyway. A clink of glasses. Through the echoey blankness, I hear footsteps and release my grip on the cat. I sink back into the sofa, staring at the ceiling. Purrl is hiding again. Gabriel must not suspect my thoughts.

A familiar freckled forearm appears in front of my face, clutching a crystal-clear glass of water. It looks good and I reach forward and grasp the glass. I can feel Purrl watching me.

'That must be some bug you've got, Milla. You look like you haven't eaten for weeks.' He watches me as I gulp down greedily. I only now realise that my throat is so dry and parched it hurts to swallow.

'So, where's the cat?' he asks, looking around restlessly. He shifts from foot to foot, glancing over his shoulder, eyes never quite focusing on me directly. He's so jittery and wary that I almost wonder if he suspects us. 'Did you read my letter? Did you get my message?'

'Yes.' I nod, and though I'm aware of Purrl watching and can't deal with the thought of her knowing

how much I doubt her, the turmoil inside is unbearable and I am on the verge of speaking out. I
look into Gabriel's unyielding eyes and try to speak
to him the way I do to Purrl. *Gabriel . . . I'm saying.
Help me get away. I need someone to take me away.*

Gabriel smiles, but he clearly does not hear me.
'Milla, love.' He comes down to kneel on my level in
a movement that is exceptionally forward considering his sober state. There's a wet, gulping sound as
he clears his throat. 'You've been a bit funny for a
long time. At first I thought it was Josh. I have to
admit I was jealous and jumped to conclusions that
I couldn't even admit to myself. But now . . . now,
well . . . I don't expect you to feel the same way too.
It's my own fault. I should have said it years and
years ago, but I was too wrapped up in my PhD and
the bird thing and all that. And, well, Milla, you
know I've always been fond of you. I've never been
any good at hiding it. I think you know . . .'

But his words don't quite penetrate. Instead,
I'm aware of a light, low hum filling the room,
gradually growing louder and louder, a call
from Purrl. A rising begin-note that extends
into *Mmmaaaaaaaaaaaaaawwwwwwwwaaaaaaaaa . . .*
She holds it long and evenly, passing it steadily
across her vocal chords. I allow my eyes to follow
the sound upwards, passing over the carpet, up the
chair, over the bookcase, till I find her. There she is
standing up on top, regal and composed. Bolt
upright, she calls to me. Her eyes gleam. They
hypnotise, they mesmerise . . . I forget everything

317

except her voice. *Mmmmmmmmmaaaaaaaaaaa* . . . she continues. *Waarrrrrrrr* . . .

Now Gabriel turns and looks round, letting out a faint gasp. 'Christ, Milla, she really is a weird thing.' He shakes his head, seemingly disconcerted, before turning back to me. He's not going to be distracted. Down on his knees again, he looks into my eyes. 'You know what I'm saying, Milla, don't you?'

My hands are gripped tightly around the glass and shaking with the tension, and as I glance upwards at Purrl, I know I must kill Gabriel. For her. For Purrl. I see the china cat at my side. Though my muscles are tensed into some sort of tetanic paralysis, in my mind I see it all. *You can do it . . . I know you can*, she's saying. In a split second, I see myself from the outside, through Purrl's eyes, leaning over, grabbing the china figure by its slender neck, gripping hard and testing its slipperiness between my fingers. Slow motion. In a dream-like haze, almost on cue, Gabriel turns his head away from me, making it easy, leaving the back of his skull open for attack, as I swing, flailing high in the air, bringing the weapon down and over, thudding it into his head, where skin splits, bone cracks and blood spurts. I can see it. I feel it. He's falling. Yes, he's falling heavily to the ground. Falling to the ground like Mina. Down he goes.

Falling like Mina . . . falling all over again . . . and we're there in the bales, just the two of us, before it happened. We've gone up to our secret hiding place

318

at the top of the high stack, clambering up the ladder, where we're not supposed to go – the place that Uncle Al always warned us against. Mina isn't that keen on going up, but I push her, tell her she's a cowardy custard, and for once she gives in. I persuade her. Partly she's worried because I'm being so quiet. I keep my mouth shut and don't chat, no gossiping. 'What's wrong?' she keeps asking, as we scale the rungs one by one. 'What's wrong?' But I don't tell her. I keep quiet, keep ascending and for once I find it's working like a dream. It's all just coming together. Before I know it, we're standing there by the edge, me facing her. She's laughing and taunting me about my silence, saying I've got a secret. 'You fancy someone!' she says. 'You're thinking about some *boy*.' I can see the blank void of the building behind her, sense the huge drop, and I know this could be my moment. I reach out a hand. I can almost see it before it happens. It's so easy, the simplest of movements. I barely feel the physical effort involved, my arm thrusting out in front, touching her chest, pushing, forcing, toppling her so easily, and suddenly she's falling, falling down to the ground. She's falling, toppling, as I watch her, not screaming, but with blank incomprehension in her eyes, head upturned in that everlasting freeze-frame of her descent. Body twisting like a cat. Her silence all the way down is everlasting. It's agonising. It chills my blood. I feel my guts knot inside me, contracting on to the impossibility of it not happening, of that momentary pause lasting for ever. Then it happens. I hear this great loud thud as body hits concrete. It's like a bomb exploding. *Bam!* That's it. Done. I crane over and see her body lying down there like a broken doll. In the eternal few seconds of silence that follow, I know it's all gone wrong.

I screamed. *What have I done?* I screamed again and began to run, stumbling across the bales, accelerating towards my sister, scuttling, clambering, slipping across the straw, almost falling on the way down the ladder, boots slipping against rungs, fear turning my body inside out as I came nearer and nearer to what I already knew. There she was. Blood gushing, crimson sticking to split-parted hair. But she was alive – she was breathing. I hadn't really killed her, though I might as well have.

No one accused me. Even when I told Mother, she said, 'Don't be silly, darling. Don't get any crazy ideas. You mustn't blame yourself like that. It was all a terrible accident . . .' And now sometimes I think maybe it was a terrible accident. Maybe even then I was just Milla the wimp, who couldn't even hurt a fly, and actually that hand never reached out to press upon her chest, to force her over the edge. No one even knew I hated her. They never asked me how I felt – only ever asked Mina to speak for us both. 'Mina's the sociable one. Mina's the bright one. Mina's the star. Mina's this, Mina's that, Mina's the other . . .' How many times did I hear it again and again and again, even after the accident? Ironically, I heard it all the more then. It could have been a dream, for all it changed.

I look down at my hands and find they're still clenched around my drink. They're shaking so hard, the water is virtually splashing out and my muscles are clenched so tight I almost imagine I could crack the glass. I haven't moved an inch, haven't even touched Gabriel. I am stuck to my seat and, before I know it, another hand is there, on top of mine, and it's Gabriel touching me, placing his fingers on top of mine. Gabriel who is still there, still alive.

'But in my own way I do love you, Milla,' he says. 'I know it probably doesn't mean that much to you. You always expect so much . . .'

Purrl spits angrily from on high. 'Betrayer,' she snarls knowingly, her voice carrying through the room . . . and as I feel the pressure of Gabriel's hand against mine, I find myself swooning, shrinking inside, shrinking back from him. I feel a heat in my blood. I feel my skin tingling, the ceiling flying up, the floor dropping out from me. I hear a loud, screeching interference rumbling in my ears. *Get away from me,* I want to scream.

'I do love you, Milla.'

Through the blur, I see Purrl's white figure, a shooting streak moving across the floor and out of the room, trailing some kind of overpowering wail which is so loud it tears at my ears. Gabriel pulls backwards, almost yanking me to my feet, but not quite. He says something . . . mumbles something . . . that I can't make out, but suspect is simply, 'What's wrong with her?' I'm not sure. Can't be sure of anything. I can't tell what's happening, other than that I now see Gabriel leaving the room, following Purrl, tracking her to the back room, which is where she has decided to take him, the back room where Josh is hidden.

What's happening to me? What is this?

I try to stand up, but can't hold it for long and find myself collapsing forward on to my hands. It feels safer there, more natural and less dizzying, though I still find I can't help panicking. I can't help feeling that all is lost. Not only is my body slipping from my control but there's no one to help. They're leaving me to my weakness. There's no way out. As soon as Gabriel finds Josh . . . I don't know. Though I know Gabriel would do anything for me, this is taking things a little too far. I try to get up again, teetering on my toes, but again falling forward. I can't help feeling there's something odd going on. My spine feels twisted. Through the back, I can hear Gabriel's footsteps. I can hear him shouting, 'Werrattt aou haolls gaiugg oaaaann kere?' Now I really can't make it out.

Even so, I can imagine . . . He knows now. He must do. He knows about Josh and I feel sick to the bottom of my stomach. There's nothing I can do. I can feel in the air that he's angry, confused. Through my skin I pick up his conflicting emotions tweaking on my antennae. I feel his footsteps vibrate through the floor, shaking up through my paws. My hairs are on end, adrenalin coursing through my veins, muscles prepared for flight,

322

to run, to escape. It's the only option. And, as Gabriel's legs appear in the doorway, I dart forward.

'Why are you making that stupid noise?' I hear this garbled human voice. 'Urgh – what has huppeeuid te hour toie? And eyiub thugtb tuiuitu nose luikee thaatee . . .'

I run beneath him. My fur brushes against his trouser leg, as he leans forward to grab me, but I keep running and he only slips over the end of my tail. I'm leaving it all. I'm leaving it all behind. As I patter along the hallway, I feel a strength and lightness in my step, a brightness hits my eyes. It's big. I smell the outside beckoning. Purrl is ahead of me, standing there on the kitchen floor, sun glancing off her blinding white back. She's waiting. She wants to lead me. She's the messenger. I see it now – she's always been the messenger. Quicker, quicker, I accelerate towards the door, pushing against the cat flap, hitting it just as it flaps back from Purrl's exit, feeling air rushing through fur, hitting the grass, taking off through the gardens, launching myself up on to the walls. Purrl's ahead of me, hurtling away like a ball of light. My beacon, flying through the air. I'm losing her, can't keep up as I blunder in my new form. I push as hard as I can, feeling the air sting in my lungs. I watch her flicker over a wall and keep following though I can no longer see her. And, as I run, I feel it all fall away, all the miserableness of human life. All those things I always hated – all a thing of the past. I'm leaving it behind: the bills, the nine to five, the self-assessment, the tax return forms, the National Insurance numbers, the credit cards, the overdraft limits, the wanting too much, the letters from my bank manager, the council tax, the shopping, the double-glazing calls, the isolation, the Jehovah's Witnesses, the monthly direct debits, the spelling mistakes, the letters from Mother, the morning-after pills, the period pains, the pregnancy tests, the split condoms, the photos of Mina, the fake suntan cream, the nail varnish, the bikini-line remover, the hairs getting stuck in the plughole, Mrs Mingerston's gossip, Ida Little's snoopings, the phone calls from Mother, the three-day diets, the cellulite, the aerobics classes, the circuit-training, the whole world of chattering desperate opinions, the bluffing, the daily depressing headlines, the nagging from Mother, getting your hair cut, shaving your legs, filing, organising, standing in queues, smart clothes, glossy magazines, the things, the labels, the products, yes, the *things* . . . having to not pick your nose, listening to Mother go on about Mina, saying hello to people you hate, shaking hands, telling white lies, telling thunking great whoppers about Mina, morals, conscience, numbers, the mind-body divide, long-term memory, responsibility . . . the lot!

'Milla!' I hear Gabriel shout, his voice distant and foreign, floating in the summer air. *Too late . . . too late . . . There's no turning back now!* Up is the only way. Climb the wall. Put it behind me. A rusted drainpipe is all there is to cling to, my salvation –

324

and it's not much. Purrl is scaling effortlessly . . . so cleanly, streaking upwards, and I follow, the ground slipping away beneath me. I reach up and extend my claws, digging but scraping away the flaking metal. I'm so heavy, body's floppy . . . pulling, twisting, skidding, collapsing, bungling. I'm not used to this, can't think how to work it, but somehow I do. It gets easier. I heave and I thrust, slipping a little, yet hauling myself up, till with a leg outstretched I can reach out. I mount the sloping wall. And I'm there, running again. I'm up. I tear across the roof-tops. It almost feels like I'm flying. I've never liked people. And I don't want to spend any more time with them. Time to stretch my paws and get out, to play in the alleys and the parks. New home, new love, new fire to sit beside, new fish to eat . . . It's all waiting for me. There, for me to take. Next stop Lady Kitty's . . . perhaps. Maybe even Gabriel's . . . Who knows? I stretch out my torso and tighten my legs for a leap.